CW00431876

A YEAR
IN THE LIFE
OF
DEIDRE FLYNN

LUCINDA E CLARKE

A YEAR IN THE LIFE OF DEIDRE FLYNN

Cover art and design by Sharon Brownlie
https://aspirebookcovers.com/

For all my readers and fellow writers who have supported and encouraged me – especially my long-suffering husband who gave me the necessary peace and quiet during the recent lockdown to write this book.

Also by Lucinda E Clarke

PSYCHOLOGICAL THRILLER
A Year in the Life of Leah Brand
A Year in the Life of Andrea Coe

FICTION
Amie – an African Adventure
Amie and the Child of Africa
Amie Stolen Future
Amie Cut for Life
Amie Savage Safari
Samantha (Amie backstories)
Ben (Amie backstories)

MEMOIRS
Walking over Eggshells
Truth, Lies and Propaganda
More Truth, Lies and Propaganda
The very Worst Riding School in the World

HUMOUR
Unhappily Ever After

Contents

MAY DEIDRE

The doorbell chimed followed by Leah's piercing screams echoing down the hallway. I was in the kitchen, still in my dressing gown and slippers, and I'd just picked up my first coffee of the day. The mug slipped from my hands, the pottery shattering on the tiled floor, sending rivulets of brown liquid in all directions.

I raced to the open front door to see Leah leaning against the wall. She was shaking, her face pale, and her arms wrapped tightly across her chest.

I looked out but there was no one outside and I couldn't see what had upset her, until I followed her finger pointing to the top step. At first, I thought it was a rolled-up bit of fur, or a carpet, until I saw the maggots crawling over the body.

It was the carcass of a very large, very dead dog. What made it even more chilling was the large spike driven into one of the staring eyes, holding a piece of paper in place; a photograph of Leah and Belinda in Cannes on one of their shopping trips, judging by the multiple carrier bags Belinda was clutching.

I put my arms around Leah, pulling her close, her body trembling against mine. Poor lamb, she had been through so much in the last few years, she didn't need more trouble; I knew how fragile she was.

Belinda rushed up. "What's all the fuss?" She looked down. "Oh yeuk, that's gross. Is it dead?"

"Of course it's dead, can't you see the worms?"

"I'm going to barf." Belinda's eyes were like saucers. "What sick person would do that to a poor, defenceless dog?"

Who indeed? The corpse was not emaciated, but the stomach had been sliced open, the intestines spilling out, coils of gut spread over the top step. A sour smell wafted up from the carcass, half-digested meat where the worms were writhing and feasting.

As I peered closer, I could see the remains of a red collar with a blank tag attached. At one time this dog had a caring owner.

I steered Leah back into the kitchen, and made her sit while I put the coffee pot back on the stove and cleaned the floor.

"I'll sort it out, don't even think about it."

"I can't ask you…"

"You don't have to ask. Leave it to me."

"If only Bill was here."

If only. Whoever had dumped a decaying corpse on our doorstep had chosen the perfect time. Leah had only moved into the villa a couple of months ago with stepdaughter Belinda and partner Bill. He'd left only yesterday for a trip back to England to settle some personal affairs, and I was here by chance while the decorators did what decorators do in my villa on the other side of the village.

Had the perpetrators chosen a time when they thought Leah was most vulnerable? Well they counted without me. I'm of the old school and as tough as they come.

"I'll throw some clothes on and get rid of it while you calm down. Want a shot of brandy in your coffee?"

Leah laughed. "Goodness no. I'll be fine, Deidre. It was just the shock. I was about to pick it up before I noticed…" She shuddered.

"Some weird person's idea of a practical joke. You're new to the area. Just some kids," I said.

I don't think for a moment Leah was convinced it was only a cruel prank, but she squared her shoulders and attempted to smile.

A pair of heavy-duty gardening gloves, a shovel, and a large black plastic bag later, Belinda and I had manoeuvred the corpse out of sight and taken it down the road to the garbage collection point. I wasn't sure if that was the correct place to put it but I sure as hell wasn't going to dig a hole in the rock-solid ground in this heat. The sun was climbing high and the sweat was already making my clothes stick to me like a second skin. The Mediterranean heat was fierce in summer time.

I was forced to listen to Belinda's constant grumbles. It was only the promise of supper in town tonight that she agreed to help at all.

"Who do you think did this?" she asked as we part carried, part dragged the sack up the road. Belinda was terrified the maggots would escape and kept dropping her side of the bag.

"I have no idea. Probably just a prank."

"It could be an enemy of Daddy's."

"Hardly," I snapped back. There was of course a good chance she was right. None of us knew the whole story behind Mason taking off the way he did. He'd represented several shady characters in court and got them off time after time. I heard it mentioned he was known in the City as the Mob's 'go to' for all legal matters. Was it only the one slip that caused him to fall on the wrong side of them?

We flung the bag into the large bin and turned to go back to the house.

"Leah won't make me go visit Daddy in jail, will she?"

"What brought that to mind?" I kicked a stone off the pot-holed tarred road onto the verge.

"Just asking."

"No, I'm sure she won't insist. Why would she?"

"He might ask to see me. But I don't want to see him."

That made sense. Jail was not the ideal residence for either lawyers or Her Majesty's officers of the law. Too many opportunities for men with a score to settle. And, word got round from one institution to another; nowhere would be completely safe. I didn't mention this to Belinda. She may well change her mind later, and want to see her father.

"Leah wouldn't make you do anything you don't want to do. Well nothing like that," I hastily amended.

"I don't want to see my brother either." Belinda stopped in the road and stared at me.

"Nor Leo," I assured her.

"Just as long as you're right." The teenager strode off

along the narrow road, in through the stone pillars, and up the gravel drive to the villa.

I felt sorry for Leah. I felt sorry for Belinda. The whole family was beyond dysfunctional.

Leah was scrubbing the doorstep. I could smell the bleach halfway up the path.

"I'd have done that."

"Deidre, it was enough you removed the poor creature." She stood up and wiped the sweat off her forehead with her arm. "Have you ever seen it around here before?"

"No. There are dozens of assorted dogs wandering around the village, but I've never taken much notice."

"I need to pick up a few bits in the shops later, so let's grab a coffee and we can ask."

"Sure."

"Maybe it was dead a long time and had been buried and someone dug it up to put on our doorstep." Belinda's voice behind me made me jump. I turned to see her spooning yoghurt from a large tub.

"Belinda, do you never stop eating?"

"Nope. I like food, and I like French food."

So did I, but, if I ate even part of what the girl managed to put away each day, I'd be the size of a house. It didn't have that effect on Belinda. At just seventeen she was taller than my five foot five, with long dark hair, a clear skin, and a figure with all the right curves and bumps in the appropriate places. As a teenager I should have looked like that. I'm not sure in our hippy era we were as worried about outward appearance. We were too busy singing and dancing and spouting platitudes about how we were going to put the world to rights and save mankind.

Get a grip, Deidre. You're pushing seventy and, while you still dress in hippy gear, you're not as young as you were. I needed to give myself a good talking to now and again. It's a cruel trick of nature that keeps our minds racing and our bodies refusing to cooperate. Well, until our minds join in the degradation stakes. Not yet, not for me. My mind is as sharp as it's always been.

"If that dog had been buried and then dug up, its fur would have been covered in soil. So no, I don't think it was buried."

"Hmmm, it was just a thought." Belinda grabbed two slices of toast, plastered them with butter and jam, and wandered off into the sun lounge.

Leah reached over to the coffee machine and poured herself another cup. She smiled at me as she sat down and helped herself to breakfast

My darling Leah, I was so fond of her. The moment my nephew James introduced us I took to her. He was still studying to become a doctor and Leah was working overtime as a nurse to support him. The wedding had been a simple affair; they were so much in love, but sensibly saving the pennies.

In the road accident a few years later, Leah lost her husband James, their two children, Brandon and Henrietta. She was the only survivor; losing part of her left leg.

I knew, when Leah came to spend time with me in Weston-super-Mare, she was in trouble. How much, neither of us guessed but, after the insurance payout, moving to the south of France was a new beginning for all of us.

I pushed the morning's incident to the back of my mind. It was a teen prank, nothing else. Even if I didn't really believe that, I would convince myself it was the truth.

We took a gentle stroll into the village, leaving Belinda to blast some indescribable noise she called music out of every window. The moment we returned I would put a stop to that. My nerves were not up to raucous rows from awkward teens.

The tall plane trees lining the road cast a welcome shade, with pink and purple cosmos and daisies nestling in the grass at the base of the trunks. I gazed up at a raptor as it circled over the meadows. The peaceful scene had a calming effect.

Leah had settled down too and chattered on.

"Madame du Pont is due at three o'clock, so I must keep an eye on the time."

"Mrs Bridge."

"What?"

"Just a quick translation into English. It doesn't have the same romantic ring does it? Is she the tutor you've hired for Belinda?"

"Yes. I was a little nervous choosing her because English is not her first language, but I understand from the Robinsons and the Telfords on Facebook that she is excellent. She got all their children through their A levels, and they also passed the Baccalaureate."

"I've heard that's a really high standard."

"So I believe, but nothing stands still, and it's impossible to judge whether the standards of any of the exams have gone up or down." Leah sighed.

"I still think you made the right choice, leaving England. It's a new start for all of you."

"I love it here. I love the warm sun…" she flung her arms out, "and I love the wide-open spaces, and the quiet country roads."

We both leapt onto the verge at the blast of a car horn behind us. Leah fell back against a tree as a low-slung, sleek, yellow sports car raced past.

"Bloody idiot!" I yelled after it.

"That was close." Leah slid to the ground.

"Are you OK?" Her battered nerves needed a rest.

"Yes, I'm fine. Just getting my breath back." She smiled bravely. "It was a close call; it missed us by millimetres."

The sun disappeared behind a cloud and the road took on a sinister appearance. The birds now flying overhead screeched like escapees from a Dracula backdrop, the tree branches threatened, and a sharp wind momentarily flattened the flowers.

Seconds passed and then the cloud floated past and once again the world was warm and friendly.

Leah stood up. "I think my breathing is back to normal, and I may take a shot in my coffee when we get to the village!"

"You're not the only one." I picked up the basket and retrieved the shopping bags that had blown out and fluttered down the road.

There was no sign of the yellow sports car when we arrived in the village square.

"Probably a mad tourist," observed Leah. "I have no idea why, but the moment people go on holiday they suddenly start behaving in a way they never would at home."

"Ah, that's because they have gone foreign." I tried to lighten the mood, but Leah only glared at me. The coffee revived us and she ordered one of her favourite doughnuts before we checked out the market stalls.

Leah's French was very basic and mine not much better but, of the few people we asked, no one was missing a large, black dog with a red collar.

"We didn't think to take a photo of it so we could put up posters."

"Don't be ridiculous Leah. Someone's pet, dead, with maggots crawling all over it! Enough to give some poor child nightmares for life."

"Goodness yes. I wasn't thinking. That would be cruel."

"And then some." I checked my watch. "I suggest we get Old Giles to give us a lift back in his taxi. It's getting too hot to walk."

Taxi was perhaps too good a name for the old boneshaker Giles was so proud of. Held together with sealing wax and string, the truck had seen better days, but Uber was not available in this rural part of the south of France. We climbed in over empty pizza boxes, bits of straw, a basket of eggs, and three sacks of vegetables. Old Giles would double up our journey with errands of his own. At least he didn't try to charge us full rate.

Back at the house we found Belinda pacing around the lounge. She had, thank heavens, turned the 'music' off, but she looked rattled.

"What's the matter? What's happened?" Leah rushed

through to the kitchen and dumped the shopping on the counter.

"Claudette tells me you've got some old biddy coming this afternoon to teach me." She glared at Leah.

"My, your French has improved," I remarked with a smirk. "How does 'some old biddy' translate from the French?"

"Very funny." Belinda paced some more. "Well, have you?" She glared at Leah.

"Yes, Madame du Pont is coming to discuss it at three."

"Come on Leah, I don't need this. It's summer time, time to park off. Why make me work?"

Leah swung round. "You've already missed far too much school, as it is. You will be taking your A levels a year late and, whether you like it or not, you *are* going to sit the exams. Whether you pass or not is up to you, but you *will* take them. So, there's no discussion."

We both stared at Leah. The meek, mild Leah had shocked both of us.

"And what if I don't want to?"

"That's your choice, but you're welcome to sit in while I chat to Madame."

"Good."

Belinda stalked off onto the terrace.

"If she's as charming to Madame as she is to you, she may well refuse to tutor her." I went to help Leah unpack the vegetables.

"Somehow I don't think that's going to happen." Leah smiled.

"What do you know that I don't?"

"Wait until you meet Madame," was the only answer she gave me. Leah turned to Claudette who had bustled into the kitchen and suggested what she could prepare for lunch.

Madame arrived promptly at three o'clock. The doorbell's thunderous chimes echoed around every room on the ground floor. "We'll have to replace them; that noise is enough to waken the dead," I said to Leah as she hurried to open the door. Seeing her expression, I could have chosen a better description.

"It didn't waken the dead dog though did it?" Belinda remarked as she floated past.

When Madame entered the lounge, I was reminded of the stereotypical school mistress of the St.Trinian era, a throwback in time. Despite the heat, she wore a severe suit, with a blouse frilled at the collar and cuffs, sensible lace-up shoes and lisle stockings. Her glasses were attached to one of those chains round her neck, and her long grey hair was neatly folded into a bun on the top of her head. Her face was sharp and pointed with a long nose and small bright blue eyes.

I stood to greet her and I could feel her eyes sweep me from head to foot, judging my long, cotton peasant skirt and loose top and the jangling bangles on my wrists. I did not meet with her approval.

Leah fussed around her like a sheepdog.

"Do please sit. Can I get you tea, coffee?"

"I'll have a white wine, large," I replied; I couldn't help myself. They both shot me a scandalous look, then Leah grinned.

"One wine, one coffee, and for you...?" She turned to Madame.

"For me I have the tea."

"Oh, I'm forgetting my manners. This is my aunt, well Deidre is not really my aunt, but she was the aunt to my first husband, my late husband that is, not my present husband, nor my present partner of course. So, we are not blood relatives but only by marriage…"

"We are old friends. Deidre Flynn," I rushed in, before Leah dug herself in any deeper. I wondered why she was so nervous; was it the result of this morning's episode?

"Pleased to meet you." Madame extended her hand. Her handshake was firm and dry. I thought I saw a brief twinkle in her eye but I couldn't be sure.

Leah bustled off to instruct Claudette. She was still finding this hard to do. She had always been an excellent and conscientious housewife and was still reluctant to delegate, even though she could afford a dozen house-keepers.

Madame settled herself on the sofa and, opening her cavernous bag, withdrew a large iPad and a stylus. Now that was a surprise. Madame was more modern than her appearance suggested.

I could hear Leah calling for Belinda, but the child had disappeared again.

"Now, I have to tell you that I cannot take Belinda alone." Madame spoke English with that delightful French lilt.

"Oh, shame, well never mind then." Belinda materialised from the hallway and plonked herself down on the couch next to me.

"No, you misunderstood, I have a pupil already, and I can take the two of you together. Her name is Sophie and she is eleven years old."

"What? A primary school child!" Belinda looked disgusted.

"Ah, but not just any child. She is very bright, too clever. I think she will be ahead of you in her work."

"At eleven, she's not even a teenager. You can't expect me to study with a baby!" Belinda jumped to her feet.

"She is what you call a prodigy." Madame was unphased by Belinda's remarks. "She is so clever for her age, and she will be taking the A levels and the Baccalaureate at the same time as you."

"Must be a bloody easy exam if you can pass it at that age," Belinda sniffed.

"Oh no, no, no, Mademoiselle, it is so much harder than your Advanced Levels. Your mother—"

"Stepmother," Belinda snapped.

"Your stepmother has shown me the reports from your school in England, and I fear we have a lot of work to do. It will take many hours of hard work."

Belinda walked across the room, spun around and came to stand in front of Leah and Madame. "Well a couple of hours in the morning maybe… if," she looked at Leah, "it'll make you happy."

"Oh no Mademoiselle, it is to make you happy. Your stepmother, she informs me, was a nurse before her accident, so she passed all her exams, so I am sure you can do also."

I was enjoying this. I saw Madame was a step ahead of her new student.

"Now, the practicalities. We will work here; I think it will be less tiring for you not to travel each day." She smiled at Belinda, whose face was thunderous.

"I will bring Sophie here with me, and we will begin at seven thirty."

"In the morning!" Belinda's face was a picture.

"Ah yes, while it is nice and cool. Then we break for lunch at two in the afternoon, and begin again at four for two more hours."

Belinda turned to Leah.

"Slave labour." She counted on her fingers. "That's eight, no, eight and a half hours a day!"

"It is only for six days in the week." Madame popped her iPad back in her bag and began to rise. "You will have the Sunday to attend mass and have a little time off. Now, I go and I see you tomorrow, bright and early."

"Yeah, whatever." Belinda was about to go into a huge sulk. Honestly, it was about time that child grew up. It crossed my mind that with all the trauma in her life it had arrested her development.

I heard Madame instructing Leah on all the materials and supplies she required for Belinda as they walked outside. I peeped through the window and was not surprised to see she drove an elderly Fiat Uno, marginally better than Old Giles' taxi, but with fewer dents and scrapes. Belinda came to stand beside me as we watched Madame fold herself into the driving seat. After a couple of false starts she was on her way.

"Deidre, Leah can't be serious, making me spend all day with that old bat. She's loopy."

"Not sure I agree with that. She's sharper than she looks."

Belinda tugged my arm. "Talk to her please. Look how nice it is out there; the sun is shining and the sea is warm—"

"And there are cute boys on the beach," I finished for her.

"I didn't say anything about boys," she protested.

"You didn't have to. I'm a mind reader, didn't you know?"

"Oh, for fuck's sake, you're no help at all." She stormed off up the stairs and I heard her bedroom door slam. If it wasn't going to create tension in the house it would be amusing.

To keep out of the way, I pottered around the garden with a pair of secateurs, much to the disgust of Jacques the full-time gardener. His glares made me so uncomfortable that I gave up and took refuge in the pool. Through the bushes I saw Belinda make for the steps to the beach. She might as well enjoy her last day of freedom.

I could have guessed that Belinda would not be up bright and early for her first lesson with Madame du Pont. Leah called her at 6.30 a.m., I followed up fifteen minutes later, and then we took it in turns every ten minutes or so. It had no effect; she was still in bed when the elderly green Fiat Uno barrelled up the drive.

I hurried out to greet them, while Leah made a last attempt to drag her stepdaughter out from under the sheets.

To my amazement Madame clambered out from the passenger side, and a young girl hopped out from behind the steering wheel. She was the cutest thing you have ever seen, with a mop of blonde curls surrounding a cherubic face and enormous blue eyes. She was the average height for an eleven-year-old, and I noticed the pile of cushions on the driver's seat before she slammed the door shut.

Madame saw the look on my face and laughed. "Yes, our little Sophie has many talents and it took her only one day to drive like a, how you say, professional?"

I could only nod as I watched Madame, closely followed by her little prodigy, sweep into the hallway and make for the lounge.

"There is coffee?" Madame called over her shoulder.

"Of course." I hurried into the kitchen but Claudette was already laying the tray. I guessed she must know Madame and her habits. Of course, in this rural village everyone knew everyone else and their family histories centuries back. I noticed she'd placed a glass and a can of coke for Sophie. I trailed behind her into the lounge, but Madame had already moved on to the dining room and was spreading out her books, files and pens on the polished table.

Sophie was doing likewise.

I turned to see Belinda in the doorway, still in her nightdress, her hair uncombed, rubbing her eyes.

"What the fuck," she exclaimed.

"*Ma Cherie!* You are late. Come. There is not a moment to lose. Every second is precious."

Belinda's gaze went from Madame to the piles of books, then landed on Sophie. "This her?" It was not so much a question as a sneer.

Nothing was going to phase Madame. "Ah yes, you have not met. This is little Sophie, my prize pupil. Say hello to Belinda."

"*Bon jour.*" Sophie smiled and her face lit up reminding me of those Madonna statues in the local churches. She walked forward, extending her hand.

Belinda gazed at it for a moment then grasped it in a

limp handshake. From the look on her face, Sophie's handshake was anything but limp.

"No, no, no, *ma Cherie!* You do not introduce yourself with a hand like a wet fish!" Madame darted forward and grabbed Belinda's right hand. "The handshake should always be firm, decisive, and not too hard that it hurts. And, never, ever should the perspiration be on the hand. Now, try again," she ordered.

Belinda looked taken aback but extended her hand to Sophie. This time she was not able to hold back a yelp as Sophie pressed even harder.

"That is so much better." Madame was beaming. "See what that says about you? I am confident. I am self-assured. I am worth meeting. Yes?"

Belinda said nothing, just glared at her.

"And now my petite, you are not dressed for learning. The body knows you are in your sleepwear, so two minutes to dress properly and then we will begin." She went to sit at the table.

For a moment Belinda hovered in the doorway massaging her right hand, then she slid out of sight and I heard her feet on the stairs.

Madame and Sophie were chattering away in French which was much too fast to follow, so I left them and went to get myself a coffee.

I'm not usually a nosy person, I'm not, but I was intrigued by the situation. I'd never seen Belinda lost for words, but it looked as if Madame could get her to cooperate, even if Leah and I failed miserably. I felt a little guilty but I was determined to hover close by and see what happened.

Belinda appeared again about fifteen minutes later in jeans and a t-shirt, and she'd brushed her hair and tied it back. She pulled out a chair, scraping the legs on the floor as if to assert her independence but, if Madame noticed it, she said nothing.

Sophie was already busily tapping away on her iPad.

"Where is your tablet?" Madame pointed to the empty table in front of Belinda. The teen shrugged.

"In my room."

"Then get it, and hurry!" Madame clapped her hands.

When Belinda returned with it Madame whipped it out of her hands and peered at the screen. "Noooo, what is this Candy Crush, Animal Crossing, Doom Eternal, Final Fantas—"

"Hey, they're my games!" Belinda made a grab for the tablet, but Madame was too quick and her fingers flew over the screen.

Belinda was frantic. "You can't take them off!" she shrieked.

"No. I can't now, because they are all gone." Madame looked very pleased with herself. "This…" she waved the iPad at Belinda, "is for studying. I will put the proper apps on for you. Now you cannot waste your time playing these silly games. You have not many hours before you take the exams. Now to work. First, we look at some English papers. We will need to study this for the homework tonight."

"Homework as well?" Belinda gasped. "Slave labour, that can't be legal."

Madame ignored her comments.

It was difficult not to smile as I crept away but,

before I left, I noticed the grin on Sophie's face. The sunlight streamed in through the window highlighting her blonde hair. With her bright blue eyes and open, friendly face, she was the closest thing to an angel I had ever seen.

Claudette laid out lunch on the terrace and Sophie joined the adults, but Belinda was nowhere to be seen. I guessed she was sulking. It wasn't like her to miss a meal, but she was probably raiding the fridge as she usually did between breakfast, lunch and supper.

I found Sophie fascinating. It was difficult to believe she was only eleven; she joined in the conversation making valid viewpoints, far in advance of her years, in fluent English.

"I read a lot," she told me in her gentle voice. "I'm reading Plato at the moment."

I saw Leah's eyes widen, but she said nothing. I studied her, hoping she had calmed down and forgotten the incident from the morning.

"Dear Sophie has a photographic memory," Madame pronounced proudly. "If she sees something, she never forgets. She is very clever."

I could see Sophie revelling in the praise.

"You will stay in France?" Madame turned to Leah.

"I'm taking one day at a time for now. I love it here, and of course we will stay while Belinda takes her exams, and then we'll make any decisions."

I noticed her fingers picking at the threads on the scarf she was wearing. Was I the only one who could sense how tense she was?

"Madame tells me you have one false leg," Sophie piped up.

Leah looked a little taken back. It was rare that anyone mentioned it, even if they noticed. Do you ever get used to losing part of your own body? I doubted it.

I wasn't the only one who was surprised at the question; even Madame looked a little shocked. I wondered if she had mentioned it to Sophie with the intention of her not commenting on it. Leah was wearing one of her long cotton skirts and tennis shoes completely hiding her prosthesis.

There was an embarrassing pause before Leah replied in a low voice. "Yes, I lost it in a car accident."

"Does it feel funny?" Sophie ploughed on. "Do you still feel as if it was there?"

I wanted to jump in to deflect the conversation, but she was a child, and children ask questions like that. They are open, honest and ingenuous.

"Just occasionally." Leah adjusted her skirt, pulling it further over her knees.

"So how far up did they cut it off?"

That was a step too far for Madame. "Sophie! That is enough for today. That is a very personal thing to ask."

"*D'accord.*" The child bowed her head, stood up, walked to the edge of the terrace, and gazed out at the sea.

"I am so sorry Madame Leah, sometimes the child, she asks the questions, they are inappropriate." Madame looked flustered.

"It's quite alright, I understand. Children will be children." Leah smiled and offered Madame the plate of a thinly sliced baguette topped with paté.

"It is not wise to tell Sophie she is a child." Madame's fingers delicately removed a slice of bread. "She does not like to be told that."

"I can imagine," I murmured, "but she is a sweet little thing."

"Yes, I am so fond of her, and for a teacher to have such a talented pupil is a dream."

Leah put her head back and closed her eyes. "It's like a dream just living here. I cannot compare it with staying in a cold, wet climate with grey skies overhead all the time."

"And the best part is we are not here for only two weeks, but for as long as we want." I added.

It was good to see Leah happy and relaxed at last, and I only hoped that this morning's incident was a one-off.

MAY LEAH

Dear Diary,

How I love my new home. It's spacious, airy, and to wake in the morning and look out over the bright, blue Mediterranean Sea is just magic. It's a bit weird having Claudette to do all the housework and the cooking. She tells me that when I entertain, she will bring in her cousin to help her. I'm not sure who I'd invite, but I guess we'll get to know a few people soon.

I still can't get my head around being not only a lady of leisure, but a wealthy lady of leisure. The amount of money paid out from the car accident is obscene. I need never work again and, as soon as Bill gets back from England, we will be house hunting in earnest. I'm happy with this villa, I wonder if the owner would be prepared to sell it? Let's see what happens in the next six months.

I will need to find something to do. I'll allow myself another couple of months to laze around and chill out and to keep an eye on Belinda. She has a year to catch up on everything she has missed for her Advanced level GCE and Madame is pushing for her to take the ~~backaloriate~~

~~bacalauriate~~ how do I spell that? baccalauréat général examination as well.

Item one. Learn to speak French as fluently as I can. That's not going to be easy at my age, but I'm going to do my best. I can chatter to Claudette but I'm not sure how colloquial her language is. How can I find out?

I must learn not to worry, that's another project. It took me years to find a balance after my mother's abuse. Then the idyllic life with James, how I still miss my soulmate and our babies. Then a new life with Mason, and look how that ended.

Now it's another new start with Bill. Oh God, will it work out this time? It all looked so hopeful and then there was the dog this morning.

No, Leah, get a grip. That was just some stupid prank from some of the local lads. We're new, foreign, and it's like a test. I'm going to put it to the back of my mind and forget it.

It's wonderful having Aunt Deidre here, she is such a comfort. I still feel so vulnerable when I'm on my own. She is so sensible, a rock and I know I can trust her.

I am going to be positive. A new life, a new start with all the nightmares behind me.

MAY BELINDA

Dear Journal,

Thought Leah was off her head suggesting I write to myself. I mean for f's sake who's ever going to read it but me? Well just let them dare try. It's private, and it's got a bloody great lock on it to keep prying eyes out.

So, here we are living on the south coast of France. It's pretty cool I guess. Can't say I miss the lousy weather. The villa is pretty nice too. My own bathroom, ha, that reminds me of those shows on the telly from America. All those rich spoilt kids had their own bathrooms and their own phones as well. Well now I got both.

There's a really great boy I saw on the beach today. Guess we would have got to speak, if Madame hadn't called me back to the slave factory. I'm gonna make plans to creep out later to see if he is still around. Wow, those abs, and that long wavy hair, but I was too far away to see what colour his eyes were. I'm sure he noticed me. He was sitting next to his surfboard on the beach and I could see him looking at me several times. I hope he didn't notice me gawking at him, but oh, he's so divine. My insides went all wobbly like jelly. He looks older than me, but I've had it with boys. I'm ready to meet a man. Think of how many females in history were married by sixteen. Leah and the other oldies treat me like a child. Sure, I guess I need to pass the exams but it's bloody hard work.

And that brings me to Madame. She gives me the creeps. It's like she can read my mind. She dresses odd too, but maybe that's because she is French. You can tell she's not English the moment you look at her. She's real strict too. I can't take a moment off to even think when she pounces like some cougar leaping from behind a rock. Her hand shoots out and her bony fingers tap the screen while she nags about losing concentration, or asking why I've not finished doing some stupid question. She even stopped me going to get a mid-morning snack. Does she want me to starve? I can't go all that time without a top up. The bloody woman doesn't even leave to go to the loo and give me a chance to sneak out. The moment my butt leaves the chair I hear "And where do you think you're going?" Ugh, I think I could get to hate her. Look, I've scribbled all down this page, but if she was looking over my shoulder she'd be screaming "And where are all the paragraphs?"

I might not like her too much but I'm not sure about Sophie. How can a kid that age know so much? Photographic memory, so what? She looks like an angel, and I hate to admit how quick she is. I'm not a total dummy, I know lots of stuff but, if Madame asks any question, the brat is in there before I can open my mouth. It's not right at that age. She's so full of herself she's not aware how much older and more mature I am. Young people these days just don't consider their elders. Ha, when she was born, I was already in big school. I need to remind her of that. It's time she showed me some respect.

I don't like the way she sidles up to Deidre and Leah either. Butter wouldn't melt in her mouth. Bet they think she's just an angel, and a bloody clever angel at that. Wonder what she wants to do after the exams? Looks as if her parents are filthy rich too. Her clothes aren't cheap. Time to get Leah to fork out for a new wardrobe, now we've got plenty of money. I mean it's only fair, I'm next to being an orphan, aren't I? Dad in prison for life and no mum. Yes, two can play the pity stakes.

I'm too tired to write any more tonight. What's it coming to when I've no one to talk to but some bloody silly book? Still it's good to vent, I guess. That stupid psychiatrist Leah made me see, kept repeating it was bad to bottle things up. So, Journal, it's you and me, and at least you don't talk back to me and order me around.

JUNE DEIDRE

The days are flying by and all is well with the world. Leah is relaxed and cheerful, the most I've ever seen her. Belinda is still grumbling about the 'slave driver' as she calls Madame, but she is getting on with Sophie now. I often see the two of them, their heads together, whispering and giggling. I hate to admit it but, even at age eleven, our little prodigy is mature beyond her years. She does come out with inappropriate comments from time to time, well in English that is; what she says in French I couldn't begin to guess.

While Belinda is slaving away at the dining room table, Leah scuttles off to the room she has converted into a study. She is working so hard on her French I am really impressed. I think it's already better than mine, but I can get by on the stuff I learned at school. I'm much too old to begin now, not at my age.

I've never been one of those judgemental people. Happy to live and let live – that was our mantra in the Flower Power days – but a few things have happened that have unsettled me. I just hoped I was overreacting and that our new found peace wasn't going to be disturbed.

The first was a conversation I overheard yesterday afternoon. I had curled up in the sunroom at the back of the house with a book, and had almost nodded off when I was aware that Belinda and Sophie were whispering outside on the terrace, loud enough for me to hear every word they said.

The subject was of course boys. Belinda was asking for information about the surfer she's been ogling for days.

Sophie's take was he was bad news. Christian was suspected of raping at least two of the girls in the village and one he got pregnant. He denied being the father and refused to take any responsibility. His parents were filthy rich – Sophie's words – and backed him up.

Belinda wanted to know why the pregnant girl's family didn't get a DNA test, and then they would have proof.

Sophie was quite dismissive on this point. According to her, they were too poor to pay and, probably, not clever enough to even know about such things. Giggling, she asked Belinda if she had 'done it'.

I think we all knew the answer to this one. I would have been amazed if she told Sophie she was still a virgin, from what I'd heard about some of her relationships. You don't go clubbing in Weston-super-Mare as often as Belinda did and remain as pure as the driven snow.

At last, the elder girl could boast about experiences that the eleven-year-old could not yet compete with. I was relieved when she refused to give a blow by blow account of what it was like; I didn't need to hear that. I didn't want to eavesdrop either but, if I moved now, they would see me and we would all be embarrassed. I lay still with my eyes closed and pretended to be fast asleep.

I was surprised to hear how honest Belinda was about her past and, although she could be the most infuriating teenager on the planet, I couldn't help but feel a little sorry for her. She'd hardly had a normal life so far.

I cringed when the story came out about Leah in the mental hospital and the information about prison, and, to quote my late mother, Belinda washed all our dirty laundry in public. Maybe the child needed to talk, to share her story with a willing listener and, from what I could hear, Sophie was entranced by every word. She asked a myriad of questions every time Belinda stopped to take a breath.

I had the uncomfortable feeling that our whole lives might well be the talk of the village by next week and I wasn't sure how these simple, rural, French folks would react to our history. We might have been better making for the south of Spain, otherwise known as the Costa del Crime. There were plenty of new arrivals there with secrets to keep.

By the time Madame called the girls in to start lessons again, I had heard enough to make me feel very uneasy. I couldn't see there was anything I could do to protect either Leah or Belinda.

The next unsettling thing happened a few days later and looked quite innocent. I heard Claudette giggling in the kitchen and, curious, I put my head round the door. She was standing by the kitchen table tearing open a brown paper parcel. She looked up and saw me.

"Look," she said in a mixture of English and French. "Is a cute *lapin bleu*."

I froze. She lifted a stuffed blue rabbit from the wrapping and tied the bow neatly around its neck.

"Where did you find that?" I gasped.

"Eeet was on the doorstep. Here, the back door." She pointed to the kitchen door. "*Est jolie,* no?"

"No, no it's not bloody *jolie,* or pretty or nice. Throw it away Claudette, now!"

"But I *comprend pas.*" The smile slid off her face and she looked close to tears.

I took a deep breath and stepped forward to rewrap the offending rabbit in the brown paper but, just as I picked it up, I heard a gasp and turned to see Leah behind me.

"What's that! Where did it come from?"

Now I had never seen the toy which had helped to send Leah on the slide into madness, but I knew the rabbit that haunted her was blue.

I swiftly smothered it in paper and pushed it into Claudette's hands.

"Claudette was just showing me the present she bought for her little niece." I gently pushed the startled housekeeper towards the door.

"But, I have not a…"

"Not now," I hissed at her, but it was too late.

Leah wasn't stupid and I had not fooled her for a moment. She marched across the kitchen and snatched the parcel from Claudette and ripped the paper off. She stared at the rabbit for several seconds and I could see the tears well up in her eyes.

"It's not the same rabbit, Leah. Just a coincidence."

"Oh, you think so? No, of course it's not the same, it's larger for a start, but it's no coincidence. Who knows I live here? Who is trying to frighten me?"

I was lost for words. I did a quick mental calculation. It couldn't be her ex-husband Mason; he was locked up for years to come, and the same for Andrea her ex-best friend. Belinda's brother Leo wasn't due for release any time soon either as far as I knew. Mason had enemies, but why would they target Leah? Would they try and claw back the money Mason had cost them from his ex-wife? Somehow, I couldn't see them playing silly psychological games like this. They would break in, beat us up, and force Leah to sign over her money.

Leah slumped onto a kitchen chair, her head in her hands. Like me, she knew our peaceful life was over. She looked up.

"The dog, on the doorstep, that was the first warning?"

"I don't know, Leah. I honestly don't know. I can't think of anyone who would want to hurt you, or why. Not now. All of them are now in prison."

At the word prison, Claudette took a hasty step backwards. I didn't know how much English she understood, but the expression on her face was not reassuring.

I went to the fridge, grabbed a bottle of wine and a couple of glasses from the shelf. I took Leah firmly by the arm and marched her outside to the far end of the terrace.

"Sit. We'll work this out logically."

As I poured two hefty glasses of dry white, I ran through all the possibilities I could think of. "They would have nothing to gain, Leah. You've tied up most of your money in a trust, and what's left over to buy a house isn't enough reason for any serious criminal to terrorise you. It has to be some local who doesn't want foreigners living here, or mischief makers, young lads out to amuse themselves."

"I can agree about the dog. It was ugly and it gave me a fright, but a rabbit, a blue rabbit? How would they know about that?"

I was reluctant to tell her about my eavesdropping episode, but it provided a plausible explanation. Sophie must have passed on the information to someone in the village, and it gave them the perfect opportunity to scare her and upset the whole family. I wasn't sure if I should mention this to Leah. Relations between her and Belinda could be rocky at times.

I was relieved when Leah appeared to accept my reasoning but, later, I remembered that at no point had Belinda mentioned any of the disturbing events that led to Leah's incarceration. Perhaps Belinda had told Sophie another time when they had been sharing secrets? It was the only possible explanation.

Life was quiet for the next two days, with no more unpleasant surprises. Claudette marched home with the rabbit under her arm. I'm not sure what she thought of our insistence that she remove it and give it to someone in the village. I noticed her give Leah some wary looks but, to my relief, she did not hand in her notice. We had been so lucky to find her and she did an excellent job.

Two days later Belinda barrelled into the kitchen waving a small, gold coloured envelope.

"Guess what! An invitation to dinner at the chateau. Look, isn't it smart?" She thrust it into Leah's hands and dived for the fridge.

Leah turned it over and read it before handing it to me. It was couched in impeccable English, a formal request for the company of… it reminded me of a wedding invitation.

"Who lives at the chateau?"

"Sophie's parents. They probably own the whole effing village." Belinda's words were muffled by the crackers she was stuffing into her mouth.

"You'll need to be on your best behaviour," I reminded her.

"I'll need a new dress," she replied, before biting into a wedge of cheese.

"Keep eating like that and we'll be buying sacks, not dresses." Leah smiled. It was good to see she was back on an even keel.

"They are really quite feudal around here you know," Belinda pronounced. "Almost like back in the Middle Ages in England. All lord of the manor stuff with the rest of the peasants breaking their backs tilling the soil in the blazing sun."

"Belinda! You can't say that! It's so politically incorrect."

"So what, it's the truth. And anyway, they won't know what I'm saying. Only Sophie and Madame understand English."

"I wouldn't be too sure about that," I added. "That is one downside to having help in the house. You need to watch what you say or it will be all round the village." I glared at her, hoping she would connect it with the family secrets she had been sharing with Sophie, but I feared I was wasting my time.

It didn't take long for Belinda to persuade Leah to drive her into Nice to raid the boutiques, since Madame had cancelled afternoon lessons. I suggested to Belinda she choose something modest since she was going to a posh dinner, not a disco. She wrinkled her nose and reminded me she wasn't growing up in the dark ages, and I reminded her that one day she would be old and wrinkly too. She laughed and said that wasn't going to happen for years and years.

I watched them drive off, and settled down for a siesta. I stretched out on the couch, book in hand, as the sun blazed through the windows into the back lounge. I could see the bright blue of the sea and the paler hues of the cloudless sky, and hear distant cries from holiday makers on the beach below. I began to doze, until the crash of breaking glass shook me awake. On the floor next to me was a rock. It had shattered the window and little pieces of glass glittered on the terra cotta tiles. I leapt to my feet and raced to look out over the terrace, but I couldn't see anyone. I listened for the sound of retreating footsteps but, apart from the odd bird cry, the silence wrapped itself around the villa.

I went in search of Claudette, but I couldn't find her anywhere. I grabbed the dustpan and brush and swept up the shards of broken glass, then vacuumed the area thoroughly. There was nothing special about the rock, probably taken from one of the lower walls between here and the beach. I hesitated before I picked it up. Could they get fingerprints off a piece of stone? Was it even wise to notify the police? It was a prank, wasn't it? Youthful vandalism? Being the new arrivals, we were the obvious target. We could handle this without making ourselves unpopular in the area, as long as the incidents didn't escalate. I needed to persuade Leah not to fret and relate it to the past. The dog and the window I could explain, but even I wasn't so sure about the blue rabbit.

As I tossed the rock over the terrace, and straightened up the room I considered concocting a story for Leah, blaming myself for breaking the glass, or a bird that had flown too hard against the window. No, not a good idea, the truth always comes out in the end. I went back into the kitchen to find plastic and tape to cover the hole. I'd ask Claudette to call Old Giles or the local handyman to come and repair it.

I tried to settle down as I waited for Leah and Belinda to come home, but I felt edgy, as if I was being watched. We'd been told there was minimal, if any, crime in the area, and I wondered how safe it would be to leave the villa unoccupied this evening. We should get it fixed now.

I phoned Leah on her mobile to ask her to pop into the hardware store in the village on her way home and ask them to send out a guy to repair the window and gave her the dimensions of the pane. She didn't question me as to how it got broken and I didn't tell her.

When Belinda bounced through the door later, she couldn't wait to show me what she'd bought.

"See how cool this is?" She held it up for inspection.

"I can't see much of it at all," I replied. "What parts of you will it cover? Not a lot I suspect."

"Get with the programme, Deidre!"

"I would if I knew what it was."

She gave me a dirty look and bounded upstairs. Leah walked in looking rather frazzled.

"Tough time?"

"I was so pleased with my French," she sighed, throwing her bag on the chair and flopping onto the couch, "but they speak so fast, and then I get flustered and forget my vocabulary. How do you say 'Have you got this in a smaller size?' when they just stand and stare at you and then go off into reams of gobbledegook. I'm just wishing they spoke English. And then I have Belinda rummaging through all these designer dresses making some very rude comments about them and I'm hoping they don't understand a word of English."

I couldn't help laughing as I went to put on the coffee. Poor lamb, she needed it.

"We went to every shop in town," she said, following me into the kitchen. "Living this close to Monaco I should have guessed the prices would be high, but I saw dresses there that would cost a year's salary to the average person."

"And what did you get for yourself?" I asked.

She looked shamefaced.

"Oh Leah, you can relax, spend what you want."

"Can't get used to it I suppose," she shrugged, and stirred sugar into her coffee mug.

That loud jangling doorbell echoed through the house and I hurried to let in the young man clutching a bag of tools in one hand and a pane of glass in the other. I ushered him into the sun lounge and then went to shoo Leah upstairs to have a shower and a lie down before getting ready for the evening out.

It was typical of Leah to purchase a second hand Ford Focus, not a vehicle that would draw attention or give the world a clue how wealthy she was. We all piled into the car, leaving early having learned that the French dine early and the invite was for 6.30 p.m.

I was relieved to see Belinda was wearing a suitable summer skirt and top, although she'd plastered on the make up with a trowel. She swore as she crammed herself into the back of the car, a good time to remind her that Sophie's parents would speak excellent English, so maybe inappropriate comments might not be a good idea.

"I know when to behave myself. You don't have to worry about me. I'll only say fuck occasionally. In French it's *merde*. Sophie taught me that."

"Why am I not surprised?" I murmured.

I heard her gasp as we drove into the south side of the village, and I noticed the blond god she had been eying up all week. Christian was strolling along, bodyboard tucked under one arm, muscles bulging, and the smallest swim shorts I'd ever seen. He was the picture of macho male arrogance.

I couldn't resist it. "I thought speedos went out of fashion years ago."

"Oh whatever, maybe in England. But they are like, so backward," Belinda shot back, craning her neck to peer at him until we drove round a bend and he was out of sight.

"He's good looking I'll admit, but then he knows it."

That surprised Belinda. "You think he looks cool?"

"In an arrogant, I'm the boss way. I pity the poor woman he gets to order around. Her life won't be worth living."

"Huh," sounded from the back seat.

We all fell silent as Leah drove in through a pair of stone pillars topped by a large lion on one side and what resembled a unicorn on the other. The road wound around beneath an avenue of trees with grasslands beyond and I swear it was almost a kilometre long. In the wing mirror I caught sight of Belinda's mouth. It was hanging wide open.

"Sheeit. This is where Sophie lives?"

"I followed the instructions exactly and it's the right place." Leah's voice was a little breathless.

The house, when it came into view, was set in a U shape, a wing either side of the main façade, in the middle of which was a massive front door reached by a flight of steps sweeping up from the gravelled drive.

Leah parked off a little to one side, only moments before Madame roared up in her beat-up Fiat Uno.

"See Belinda, not the shabbiest car in the park," I laughed.

A moment later a whoosh of gravel and a silver Rolls Royce convertible swept past and parked on the other side of the entrance.

"Bloody hell," was Belinda's reaction. "That's a Rolls Royce, isn't it?"

"Yes, it's got the flying lady called the *Spirit of Ecstasy* on the front. That model is the Dawn Convertible." We sat there like country bumpkins for a moment.

"Fuck me, how much does one of those cost?" Belinda asked, as we opened the doors to get out.

"Most of them are custom built, or have extras designed for the buyer, but I guess they start around three or four hundred thousand. Pounds, that is."

For once, Belinda was silent, and then Madame hurried over to her and gave her a sound kiss on both cheeks. This continental greeting took some getting used to, and I could see Belinda cringe at the familiarity. She would have to accept it in time.

To our horror, we noticed that all the other guests were wearing evening dress. I could have kicked myself for not doing a bit of basic research beforehand. Once, it was the custom to dress for dinner but, after the ravages of two world wars, most places had relaxed the rules. Maybe there was a little truth in Belinda's comment that modern ways had not penetrated as deeply into rural France?

I saw Leah put on a brave face, taking it all in her stride.

The front door opened and Sophie, dressed in a long evening gown, and looking way older than her eleven years, came barrelling down the steps. She stopped and gave Madame a quick bow, then flung herself at Belinda. "I am so happy you are here. Now it is not only me and all the adults with their boring conversation." She rolled her eyes upwards and the girls laughed. They made a strange pair; Belinda so much older, Sophie so much more mature.

The little hostess grabbed Belinda by the hand and marched her up the steps. The other couple had by now disappeared inside and we trailed slowly behind, Madame chattering all the way, explaining how many generations the family had lived here, how they had survived the French Revolution and how much of the neighbouring land they possessed.

At the top of the stairs, we were met by a man in uniform I took to be a butler of sorts. He gave a slight bow, offered to take our wraps or coats and waved us into the hall.

"Sophie!" A voice came floating down from above.

"*Oui Maman.*"

"*Viens ici.*"

"Won't be a moment." Sophie let go of Belinda's hand and raced up the stairs.

Belinda wandered over. "Look at the fucking size of this hall! It's bigger than our whole villa."

"Not far off," Leah replied. "And watch your language!"

Madame had disappeared and the three of us stood awkwardly not quite sure where to go. There was plenty to look at. On either side, at the bottom of the grand staircase, stood a full suit of armour, and every inch of the walls was covered by oil paintings. I guessed from the family resemblance they depicted previous ancestors. Along the edge of the black and white tiled floor were placed small tables with even smaller, spindly chairs. I could see at least six heavy, polished oak doors leading off the hallway.

Belinda did not stop muttering. "Bloody hell, stuff must be worth a fortune. Sophie's family is rolling in it. Bet she can trace her ancestors back generations, and they taught us in school they'd chopped off the heads of all the gentry in the revolution. They were wrong. Fuck me, just look at all this and we thought we were rich."

"Will you stop swearing," Leah hissed at her. "Behave yourself. It is impressive, but take it in your stride. Relax."

There was no stopping Belinda. "Can you imagine having all this space to run around in? You could get lost in here. And, did you notice there were two more buildings either side of the front door. Wonder how many rooms they got?"

"Well I can't see a guide book anywhere, and it would be very rude to ask." Leah was getting agitated.

I turned to see if the butler person was in sight, but he too had disappeared. I wondered how long we were going to be left standing like lemons in the hallway.

I suddenly noticed that Belinda had her phone out and was taking videos of the hallway.

"Put that away." I growled at her.

She shrugged her shoulders and ignored me. "My old friends will never believe this. Geez, I need proof, don't I? Hope they won't think it one of those boring tourist venues. 'This, guys, is where your friend Belinda dined last night. Some pad, eh?'"

Leah reached out and snatched the phone off her, and Belinda's hand shot out to grab it back when there was a flurry at the top of the stairs and an elegant lady whom I took to be Sophie's mother hurried down to greet us.

"Ah *je suis désolé*. Where is Barnard? It is so bad you wait here. Come."

She grabbed my hand and gave it a hearty shake, before moving on to take Leah's and then Belinda's, all the while repeating how sorry she was.

Preceding us, her long green evening dress billowing out behind her like a ship in full sail, she waved us through one of the doors into a grand salon. It resembled those I'd seen on conducted tours in many English stately homes. A large roaring fire in a massive stone fireplace, despite it being June, and sofas, tables and chairs dotted around the rooms. Dressers held porcelain pots which I doubt were from Ikea, and yet more family heirlooms were stuck to the walls.

The other guests were standing close to the fireplace sipping sherry. A middle-aged woman, in what I can only describe as a French maid's outfit approached us, thrusting her tray under our noses.

Before Leah could stop her, Belinda reached out and grabbed a schooner and knocked it back while Leah and I helped ourselves. Before the maid, who didn't look that steady on her feet, could move away, Belinda had commandeered a second glass full of sherry.

I could feel the waves of anger radiating off Leah, but now was not the time or place to take her stepdaughter to task.

Sophie's mother spun round and, pushing Leah forward, made the introductions. "Madame du Pont you know of course. You must meet Monsieur and Madame Fenton. They have also come to call our *belle France* home.

"Call me Humphrey, and my wife Margaret. Very pleased to meet you." There were handshakes all round.

"And here is Madame and Monsieur Morrison."

"Please, Daniel and Geraldine."

"It's a pleasure." More handshakes.

"I am so sorry but Monsieur le Marquis will be late to join us, the business it is so much."

It was difficult to take my eyes off Madame la Marquise as I now learned her title. She was a peacock in her shimmering dress and high heels, always moving as if she dared not stop. Every sentence was accompanied by arm waving and her laughter spilled out like water trickling over a waterfall. Like an animated puppet she encompassed each one of her guests, putting everyone at ease. I almost forgot we had not dressed for the occasion, if only we'd known. We possessed suitable attire but it was still hanging in the wardrobes at the villa.

Belinda's face lit up as Sophie bounced into the room. The elderly maid did not offer her sherry, but rather a small glass of pale pink liquid. I guessed it was watered down wine. I was alarmed to see Belinda dive for another large schooner of sherry. The child would be legless if she carried on that way.

I was pleased to see how relaxed Leah was, chatting to Geraldine Morrison.

"We came and spent all our holidays in the area, then we bought a holiday home and, when Daniel retired, we couldn't wait until we came to live here."

"We've moved into a much larger place now," Daniel added, butting into the conversation. "Are you looking to buy?" he asked Leah.

"I was planning to, yes. I'm renting for the moment."

"We're also renting," Margaret Fenton added. "We've searched high and low but can't find exactly the right place."

After a few minutes of small chat, the butler appeared in the doorway to announce that dinner was served and we all followed him into the dining room.

"Well fuck me!" Belinda exclaimed staring at the polished table which appeared to stretch for yards down the room beneath the chandeliers. The crystals caught the light, reflecting off the glasses and the silverware.

"Will you stop it!" Leah hissed.

The teen shrugged. "Whatever."

I got a sinking feeling in my stomach. There would be more wine with dinner and Belinda had had way too much to drink already.

Small cards placed at each serving told us where to sit, and I was alarmed to see that Sophie and Belinda were next to each other, way out of reach. Neither Leah nor myself would be able to rein her in if her behaviour deteriorated.

The food was excellent, as you would expect. I wasn't sure what each dish was, but it tasted divine. As so often happens, there was a lull in the conversation as we were drinking the soup and Belinda picked up on a remark Madame la Marquise made to Humphrey Fenton about the difficulties in maintaining such a large estate.

"The chateau, it is so old, always there are so many works to make it is a battle all the time."

"We have lots of old piles in England too," a voice rang out from the bottom of the table. "You should invite the tourists in. Charge them fifty Euros a head for a tour and you could rake in the cash."

There followed one of those silences as everyone looked in horror at Belinda who was oblivious to her faux pas. She continued to make it worse. "Some of them have attractions in the grounds as well; old steam traction engines, fun fairs, even zoos and wildlife parks. You have to pay to go into those separately, so that's more money."

I glanced at Sophie's face, even she looked alarmed.

Leah rushed in to fill the gap. "I don't think everyone understands your sense of humour Belinda. I'm sure Madame has no such ideas."

"*Non!*" Madame la Marquise took a long gulp of wine.

Daniel Morrison turned to Leah. "Brand. Did I hear correctly that's your surname?"

"Yes." Leah's voice was barely above a whisper.

"Any relation to Mason Brand?" Daniel picked up his wine glass but never took his eyes off Leah.

"I was married to him, but the final divorce papers should be through any day."

"Do you know him?" I asked, staring hard at Daniel.

"Not well." He dropped his eyes as he speared the duck on his plate.

"Daddy's in prison," Belinda's voice floated out. "For life," she added with a deal of satisfaction, and downed more wine. I watched, my heart sinking, as the ever-attentive butler replenished her glass.

Leah beckoned to him and he came, prepared to pour wine for her, but Leah placed her hand over her glass. She tried to whisper not to give Belinda any more drink, but I don't think he understood.

The only person who was enjoying herself was Sophie. She was bright red in the face from holding in the laughter, but the tears of mirth streamed down her cheeks. Her shoulders shook as she slid down in her chair aware that her maman was not amused in the slightest.

By this time both Leah and I were wishing the ground would open up and swallow us both. I was reluctant to take the lead. Should we get up now and remove Belinda before she could do any more damage, or hope things wouldn't get any worse?

They did.

"Prison, oh my!" Margaret Fenton's eyes were like

saucers. "You poor thing," she added, as if to excuse her rudeness.

"Yup, for murder, and they don't let you out easy for that, even in England." Belinda's voice penetrated the silence again.

"Uh, quite." Margaret's hands shook as she sliced into the caramelised onion.

Leah went on the offensive. There were occasions when she was a lot tougher than she looked.

"How do you know my husband?" she asked Daniel, making eye contact.

He paused, and I noticed a slight tic at the corner of one eye. "Early business dealings," he replied abruptly. He turned to the Marchioness. "What date is the village fair this year?"

Margaret Fenton nudged my arm and whispered in my ear. "I didn't realise, didn't make the connection. The trial was all over the newspapers, dreadful story. So that's the poor prison widow. You a relative?"

She startled me. We were dining in style, in a chateau hosted by the nobility, but gossip and curiosity were the same the world over.

"Not a blood relative no, but I'm very fond of Leah. She's been through a lot and I respect her more than anyone I know."

"I thought I saw her in the village with a man. A brother?"

I sighed. It was impossible to avoid such direct questions without being rude, and Belinda had done enough damage already.

"A friend." I hoped that would be the end of it. Before

Margaret could grill me further, I was saved by the late arrival of Jules Lampierre, the Marquis.

He was as charming and elegant as his wife, full of apologies in almost flawless English for his unforgiveable behaviour to their guests. He'd been out on the farm attending one of his prize mares giving birth. He had high hopes the foal would take the Arc de Triomphe at Longchamp.

I heard Sophie telling Belinda that was the most prestigious race in the French horseracing calendar.

The rest of the evening passed without any more embarrassment, if you ignore the fact Belinda had passed out at the end of table. Her head had slumped onto her arms resting on her side plate, her hair spreading out over the tablecloth.

"I must apologise for my stepdaughter," Leah said as we left the table. "She is not used to sherry, or wine, and I think it was all a little much."

"We quite understand," Geraldine Morrison smiled at her. "We also have trouble with the boys when they come out."

"No, we don't," Daniel contradicted her.

"But darling…" She got no further as he took her arm firmly, much too firmly I thought, and frog marched her out into the hallway.

Madame du Pont, who I don't remember uttering a word all evening, whispered in my ear. "No lesson tomorrow. I think Belinda will sleep late, no?"

I put my hand on her shoulder. "Thank you."

She grinned, and together we went to help Leah prise the unconscious teenager off the table.

There was total silence in the car as we drove home, except for a few snores from the back seat.

As Leah drove in through the gates and up the gravel drive, I saw that Claudette must have left the exterior lights on before she left, but she would not have left the front door wide open.

JUNE LEAH

Dear Diary,

I should be asleep in bed by now. Its late, but I'm so wound up I know I'll just lie there and worry.

What a month, my head is in such a whirl. I'm damned if I want to rely on a man to help me. I wanted to scream when Bill phoned to say he was flying to Melbourne to help his daughter who was going through a difficult divorce and he'd be away longer than he expected. Deidre is a great comfort and so sensible and down to earth, but I still feel vulnerable depending on another woman.

I love it here in the south of France, and the villa is beautiful with its views over the Mediterranean Sea, which really is bright blue most of the time. But I can't shake off a feeling of impending doom. Am I being paranoid or do I have a good reason to be fearful?

Let me list the events. That blue rabbit unsettled me more than I let on. It wasn't identical of course to the one that frightened me in the London house, but what are the chances of a stuffed toy, of the right animal and the same colour appearing on the kitchen table here in France? I could see Deidre was doing her best to gloss over it but I think she was rattled as well. I hope I never see it again. It's not as if I could go to the police and report it. That would be a very good reason to lock me up in the nearest mental home.

If someone told me a year ago, when I was living in a flat in wet and windy Weston-super-Mare, that I would be dining with minor royalty in a French chateau with a butler pouring my wine, I would have laughed. I wandered into a different world for a few short hours, spoiled by Belinda making a scene and embarrassing us all. Why can't that child keep her mouth shut? Yes, she's been through a lot, with both her mother and father, and then the trouble in Weston, but she's still such a child, arrested development they'd probably call it. I wonder if Sophie will be good for her? The child is wise beyond her years, but my greatest hope is she will spur Belinda on to work hard for these wretched exams. She has really fallen behind and I can see she's struggling under Madame du Pont's discipline. That woman is a slave driver, even I have to admit that. She was very quiet last night, but perfectly at ease. She's probably part of the *noblesse oblige* herself. I didn't enjoy the experience, except the food was divine. We were dressed all wrong of course, how were we to know? They should really have said formal attire on the invitation.

Quite apart from Belinda's insufferable comments, Daniel Morrison knows Mason. How? Was Mason his lawyer? Is Daniel another client my soon-to-be Ex argued an obscure point of law that allowed him to escape prosecution? Or, is he one of those who threatened him and forced him to flee abroad? I doubt he'll tell me. Is the south of France home to a criminal element?

Then tonight we came home and found someone had been in the house. That gives me a real creepy feeling. Nothing had been taken, except some of Belinda's electronics, so she tells us, but they left such a mess behind. It has to be more teen pranks, throwing food on the floor and spraying paint on the walls; it's the sort of thing they do. I have no idea what the words they wrote mean, so that's lost on me, and I'm not sure I want to know. It was pure destruction. I'll have to get in professional cleaners. It would take days for us to clean it all up. I wonder what Claudette will say when she arrives for work in the morning? I can only hope she won't hand in her notice and walk straight out. I wouldn't blame her. I can't imagine what she thinks of us.

JUNE   BELINDA

Dear Journal,

I don't fucking believe it. Some scum broke into the villa and made a bloody awful mess. Geez, I thought they were nice people around here. It's as bad as it was in London and Weston. How dare they!

The bastards have taken my old phone, my iPod and my iPad and my standing charger. All my stuff is on the cloud but some greasy filth is probably pawing through my photos right now. I must put a block up soon, but it's hard to think straight. There are a dozen men inside my head all hammering away. Wow their wine is strong, or was it the sherry? I haven't drunk much for a while; Leah would notice if I flattened the wine. But hell, they were tiny glasses.

I had no idea Sophie lived in such splendour and she must have one of those titles or something like her mum and dad. She never said. How'd you get around in a place that size? Bet they've not been in some of the rooms for weeks, no, years. I'll get her to give me a tour. Now, there's a thought. I've told her lots about my life, but I don't know anything about her. Time to give her the third-degree next time I see her.

I could feel Deidre's eyes boring into me at dinner, and Leah wasn't much better. What does she expect? I think she was just as rattled. If we knew we had to tart up, then I could have got her to get me that cool dress with the sequins that went right down to the floor. Of course, she didn't like it, moaning about how it all but let my boobs drop out. Like to see those old fuddy-duddys' eyes pop out too.

So, we sit there like lemons in semi-smart gear, and they're all togged out in clothes suitable for the Emmy Awards. Good thing Madame was also a guest and let me off slaving over a hot book all day and give us time to go shopping.

At least all the guests spoke English, but I couldn't hear everything they said as Sophie was whispering in my ear most of the time, well as much as I remember. The last part of the evening is a bit of a blank. Don't remember how I got home, was a bit out of it but, seeing what those bastards did to my room, then I was mad. I'll grill Sophie and see if she can spill the beans. She must know everyone in the area, and I guess most of them work for her father. Now, there's a guy; her dad is one cool dude, and loaded as well. And I thought we were rich, hell we're paupers, even with all Leah's insurance money. She's so bloody tight with it. Why can't we have a decent car, like that Rolls Royce that the other couple came in? That is really cool. Everyone would take notice of us then. No, she has to get a scruffy Ford Focus that belonged to someone else before us. How cheap can you get? Hey, you got money, you flaunt it.

Fuck, my head hurts, but I'll have to get up; I need to check my old phone is blocked. If Madame turns up, she can go take a hike, I'm not bashing my brains out over any sodding books today. I'm only going to write it here, but she freaks me out. There's no getting past her. She sees everything, I swear she can read my mind. She even warned me off leading Sophie away. I think she means astray, making her behave badly. Poor kid never had a chance to have any fun. Bet they're as stuffy every day like last night. Wonder if they will ever ask us to dinner again? Probably not, but I'll get Sophie to take me round the house. That should be a laugh.

JULY   DEIDRE

Breakfast the following morning was a very solemn affair. Leah crept in like a wraith and said nothing as she fiddled with the coffee pot. Her hair, still wet from the shower, was tied back with an elastic band, and her orange t-shirt clashed horribly with the red shorts. Her shoulders were hunched like the first time she had sought sanctuary with me in Weston, and her hands shook slightly as she pulled the mug from the machine.

I walked over and, taking it from her unsteady hand, I placed it on the table before giving her a big hug. "There, there. It's going to be fine. I'm here and I'm not leaving, not before Bill gets back."

She pulled away. "Really? Even when the decorators have finished?"

"My place is not going anywhere, unless we all move over there while they repaint this place."

We looked at the graffiti spread across the walls. "Bright colours." Leah attempted a giggle.

"Budding art students maybe?"

We both laughed, but it was forced.

Belinda stomped in and made for the fridge. "What's to eat?"

"Wet cardboard suit you?" I asked. "At the rate you eat would you know the difference?"

"Oh, very funny." She grabbed cheese, ham and a tomato, then raided the bread bin and liberated two croissants. "Sophie tells me they would never have fried bacon and eggs for breakfast in France. Weird eh? Leah, I need to borrow your tablet or laptop. Those bastards took mine last night and Madame will have a cadenza when she finds all my work gone."

Leah whirled round. "You've lost all your work? Gone – all of it?"

"No, don't be silly." Belinda waved her knife around like a conductor's baton. "It's all up there in the cloud but I need to get it back down again. And I need a new tablet and a laptop." She plastered the cheese on the pastry and hacked off several slices of ham.

"What a good thing Leah didn't buy you that Airbook you were after."

"Not yet." Belinda took a huge bite, her cheeks filling out like a hamster.

"It won't be today." Leah finished off her coffee and helped herself to some of Belinda's ham and cheese.

"Hey!" she protested.

"Share or go without," her stepmother snapped.

"Huh. Don't shout, my head's in agony."

"As you may have guessed, Madame du Pont is giving you a day off to recover from your hangover."

"I'm not hungover!"

"Of course you are. Look at you. You were out of it last night. You passed out at the table."

"I didn't!" Belinda stared down at the table, hiding behind a curtain of hair.

"You don't have to believe me. Ask Deidre, ask Sophie."

"Sheeeit," was the only reply as Belinda continued to stuff food into her mouth.

"We're all in the same boat," I said brightly. "Lots to clear up. We can't leave it all to Claudette. And it will give us a chance to see what else might be missing. Strange Belinda, they took your laptop and not Leah's?"

"Yeah well. Probably, 'cos it's got more interesting stuff on it."

"It wouldn't happen to be on the cupboard over there, would it?" Leah's sharp eyes didn't miss much.

"Oh fuck." Belinda was not pleased. "Well they did take my iPad and my iPod. I need to get new ones."

I looked at Belinda's face. She was lying. When we left the villa last night, we had left money lying about, Leah's bracelet was on the sink and my mobile phone was on the coffee table. It was all there when we got home. I had a strong feeling that nothing had been stolen. Why? The invaders had caused damage but they had not taken a thing. Maybe they didn't need the money or preferred not to handle stolen goods. Were they rich kids having a laugh? I hoped that was the case and it wasn't something more sinister, but I couldn't shake off the feeling of doom that surrounded the villa and its inhabitants.

Leah managed to track down a company in Cannes that sent a team of three workmen who scrubbed and painted at a frenetic speed and had the place back to normal in two days. If I understood their foreman, this job was a pleasure. Often, they had to clean up after a corpse had been found days or weeks after death, or the criminals had smeared faeces over the walls and furniture. His opinion was these scoundrels as he called them had, in comparison, been very kind. I wasn't sure I agreed with him.

All went quiet for a couple of weeks, but I determined to find out more about the guests at the dinner, and the best person to ask was Madame du Pont. I saw her relaxing in the sun lounge one siesta and took her a cup of her favourite coffee and a plate of biscuits.

"How is Belinda doing?" I asked, settling opposite her.

"She is improving, but I remind her every day to concentrate, to think, to complete the tasks. They are lazy in England in the schools, no?"

"Some are, I guess. Others work very hard."

"I see on television that pupils are very rude to their teachers. Here in France we respect our *professeurs* and obey them."

I hated to agree with her but there was truth in her words. "I'm sure Belinda respects you."

"Hmm." Madame was non-committal.

"Is it too early to tell if she will pass her exams?"

"We have some months yet." Madame evaded the question.

"Did the Morrisons mention at dinner the other night, they have children here too?"

"Two boys, they are fifteen and seventeen."

"And they go to school locally, or have a private tutor like Belinda and Sophie?"

"No, they attend a boarding school in England. They are here in the holidays."

"I think it's a shame to have children and then send them away for most of the time."

Madame gave a shudder. "Not those two. They are, how you say it, 'hell on wheels'. They give their parents much worry."

"Oh dear." I pushed the plate of biscuits towards her and smiled as she leaned forward and took one. "Difficult to get into mischief in this rural part of France?"

The *professeur* became more animated. She sipped her coffee and settled back in her chair. "They are very naughty. One time they drove away in the truck for Old Giles and, when it had no more petrol, they left it in the middle of the street in Cannes."

I gasped putting my hand to my mouth. "Goodness!"

"And that was not the worst. They stole two of the hunting dogs and then made them to fight. One died."

"Oh, that's dreadful." This time I was shocked.

"There have been complaints too about them harassing the village children. And also, they stole all Madame Couterie's washing and dumped it in the river. Poor woman, she washes for people in the village, and it gave her a lot of work."

Before Madame could list all the criminal activities the Morrison boys had got up to, I steered the conversation in the direction I wanted to take it. "Those poor parents, how do they cope?"

She shrugged and twisted her necklace between her fingers. "They think it very funny, but then the local families became very angry and they went to talk to them."

"And did that help?"

"I don't know. I don't think so. There have been more incidents since then. If it happens many more times they might be asked to leave. But they are rich," she continued, "they spend a lot of money in the village and employ many people."

"They have a chateau like the Lampierres?"

"Oh no, no, no. But their house is very large and they have much land and their wine is famous and it has won a lot of awards. But they bought the winery with the house. I do not think they know a lot about making wine; they employ many people to grow the grapes and mix the blends."

"Have they lived here for a long time?"

Madame thought for a moment. "No, perhaps five years."

"Looking at the prices for property in this area, they must, indeed, be very wealthy."

Madame leaned forward and lowered her voice. "It is said that they were connected to the criminal gangs in London, with drugs and fraud, and that is why they came here."

I pretended to be less interested than I was, but I immediately wondered if that's where the connection with Mason came in. Had he defended them at any time in court? I decided to go through the paperwork that Leah had packed up from the London house and see what I could find.

"Are their boys here at the moment?" I wondered if they'd been responsible for the damage to the villa.

She put her head to one side and thought for a moment. "I don't think so, but it is possible."

Another thing to check. Was it British half term a couple of weeks ago?

I was about to grill Madame about the Fentons, the other couple from the dinner, but she glanced at her watch, jumped to her feet, and announced it was time to get back to work. She swept out of the lounge, her voice cracking as she shrieked for Belinda and Sophie to come quickly.

I waited until Leah had taken Belinda into Nice, on yet another shopping trip. Belinda was always keen to help relieve her stepmother of her insurance money. There had been a big row with Madame, but this time, Belinda won. She threw a typical toddler temper tantrum and insisted on taking the day off.

Claudette had asked to go home early as her elderly mother was not feeling well, so I had the villa to myself.

I didn't feel at all guilty; I saw this as a way to protect Leah. It could explain the break in, and also put us on our guard with the Morrisons. A couple of times Leah had mentioned that she had run into Geraldine Morrison in the village and they'd had coffee together. They were, she told me, becoming great friends. I had my suspicions about that after my talk with Madame.

It was several days before I got a chance to creep upstairs where Leah had stored Mason's paperwork. She'd not put the London house on sale; Leo would be out of jail in a few years and it was his family home. She had removed personal stuff on the advice of Mason's lawyer but, as far as I knew, the house was standing empty. It wasn't up to Leah to let it out, and she didn't want to get involved anyway. Some official, apparently representing Mason's law firm, told her what to take and said they would travel over and collect anything they might need. I did wonder why they didn't ask for the paperwork to be returned to the office. Did they know how many files Mason kept at his house? Probably not. He was the head of the firm and he didn't have to share information with his employees. They simply acted on his instructions after he was locked up and Leah, of course, also did as she was told.

If it had been me, I would either have laid out all the documents on the tables and kitchen counter tops in the London house, or I would have burned the lot. Leah followed orders and, along with her personal belongings, had the files transported to the villa and locked them away in the attic.

It had taken me a while to find the key. I peeked in Leah's drawers in her suite but drew a blank. I went back down to the kitchen and sorted through the key rack. Leah didn't have a deceitful bone in her body, why would she hide it? The huge bunch of keys jangled as I marched back up the stairs.

The extendable ladder creaked as I yanked it down, climbed the wobbly steps and, after a frustrating ten minutes, I found the one which unlocked the trap door and pushed it up and over.

The air disturbed the dust which made me sneeze. I eyed the piles of boxes stacked neatly on the floor. It was going to take time to go through them all, and I considered asking Leah to help, but I didn't want to worry her. She didn't see the Morrisons as a threat, and I wasn't going to undermine her confidence in forming a new friendship with Geraldine. Leah was wary of making friends, with very good reason.

I started with the box on the far left. The cardboard was sturdy and the lid slid off with a loud sucking sound. Inside was a bundle of files, I opened the first one. It contained a lot of personal stuff relating to Mason and made for fascinating reading. I found copies of his birth certificate, and one for a brother, Michael. I didn't know he had a brother. He also had a sister, Jay, and I wondered where they were. Did Leah know? Perhaps she had met them at the wedding.

Digging deeper I found old school reports, saw that Mason had been expelled from at least two schools and then the surprising discovery that at one point, when Mason was about fourteen, his parents had won a lot of money. I read a letter in which his father had confirmed they wanted no publicity, despite the incentives offered by the competition organisers.

Earlier photographs showed them standing outside a shabby terraced house in Bradford, but in later ones they were seated in the garden of a fair-sized house in the suburbs of London. They had changed their lifestyle, moved up in the world, and sent Mason to a boarding school. There was no mention of Michael and Jay. What had happened to them?

I repacked the first box and started on the second one. This one contained legal files, correspondence, police reports, lists of witnesses, signed statements, court dates, and more. I checked the defendant's name. Wilkins. On to the next.

The time flew past as I checked each file, put it to one side and went on to the next. I counted the boxes, fifteen, and I had only started on number three when I opened a file near the bottom and found what I was looking for.

'Pertaining to the arrest of Daniel Alexander Morrison, of 15 Orchard Road, in the… charged with… on the…'

My eyes flew over the words. And there it was – counsel for the defence: Mason Brand & Associates. Had Mason won the case? I flicked through the papers furiously and then I heard the brakes on Leah's car squeaking as she turned into the driveway.

I feverishly stuffed the files back into the box, tucked the bulky Morrison papers under my skirt, and scooted down the stairs. I only just managed to replace the keys before Belinda skipped into the kitchen clutching armfuls of branded carrier bags.

"Hey Deidre, you should have come, bought something more up to date." She nodded at my cotton shirt and long Indian style skirt. "They even had stuff for old people too, and some of it was quite cool."

I held my tummy in to disguise the bulky paperwork I was hiding and only nodded as I made a rapid exit from the room.

"Hey, you're not upset I called you old, are you?" Belinda's voice floated up the stairs behind me.

"No. Just uh, going to the loo. Back in a moment." I hoped that would satisfy her, as I wiped the sweat off my forehead. This sneaking around made me feel very uncomfortable.

I looked around my room. Where could I hide the files? Under the bed, top of the wardrobe, bottom of a drawer? In the end I dragged my suitcase out of the dressing room and packed the papers inside the lining and zipped it up. A professional thief would find it with no problem but it was the best I could do. Now I needed some peace and quiet and privacy to read it all.

Belinda picked up I was distracted at dinner that night. She was doing her best to persuade us to go out to the cinema.

"But all the movies will be in French," Leah said.

"That's the whole point. We should choose one that we have seen so we'll know the story. It's got to be good practice, Leah. Come on, don't be such a drag." Belinda was determined to get her own way.

Leah glanced at me. "You'll come as well?"

It was the last thing I felt like doing. I wanted to start combing through all that paperwork and go raid the boxes to see if there were other files pertaining to one Daniel Morrison, but one look at her face and I couldn't refuse her. While Belinda had bounced back quickly after our home invasion, it had left the adults on edge.

We all piled into Leah's little Ford and set off. The evening was a success; the comedy had us all laughing, even if we missed part of the plot, and Belinda positively glowed when she persuaded Leah to stop off at a fast food joint so she could get greasy chips and a hamburger.

As I wriggled down in bed that night, eyeing the suitcase in the corner, I knew just where to go to study the papers. I smiled as I closed my eyes and went to sleep.

We were all woken by an enormous bang from outside at the front of the house. Leah and I bumped into each other as we came flying out of our rooms, pulling on dressing gowns, then flew down the stairs.

I grabbed a knife and a broom from the kitchen and

held on to Leah's arm before she opened the front door. Neither weapon would be much use, but it was a comfort to be holding something.

The moment we eased open the front door, the heat slammed into us like hitting a brick wall. Another explosion rocked what was left of Leah's car as the flames licked over the paintwork.

She gasped and fell back against the doorframe.

I peered into the darkness but the bright light from the fire made it impossible to see if anyone was out there. The noise of the metal engine parts crackled and spat, drowning out any footsteps or sounds of a car driving off in the distance.

Belinda arrived and stood staring. "Oh sheeeit! What a fuck up."

"I guess that's one way of describing this. Leah, you're going to have to go to the police now."

She nodded, and I saw the tears running down her face.

"Bloody hell. How long will it take to get another car? We can't be stuck at home without getting around. Be like prisoners."

"We've still got my car, so we're not locked in," I said. Trust Belinda to think of the practicalities.

"Hey," the teenager brightened up. "Say Leah, can we get a proper car this time, a sports car, like that yellow one that goes past? Now that would be real cool."

"Do you know who owns that car?" I asked her, remembering how it nearly drove us off the road.

"Nah, but it's so French, and so summery, and they can go like the clappers." She paused, and then she took a step outside and looked at the burning wreck. "Who would have done this?"

I think it dawned on her that we were a target; that our lives might be in danger.

"Who would do this?" she whispered. "What have we ever done to them?"

I dropped my makeshift weapons on the floor and put my arm around her. "I don't know, Belinda. We must hope the police can find out and lock them away."

"How come I'm surrounded by jail birds?" Her voice wobbled as her bravado drained away and she cuddled closer and began to sob.

I put my other arm out and gathered Leah into the group hug and we stood together as the flames burnt down before us.

We saw car lights appear at the end of the driveway and looked fearfully as they drew closer. Several of the neighbours had come to see what was happening. They chattered away like starlings as they got out and observed the burning wreck. Much shaking of heads and tutting but whether they came to either gawk or offer their condolences, I couldn't decide. They all looked shocked, and I hoped they were not planning to go to the mayor to have us moved on.

One tall man, dressed in a pale blue shirt and blue trousers, stepped forward.

"We don't need to call the police Leah; they are here already."

He bowed his head and introduced himself as Monsieur I'agent Francois Ecole, gendarme.

We pulled apart and led him into the house.

Leah rushed off to make the coffee, bumping into Claudette who had also arrived with the crowds now gathered around what was left of the Ford. There was much discussion in rapid French and lots of arm waving. I could only guess they were suggesting the cause and effect.

Leah returned to the lounge and sat next to Belinda on the couch as the gendarme pulled a notebook and pencil from his pocket.

"My English she is leetle," he apologised. "but you can tell me how…" He waved towards the front door.

"I have no idea. We went to the cinema and then we came home and we went to bed. Then bang! The noise, and we saw the car on fire."

"You did not see the people who do this thing?"

We shook our heads.

"We were all fast asleep," Belinda stated, and it was only then that I noticed she was not in her nightclothes but dressed in jeans and a sweatshirt. Had she been planning to creep out, or did she stop to get dressed before rushing out to see what caused the explosion?

Francois Ecole looked at her jeans for a moment but didn't pursue the question I was longing to ask.

"I am so sorry Madame Brand for your loss. Can you to please tell me if you have any enemies? You know someone who does not like you? Who wants to hurt you?"

"No, no I don't." Leah's reply was convincing. I'm not sure that was the truth. This was a step beyond a teen prank, wasn't it?

"Tell him about the break-in too," urged Belinda. She turned to the gendarme. "They smashed their way in while we were out to dinner at the chateau, and they painted rude words on the walls and threw all our stuff around."

"Yes, I know. You have the Belize brothers from Cannes to make it all clean again."

Of course, we should have guessed that everyone in the village and beyond would know everything. In rural parts gossip was rife.

"It's just a prank, right?" Leah asked.

Ecole's brow furrowed. "Prank? This I do not know."

"A joke, or vandalism," I explained.

"Ah, no. This ees serious. This ees not a joke. You have nothing else to tell me? The time?"

Belinda looked at her watch.

"No, idiot, the time we heard the explosion." Leah sighed. "We were all in bed by midnight, and it was some time after that."

"It was close to two am," Belinda said.

The gendarme nodded at her and scribbled in his book. He eased himself out of the chair. "Please not to touch the car, tomorrow or soon; the forensics they will come to look at it." He reached into his pocket and pulled out a card. "My brother, he has a garage in Cannes. He has good cars to sell. He will sell you another very soon."

I bet he will, I thought. "We will need a case number, for the insurance claim," I said out loud.

He walked towards the door. "Come to the station tomorrow. I will give you a number. Now I am not at work."

"That's bleeding obvious," muttered Belinda and, in case she said more, I gave her arm a hard squeeze and growled at her.

We straggled after Francois Ecole along the hallway and out of the front door. Only half a dozen neighbours were still hanging around the bonfire which was now little more than a pile of ashes floating over the scarred metal shell. They flocked towards the gendarme badgering him with questions. More arm waving, more raised voices; they hustled around him as he climbed into his car and drove off. Looking back at the house, the door firmly closed, the show was over and the last few left.

Claudette was nowhere to be seen, so we guessed she must have walked home across the field. We checked all the doors and windows were firmly locked and went back to bed.

The following morning everyone was very subdued. The car wreck, right outside the front door, sent shivers down my spine. Even if it was local lads having fun, the Brand villa was their main target and that was not a comfortable thought. Why us? Had we upset any of the local boys? I briefly wondered if Belinda had, as she would describe it, pissed them off?

Madame du Pont drove in with Sophie and they both scrambled out to peer at the burnt-out wreckage, tutting and exclaiming in rapid French. They had of course heard all about it on the grapevine and they were full of apologies for the terrible acts of their fellow citizens.

Madame clutched Leah and poured out streams of unintelligible words, her distress littered with *je suis désolé* over and over again. She was sorry, we were sorry, but who was not sorry?

We left Belinda giving them a dramatic blow by blow account of the events from last night while Leah and I first went to the police station to sign official statements, and then drove into Cannes to find the car showroom belonging to Francois' brother.

"Thank goodness your car was parked in the garage, or they might have set light to that as well," Leah muttered as we walked up and down the row of cars, their paintwork glistening, their tyres boot-polished black.

I stopped by an open topped British Racing Green MG.

"Not a chance!" Leah laughed for the first time in hours. "You're as bad as Belinda. No, I'm going for sensible. Maybe an SUV with one of those alarm systems that scream if anyone gets too close."

The other Ecole brother came hurrying over. Of course, he had heard of the terrible accident. The Madame was a victim and we were subjected to lots more *désolés*, arm waving and words spilling out so fast the locals would have struggled to keep up.

At first Leah battled to communicate with her new found French, but Berlinda had downloaded a translation app on her phone, and that made the negotiation a simple process.

Two hours later we drove away with promises ringing in our ears that we could come and collect tomorrow; all the paperwork would be completed and Madame could drive away in her new car, which was the very best choice at the very best price of all the cars in the garage.

"I'm exhausted." Leah resembled a piece of wilted lettuce.

"Let's stop for lunch and try and make sense of all this."

We settled down at a pavement café, ordered our food and sipped a glass of wine.

"What do we know? Let's make a list." I pulled out my notebook and began to write. "We had a rock thrown through the window."

"A break-in where they sprayed the walls and wrecked the place."

"The car torched."

"And the dead dog on the doorstep."

I'd forgotten that, and added it to the list.

"And we've not heard of any other similar damage from other people in the area?"

Leah shook her head. "No, I asked Geraldine, and she said everywhere had been very quiet."

"Who could be targeting you, wanting revenge? Let's list names as well."

I saw tears appear in the corner of Leah's eyes.

"I don't know."

The waiter came over with the food. Fish for Leah and a salad for me. We assured him that would be all. I continued to scribble as we ate.

"Mason must be top of the list. He's furious you're still alive and collected all the money, and he wants to get back at you."

"But Deidre, he's in prison."

"Many prisoners have outside contacts, a third party who owes them a favour."

"I doubt Mason has enough money to make it worth their while to come and terrorise me. And I suspect he has more enemies in prison, those he defended and failed to win their case."

"OK, so maybe he's not top of the list and, even if he's a model prisoner, it's unlikely he'd be out in less than fifteen years."

Leah speared a bean and paused. "I'd be more likely to think Leo would be spiteful."

"He won't have the money either. Sure, he'll be furious he didn't get his hands on your money, but I'd think his resources outside the prison walls would be even less plausible than Mason's reach."

We both sat for a while.

"Andrea?" There was a wobble in Leah's voice as she said the name.

"Your ex-best-friend? She's more likely to find another victim to con. No, I think we can cross her off, but I'll put her name down anyway."

Leah glanced at the notebook. "Oh dear, I do have a lot of enemies, don't I?"

I patted her hand. "I know it sounds ridiculous, but don't take any of this personally. You are a very rich woman. To be honest they don't care about you, it's the money they're after. A few million goes a long way, even these days."

"I'm not sure I want all this cash," Leah sighed. "It's not as if I wanted to buy planes and jet skis and mega yachts."

"Belinda would like that," I replied, and we both laughed.

"Another couple of years and she will be off." Leah wiped her hands on her serviette and took a sip of wine. "Deidre, you don't think Bill is involved, do you?"

I was tempted to immediately say 'no way', but I

wanted to think first. "I don't think so for one minute. No, it's very, very unlikely. You know I'm a little fey, and I've never had any vibes he's anything sinister. No, I think Bill is straight-up. Look Leah, it's more likely to be an ex-client of Mason's. If one of them feels cheated, they may well come after you for what they feel is rightful compensation."

Maybe I should not have said anything, but I saw her face turn pale and her hands shook, and her wine glass rattled as she dropped it on the table.

"The boxes," she said. "Mason's papers, do you think the answer is in one of those?"

Now was the time for me to confess. I nodded and told her how Daniel Morrison's remark at dinner had tempted me into beginning a search.

Once we had a plan, Leah bounced back. "You've given me hope, Deidre. I'm not going to sit still and be a victim. We're going to find out who is doing all this stuff and fight back." She wiped away the tears and sat up in her chair. "They have no idea what they are up against. No one is going to drive me into a snivelling wreck again."

I breathed a sigh of relief. This was the girl who had married my favourite nephew, James. She had courage, and I was going to do everything I could to help her.

JULY LEAH

Dear Diary,

I have taken on a new lease of life. I am going to be strong and not let these whoever they are get me down. Deidre is such a comfort, a rock-solid person, and she's keeping me grounded and given me courage. Neither Mason, nor his cronies have any right to my money. Since Mason ran out on me, I've not taken a cent from him and I'm looking after his daughter for free, now I think of it. I've never hurt him in any way. Hell, I've put up with a lot, but no more. As for his sleazy friends, they don't deserve my money either. Maybe they think Mason had stashed away the proceeds of his rotten law firm and that's the money I have access to. Well they're wrong, and if we find out who it is, I'll tell them. Not sure how I'd do that, but I'll think of something.

Tomorrow Deidre and I will start combing through all those files. She did mention there may be more back at Mason's old law firm. Maybe he's running that from jail, who knows? But there was a reason he kept this paperwork at home, and maybe it will give us some clues.

I'm quite excited about my new car. I feel quite brave

paying so much for another, and I've not had to wait for the insurance payout either. First car I've ever had that is bright red. Glad I'm still sensible though and bought a pre-owned. New cars lose so much of their value the moment they are driven out of the showroom. I do hope no one destroys this one. We'll squeeze both into the garage at night.

Please let August be a quieter month than June and July. All I want is a peaceful life.

JULY   BELINDA

Shit me, there's never a dull moment in our lives. I never knew a car would burn like that. Bang, whoosh, crackle, the noisiest thing ever. Guess it was the petrol that made the explosions and then bits of hot metal flying everywhere. No big loss, stupid kind of car to have when we're so rich. Bet a Rolls Royce wouldn't have gone up like a Guy Fawkes bonfire. Changed my mind about Leah getting one of those. Staid and stuffy. I hope she chooses something decent, a sports car I can drive next year. It sucks here in France, really pisses me off. If we were back in England I would be driving by now. I couldn't believe it when Leah said you had to be 18 to get a licence in France. How bloody backward can you get? At 17 you are perfectly mature and sensible enough to drive on the roads. Another whole twelve months! That's like forever to wait.

I asked Leah if we could go back to England and let me take the test and then I can come back and drive here. But she said it doesn't work like that, still have to be 18. How rotten.

Sophie is pretty amazing for an 11-year-old. I can't

believe she likes the same things I do. She's tall for her age, so it's easy to forget she's so much younger. She's into clothes, and she spends a fortune on them too. Her mother got her a new skirt last week and it was over 500 Euros. Can't see Leah shelling out that much for one skirt. The top to go with it was even more.

She's also interested in boys. I wasn't when I was only 11. Thought they were rough and smelly and violent. At school they'd pull your hair and thump you and shriek about lavatory jokes. I haven't met too many French boys yet, but Sophie tells me they are mature and very deferential – cool word, eh? Sophie knows lots of cool words like that even in English. French guys are super polite to women and very well behaved. Her dad is sure cool. But then he's sort of royalty and that makes him extra interesting. He's like one of those older Hollywood stars, all sex and twinkly eyes. Her mother is a bit stuck-up though. I'd like to see her bend over; she's always standing so straight as if she had a steel rod down her back. Sophie says that her mother is always on at her to stand up straight, but she doesn't want to look all starchy like her *maman*. Sophie is an only child, no brothers or sisters. I asked her if that means one day the chateau and the farm will belong to her. She said she didn't know. She thinks that women can inherit ordinary property but, when it comes to large estates and titles and things, it might have to go to a male relative. She hasn't asked her parents as that would mean they have to die first and that's a bit rude. I think Sophie has a title too but when I asked her about it, she clammed up. Maybe I'll ask Madame.

Madame! What a slave driver. If she was a teacher in

England she'd be sacked by now for cruelty. She gives us masses and masses of homework. It doesn't leave any time for fun or Candy Crush or telly or anything. She can read my mind, I swear it. My French is like pretty good now, but the bloody woman even criticises my English as well. Come on, how come she gets away with that? It's my language, not hers. We did get her talking about the time she spent in England. She says she was only there a year and, in that time, she was like really fluent and even got to speak slang words too. I must find some sentences that she won't know. All the other French people put their words in the wrong order when they speak English, it's real funny.

I saw Deidre looking at me when we went to watch Leah's car burn. She noticed I was dressed, though I don't think Leah did. I wasn't about to tell her that Sophie and I had arranged to meet up and go to this club place in Nice. Sophie borrows this scooter which no one ever uses and she was going to come and collect me in the lane outside. Now her dad lets her drive around the estate, but he won't let her go on the public roads even though he says she's a really good driver. Shit me, she's got years and years to wait to get her licence. I guess she got scared off, when the car exploded, and went back home. We'll plan it for another night. Can't wait. Sophie knows all the local boys and her parents don't breathe down her neck like Leah does. Wish I had neat parents like Sophie does.

AUGUST   DEIDRE

I felt better after confessing to Leah that I had snooped and checked out at least one file from the boxes stored upstairs. We agreed we'd start right after breakfast, as soon as Madame and the girls were busy in the school room.

Leah had bought extra tables and chairs from a furniture store in Nice, and a couple of bookshelves and a large whiteboard and all the accessories. Madame had been quick to give her a full list of necessary items. This included special window blinds that Old Giles' son Henri was instructed to install. I didn't think Henri looked a day younger than Old Giles, but maybe that's due to the hot Mediterranean sun. Of course, I should have guessed that Old Giles, and in turn Henri, was related to Claudette. In fact, apart from the new expatriate arrivals, everyone in the village was related to everyone else.

As Leah turned the key and opened the trapdoor to the attic room, we were met with a hot blast of stale air. The dust lay thick on the bare boards and I reminded myself to bring cushions with me next time. It was going to take several days to go through all the files if we did the job properly.

Leah pulled up the ladder, lowered the trap door, and locked it behind us. The fewer people who knew what was in here the better. We might be sitting on a time bomb.

"I've had a good think about the break-in," Leah said, as she settled down on the bare planks. "It's possible they wanted this stuff and, when they didn't find the boxes, they got mad and made all that mess."

I knelt down carefully, and folded my cardigan into a cushion. "I don't agree Leah. Professional thieves don't break in carrying aerosol paint cans in their pockets."

"They might if they wanted to cover their tracks, make out it was local vandals."

"Then why not pull down the ladder and break into the attic and search up here as well?"

She thought for a moment. "Maybe they were disturbed. This trap door is pretty solid, I'd not like to try and kick it in, even if I noticed the ladder above me."

"Nor I. People so seldom look up do they? They might not even have noticed the ladder on the hall ceiling."

We got to work. Leah was fascinated reading the personal papers, amazed to discover that Mason had siblings. There were no death certificates for his parents and we wondered if they were still alive. And his brother and sister, there had never been any mention of them either.

It was hot, dusty work and by lunch time we had only combed through three of the boxes. It was pretty boring stuff. Warrants, and claims and counter claims and appeals and witness statements and lots of long-winded legalese neither of us understood.

"What a complete waste of time and energy and

money," Leah grumbled. "Why can't they just operate the courts like Judge Judy? Quick, to the point and sentence, over and done with."

"I have no idea. Jobs for the boys I guess." I was reading screeds of papers where a whole case had been dismissed due to one police officer having not read rights or getting the correct form signed before removing the drugs as evidence. It was ludicrous; the dealer was blatantly guilty.

"It's a cat and mouse game, nothing to do with justice or obeying the law." Leah sat back on her heels, her hair hanging in tendrils as the sweat poured off her face. We'd agreed not to open the window and draw attention to the fact we were up here in the attic room. Above us the heat radiated down through the tiled roof and the occasional scurry among the wooden rafters reminded us we were not alone.

"It all makes money for the lawyers, and practically no one else."

"Can I complain?" Leah sighed. "I lived in the lap of luxury for years on the proceeds. Mason never even questioned what I spent."

"He wouldn't need to with you, you will always be careful," I reminded her. "And, don't forget," noticing the guilty look on her face, "we know that most of Mason's paying clients were connected to the Mob, and I'm sure they terrified a lot of poor, innocent people in order to amass their fortunes."

"Deidre, when I married him, I thought I knew him. I had no idea he was mixed up with the wrong kind of people. He was so respectable; a member of the golf club, the Chamber of Commerce, Round Table, such a well-respected businessman who headed up the best law firm in the area."

"Perhaps someone got to him later. Did it ever occur to you that he was coerced into defending the lowlifes?"

She thought for a moment. "No, it didn't. Maybe that's why he changed, got aggressive, domineering and distant."

"Could be. Without that, you would still be one happy family. Well," I added, "if Belinda had a sunnier nature."

We laughed. "Belinda! She's not changed one bit. A couple of cheerful, relaxed interludes, then back to the angry and sullen teenager from hell."

We turned back to the files, and it was only the sound of the broken exhaust on Madame's car departing that had us leaping to our feet and scrambling back down the ladder.

"What have you two been doing?" Belinda's voice made us jump. We were both filthy dirty and Leah had cobwebs in her hair.

"Cleaning," I said. It was the first thing that popped into my head.

For once Belinda did not follow through. She had news.

"Claudette's cousin has a dog and it's just had puppies and she said I can have one. Can I? Can I please?"

Leah leaned back against the wall. "I think it would be nice to have a dog Belinda, but right now is not a good time. Let's wait until we're settled in our own place and then, if it chews or damages stuff, it won't matter."

"That could be months, years! I want one now!"

"Belinda, not now. Please be sensible. The garden, such as it is, isn't even fenced, so what if it ran away?"

"It wouldn't. I'd watch it. Leeeaaahhh, I've never had a dog of my own."

"We had Zeus."

"Oh yeuk, that smelly old thing? Only Daddy ever liked him. He was gross. This puppy would be mine."

"I didn't like Zeus either." Leah glanced down at her prosthesis; was she remembering the times Zeus bit her leg? "The answer is yes, but not yet."

Belinda marched off, flinging words behind her. "Never let me have anything. No one cares about me. All anybody in this family thinks about is themselves. Soooo selfish! I don't matter. I might as well be dead."

It was difficult not to laugh. "Have you suggested to Belinda that she should go on the stage?" I chuckled.

"There are days when I wished she would just go away, anywhere." Leah ran her fingers through her hair, brushing the dusty cobwebs off on her skirt. "Let's go and have supper."

We didn't get very far with the files in the next few days. We knew that France shuts down for the month of August and I know Leah was expecting Madame to also take a long break, but no, she announced that she would only give the girls two week's holiday, and then left them with so much homework it's doubtful they would have time for much else.

Belinda of course threw a wobbly, and even Leah had to agree that she did need a break, and offered to help her complete some of the assignments.

In return, she was informed that her stepmother couldn't possibly understand the complexity of the work at this level of education and thanks, but no thanks.

I thought Leah was very patient, considering she had passed her Advanced Level General Certificate of Education in England in Biology, English and Physics. She then went on to complete her three-year training as a nurse and, before the accident, she was a staff nurse at a large hospital outside London.

Had it been me, I would have rammed those facts down Belinda's throat, but gentle Leah only smiled and told Belinda that was fine, and maybe if she got up early to work for a few hours she could then hit the beach and kick back.

The response she got was a lot of eye rolling and a 'Yeah, whatever'. And a reminder that 'no one ever gets up early on a holiday'.

At that point Leah gave up and left her to her own devices. What can you do with a teen who refuses to cooperate? Too late for the naughty corner, or a grab and tuck under the arm and carry them off to confine them in their bedroom. Grounding, or confiscating, or reasoning are your only options, and none of those were working with Belinda. I guess she was as bloody minded as her father, though I had never met Mason.

Belinda dragged around the house for a couple of days in a sulk, banging doors, slamming cupboards, raiding the fridge, and turning up the sound on the television so that people in the village could listen in to her chosen programme as well.

Leah was on the point of buying the child her own set for the bedroom before I stopped her. "A reward for her bad behaviour? I don't think so, Leah."

When no one was looking I loosened one of the

connections on the back of the television and that solved the problem for the moment. Belinda of course demanded that we buy a new set, but we both ignored her pleas.

I was relieved to see Sophie arrive on her electric bicycle. I could already guess that Belinda would be whining to have one of those too. I was surprised that an eleven-year old was legally allowed to ride a powered bike, but when I sneaked away to google it, I couldn't find an answer. She wasn't wearing a helmet either, but then she didn't have to cross any major roads and, if your dad is the local Marquis, I guess it didn't really matter.

The two of them disappeared and, catching Leah's eye without saying a word, we grabbed the key and climbed the ladder into the attic room.

The heat up there in August was intense and soon we were both dripping in sweat and constantly wiping our hands dry as we shuffled through the paperwork.

Leah had brought her tablet and was compiling a list of names of all the clients we found.

"Let's mark those who had a successful outcome," I suggested. "They would have less reason to hold a grudge against Mason."

"That's a great idea, Deidre." She scrolled down the list and typed in a star against several of the names.

I pulled another box across the floor towards me. "He was certainly a popular lawyer."

"Yes, for all the wrong reasons. You wouldn't believe how often he appeared on television standing on the court steps with some fat thug beaming from ear to ear. Let off usually on some obscure point of law."

"While the whole world knows they are as guilty as

hell." I tucked a stray lock of hair that hung down over my face.

"Exactly. I know what I would do. Rewrite some of the laws and give the police more powers."

I nodded as I flipped open another file. "Here's a second one about a case against Daniel Morrison. He was a busy man." I put it to one side so we could study it later.

I have no idea what Claudette thought we were up to, closeted away in the attic room every time Belinda disappeared with Sophie. If we'd waited until she'd gone home too, we wouldn't have finished the task before Christmas.

Through the small window set in the tiled roof, we could see a small area of the beach. Occasionally we noticed Belinda and Sophie wander down carrying towels and a beach umbrella. This area of the coast was not popular with tourists; it may even have been a private area solely for residents, but I'd noticed a few local boys carrying body boards, which I considered ludicrous. There is little or no tide in the Mediterranean, but perhaps it was part of the image and they used the boards as a macho form of Lilo.

Leah and I took a few days out from our attic-scrambling as she called it. We drove east to Cannes a couple of times and then in the opposite direction, past Nice to spend a day in the Principality of Monaco. We played tourist, catching the bus up to the palace, and were lucky enough to see the changing of the guards in their white uniforms. We ambled around the cathedral, the resting place of many of the ruling Grimaldi family including that of Princess Grace.

"From Hollywood to princess," I whispered in Leah's ear.

"The whole place blows you away," she said, as we descended the old streets towards the port.

"You can feel the money." I observed a young man so impeccably dressed you could tell he didn't shop at Primark.

The buildings huddled together on the cliffsides, among the most expensive in the world, dwarfed Leah's new found wealth. The mega yachts in the harbour were breathtaking and we hovered for a while by the fountains, watching people go in and out of the casino.

"Come." I grabbed Leah's arm.

"Goodness no!" She pulled back.

"Nonsense. We can't come to Monaco and not have just one little flutter. You can write in your memoirs about that day you gambled in the casino at Monte Carlo."

"I won't be breaking the bank, though," she replied.

The decorations inside were not to my taste. Too much glitter and gilt verging on gaudy, but it suited the venue. The multi-coloured glass ceiling was very impressive as the sunlight filtered down in a rainbow of colours. They charged us ten Euros each to go inside, and the lowest bet was five Euros. After observing several tables, most patrons were betting upwards of fifty or a hundred Euros a time. We changed our minds. It was a different world, a different culture, and not one I would want. So far from my Flower Power youth when simplicity was the key.

Leah clutched my arm as we went back outside into the bright sunshine and the crowds. "With all my problems, I'm happier than some people I've noticed here."

"I don't think the hard part is accruing the money in the first place. The problem is keeping it," I said.

"I have no intentions of wasting any of mine, or radically changing my lifestyle. Do you know, Deidre, I even envy Claudette a little?"

"What? Why?" I gasped.

"I know what you'll think, but I miss my house-keeping. It's still strange to have someone come in each day and clear away all our mess."

"Are you thinking of getting rid of her?" My heart sank. For all I talked about simple living I've always hated cleaning and scrubbing and ironing and other household tasks.

Leah laughed. "No, of course not. I must learn to relax."

"How wise. Let's find somewhere to have a bite to eat before heading back."

The noise of the music assaulted our ears as we drove back through the gates, too loud for anyone to hear us arrive. The front door was wide open and inside we saw Belinda, Sophie, two other girls and four local boys aged anything from sixteen to twenty. They were gyrating in the middle of the room except for one couple who were writhing around on one of the couches, lips joined and bodies melded.

Belinda's face dropped when she saw us, and she dashed over to turn off the music. Arms dropped, feet froze on the tiled floor, in the silence they all turned to look at us.

"Where is Claudette?" Leah asked quietly.

"Gone back home. Her mother is sick again." Belinda addressed the floor.

"I see." Leah turned and walked into the kitchen. I admired her control and the way she was handling things.

One by one the guests shuffled and stumbled out of the front door and off down the driveway, not stopping to say goodbye, or apologise. From the kitchen, I could see the door to the liquor cabinet was wide open. From the half-filled glasses making rings on the polished tables, to the crunched crisps, crackers and crumbs floating on the spilled liquor on the floor, we had disturbed the party in full swing.

Left alone, deserted even by Sophie, Belinda came barrelling into the kitchen ready for a fight. She stood in the doorway, hands on hips.

"So?"

"Yes?" Leah looked at her and smiled.

The teen was taken aback. She swayed slightly, not completely sober, and then she made a run to the downstairs toilet and the sounds and smells wafted through as Belinda disposed of copious amounts of alcohol into the plumbing system.

Leah followed her inside carrying a wet towel and I heard her suggest Belinda should go and lie down until she felt better.

I wanted to laugh. The child was confused. She was expecting a huge row, screams of disapproval and accusations from her stepmother and that hadn't happened. Something was wrong, but she was in no fit state to work it all out.

Holding her arm, Leah helped her upstairs and onto her bed leaving a bucket by her side and shut the door.

"We can't blame Sophie," she sighed. "Belinda was a

handful in London and in Weston." She took a brush out of the cupboard.

I turned from filling a bucket with hot soapy water in the sink. "You've done what you can Leah, and no one could ask more of you. The future will take care of itself and, if Belinda is going to end up on the wrong side of the law like the rest of the family, frankly there's no way to stop it."

"One good thing…" Leah twirled the brush handle in her fingers, "she knew I wouldn't approve, so she's aware of the boundaries. Knowing right from wrong is a good step in the right direction. And it's not the first time she's been drunk. Also, she was at home. I lost count of the number of times the police rang the doorbell in the early hours after picking her up from outside some club or other."

She went to fetch the mop from the utility room, almost bumping into Claudette as she popped her head round the back door.

"Oh, *je suis désolé Madame. Oh Mon Dieu!*" She caught sight of the state of the lounge and then the mess in the kitchen.

"We'll give you a hand," Leah said, to be met with total confusion.

I had to laugh. "Claudette, Madame means we will help."

"Ah, *D'accord.*" She pulled cleaning cloths from the cupboard, then began collecting the glasses and plates.

"If it wasn't for the fabric on the furniture, I'd be tempted to get a hosepipe and sluice the place down." Leah swung the mop into the bucket and wrung it out.

Belinda did not appear for supper that night, nor did she come down to breakfast.

Madame du Pont arrived promptly at 7.30 a.m., her little green Fiat Uno popping, rattling and swerving up the road and in through the gate posts.

Sophie jumped out looking as fresh as a daisy, none the worse for wear, but maybe she didn't drink too much the day before?

"Where's Belinda?" she asked, as she raced into the hallway.

"Still in her room, I believe." Leah stared hard at her. "How are you feeling this morning?"

"Fine. Why wouldn't I be?" Sophie replied.

"Just a thought."

"I'll go get her, or Madame will be shouting at both of us." She ran upstairs and banged loudly on Belinda's door, before flinging it open and disappearing inside.

I grinned at Leah and shook my head.

Madame gave us a nod as she manoeuvred her large carpet bags into the study. Belinda had protested when we referred to it as the school room, as 'belittling'. The name change she agreed to was library or study.

Leah and I took our coffee out onto the back terrace. We'd leave it to Madame to prise Belinda from her funk and press her nose to the grindstone.

There was a roar from the front of the house. "Old Giles," said Leah. In the peace of the French countryside we'd learned the different car engine sounds.

She was right, a few moments later Giles appeared at the back door looking as white as a sheet, calling for Claudette.

Leah jumped to her feet and went over.

"Giles, what is the matter? What's wrong?" She took his arm and gently led him over to the table and lowered him into a chair, while I went to find Claudette. When we returned it was to see Leah looking as upset as Giles.

"What is it?"

Leah pointed to Giles who handed me his phone. I gasped. It showed a photograph of a baby in a pram. It was just possible to see it was outside the boulangerie in the village. Not an unusual sight except that the baby was covered in blood. Its throat had been cut from ear to ear.

I gasped and sat down as I passed the phone to Claudette who'd come running out of the house. She took one glance and wailed loudly.

"When?" gasped Leah.

"*Hier*," said Giles. Yesterday.

Claudette was in floods of tears, her body shaking as she staggered backwards and fell onto the stone wall at the edge of the terrace. "*Porquoi, porquoi?*" she shrieked. Why.

The commotion was enough to bring Madame du Pont hurrying through the back door. "What is the problem? I cannot teach with all this noise."

No one said a word, as the phone was passed on again. Madame screeched when she saw the picture.

"Who would do such a thing?" Leah whispered.

"Do you know the baby, is it from the village?"

They all shook their heads.

Belinda peered over Madame's shoulder and shrieked when she looked at the phone. She snatched it out of the teacher's hand and scrolled across. "Oh shit, there are lots more, look."

There were at least twelve other pictures taken from different angles, close ups, and one taken from the other side of the road which clearly showed it was our bakery in our village.

Old Giles wiped his arm across his eyes and then took back his phone. He walked as briskly as he was able back to his car and drove off, scattering the loose soil and creating a cloud of dust behind him.

For several moments no one moved. I think we were all stunned and it was almost possible to see the veil of fear that fell over us. A murder is horrific at any time, but to kill a defenceless baby, that is a step too far.

"If the baby is not local, I wonder if the killer lives here?"

I shot Madame a look. Had she forgotten the children were listening but she ignored me. "This is the barbaric," she added. "And too in daylight."

"Surely someone saw something?" Leah asked.

There were several more moments of stunned silence then Madame stood up, straightened her shoulders, and marched her two pupils back to the study, clucking like a mother hen.

Claudette too dragged herself to her feet and shuffled back into the kitchen. Her shoulders were stooped and we heard the occasional sob as she resumed cleaning the windows.

"I refuse to feel paranoid, but I question why life cannot run smoothly. Okay, I know this is really nothing to do with us, but we've never heard of any trouble in the village before. I've lost count of the number of people who say they never lock their doors, but it's one disaster after another." Leah sighed.

I took both her hands between mine. "You're strong Leah, stronger than all of us, most of us have never been tested like you. I'm so proud of you."

She smiled as she withdrew her hands to cradle her half empty coffee mug. "To be safe, I suggest we do lock our doors from now on. This is the first what – accident? It's not been on our doorstep, but we don't need any more disasters."

I could only agree with her.

AUGUST LEAH

Dear Diary,

I have fallen in love with this part of the world, despite the weird and unsettling happenings. Every morning, when I draw the curtains, I gaze out over a bright turquoise sea, and even on the odd occasion it turns grey it is still beautiful. Most days the sky is a dazzling blue, the hedgerows a brilliant green, and there is just enough rain to save the undergrowth from turning that dusty brown. The almost sandy beach with its tiny, tiny stones glistening and sparkling in the light, and the cliffs at the far end which dive almost vertically into the sea, are breathtaking.

The birdlife is also prolific. I know nothing about birds whatsoever, but I've noticed so many different varieties. I look skywards and see the shadows caused by the large raptors soaring overhead that are so rare now in England.

I love the villa too, the shiny brown-tiled floors, the chintzy covers on the cottage furniture, the space and the way the glass curtains open out bringing the garden and the terrace indoors. How can I fail to be happy in such a paradise?

Yet I am getting jittery. I eyed up the Valium tablets in my bathroom cabinet this morning, but I'll resist taking them. That would be too easy and my sixth sense warns me to stay alert.

Another month gone by. Bless Bill, he writes almost every day, but I collect the letters in batches at the *bureau de poste*. If the franking isn't clear I get to read them in the wrong order. I've been tempted more than once to write and cry out 'Come back now!' but of course I can't do that. I have Deidre, and she is a comfort and a rock of sense. I wish she was a little younger. She is very sprightly for seventy, a good age but it slows you down and I can see her thought processes take longer.

I'm not sure I can protect Belinda if she gets into trouble here. She's so headstrong and will have her own way. Dear God, does criminality run in the family? Is it in the genes? I don't think Caro, Belinda's mother, was a law breaker, but perhaps it's the mental makeup that causes anti-social behaviour.

I didn't think Belinda could kick over the traces here, in rural France. There are no nightclubs nearby, no shopping malls to loiter in, and the bars are drinking holes for the elderly village men and would not welcome a young, rowdy crowd disturbing their peace. When not discussing local politics, they are all glued to the TV sets watching the football.

Deidre and I are halfway through the boxes in the attic. So far, we have a pile of files and folders on twenty clients Mason did not manage to get off. Whether they hold a grudge it's hard to tell, but why would they target his daughter and me when they could get him beaten up or even killed in jail?

I've begun to haunt the *bureau de poste*, not only hoping to get letters from Bill, but also for those final divorce papers. Why is it taking so long? We've been led to believe that it's so quick and easy these days. My patience is wearing thin.

I felt mean telling Belinda no dog, not yet, but it makes sense for the moment. Was the party an act of revenge? Where did she find those kids? I'll try and chat with her about them and find out more. Perhaps I'll get to meet them and maybe the parents too. I'd like to widen my circle of friends here. Need to work more on my French but it's so hard when you're older. I keep forgetting my vocabulary and I get my tenses all mixed up. I get some very strange looks when I go to the market and then the stallholders burst out laughing. I'm happy to be entertaining, but that's not the idea. They are very kind and reply to me in broken English, and somehow we get by.

I could sense a change in the village when I went to the market yesterday. No one was laughing, everyone looked fearful. The death of that poor baby has shaken everyone. I can't imagine how that bereaved mother felt when she walked out of the shop and saw her child. There is a sense of oppression, a cloud hanging overhead. It may not have been anyone from the village, but I feel a target. None of the shopkeepers would look me in the eyes. Their manner was brusque, not a smile in sight.

They wouldn't suspect our family, would they? Just because we are the new arrivals in the area? Can't say I blame them, Claudette told me there had never been any trouble like this before. She's still friendly, but then employment opportunities in this area are few and far between. She's aware that the Brand family have been the target of the other attacks, but killing a baby is in a whole different league.

Let's hope September will be a better month. Perhaps the answer is in those files.

AUGUST BELINDA

My Journal,

Just my bloody luck Leah arriving home and breaking up the party. We were all having a really cool time and I'm sure Christian was eying me up. I think he really fancies me which is so radical. You don't see abs on any of the English boys, but then Christian is 22 so he told me. He's a lifeguard down on the coast but lives in the village. I gave him the eye several times and danced with the other guys just to make him jealous. I'm sure with a bit more encouragement we can get it on.

Sophie knows all the cool kids around here, but then it's her home, she's not moved around like me. I can't believe the French guys take an interest. I mean I know I keep banging on about her only being eleven but the guys in England wouldn't even give her the time of day. But then I guess it helps if your dad is the local chief. And if Sophie is an only child, she's going to inherit acres of land and that bloody great chateau and all those racing horses.

She says that all her dad talks about is his precious horses, he's hooked on them. Her mum doesn't seem very happy though, wonder why? Probably not happily married. Sophie says that divorce is difficult as the Catholic Church does not approve and, in those circles, it's not acceptable but frowned on. You wouldn't catch me staying with someone I didn't love any more. Hell no, I'd get out and find someone better.

Anyhow, Sophie was getting pretty hot with this guy and I googled the age of consent in France and it's 15. So, it's okay for me but still against the law for her. It just sucks you can get it on three years before you can drive a car.

If I can't have a car then I must work on Leah to get me a scooter. That would be even better than Sophie's electric bike thingy. Good excuse to ask Christian if he can soup it up, make it go really fast. I can guess Miss Spoilsport will insist I have something that's safe and slow. She's getting to be a helicopter parent, always hovering, breathing down my bloody neck.

Wish I had parents like Sophie's. She can do anything she wants. They never check where she is or what she's doing. They don't bug her all the time and look how grown up she is. You would never believe she is only eleven. Heck if you'd told me my BFF would be six years younger than me, well OK, only five years now as it's her birthday next month, I'd have told you to get off! Pity we are not the same size as she has some radical clothes and she said I could take what I wanted. We had a good giggle in her room, no wait, it's not a room but a whole suite in the chateau. There's a room to sleep in which is *ensuite* of course, and would you believe she has her very own jacuzzi in there. Then she has an enormous sitting room and another room just to do her homework. When I tried to open yet another door in her '*appartement*' as she calls it, she flew at me and told me that was her private place and to butt out. That's fine with me, no problem, but she scared me for a moment she was so furious. I don't care what she keeps in there, no problem, no worries. Anyhow, we went back into her dressing room, and did I mention she has this enormous room just for her clothes, shelves and shelves and shelves of them. And shoes, I've never seen so many in my life, more than they have in the shoe shop in the village.

A couple of tops were large enough but I wasn't sure about taking them though Sophie was very insistent. I could just see Leah having a hissy fit. Some rubbish about us not being able to afford to buy clothes. But man, these were like really special, expensive clothes. Sophie said I was stupid as her mother wouldn't even know. She gets most of her stuff online from the top end shops and then more when they go on trips to Paris. She's invited me to go with them next time, wonder if Leah will let me? Mind, at my age she can't stop me but then I'd not have enough money to spend. That sucks. Maybe I should get a job? Nah, when would I have time? Madame bloody du Pont keeps us at it all day and all bloody night. Fuck me, the amount of homework's too much. And, if you upset the old bat, she raps your knuckles with a ruler. That would not be allowed in a British school. Be had up for child abuse and the teacher made to apologise and then get fired.

Real shame about that baby. Who'd do something like that? Must have a sick mind. It's pretty creepy round the village now. People looking bug-eyed at each other. Hope they don't think it has anything to do with us because we're new here. Got some huge death stares from the old witch in the café and she banged down my hot chocolate so some of it spilled over on the table and the churros fell off the plate. Won't go there again, but there aren't too many cafes in the village and she does the best chocolate dips for the churros.

Those pics were dead gruesome though. And they didn't find the knife, so Sophie tells me, and it must have been covered in blood. Imagine, putting a knife covered in blood back in your pocket. Yeuk!

Time for bed, to dream of Christian and feel his abs pressed hard against me, bliss.

SEPTEMBER DEIDRE

The howling began before dawn. It was still dark when the cries woke me up. They were bloodcurdling, but I leapt out of bed without thinking of the danger. I had only reached the top of the staircase when Leah came flying out of her room, hair mussed, tying her dressing gown around her.

"What is it?" she asked. "God, it sounds awful. Something being murdered?"

"I've no idea, but let's go investigate together. Whatever is making that row is in a lot of pain." I gave her a reassuring smile though I wasn't feeling too brave.

We tiptoed down the stairs, and into the kitchen.

Feeling her way in the dim light, Leah reached over to the knife block, and removed two of the largest ones. She handed the carving one to me, while I grabbed the large rolling pin Claudette had left on the draining board.

We sidled up to the back door. Leah tried to turn the key then gasped.

"It's not locked!"

"It must be. I checked it before I went to bed and I was the last one up." A shiver ran down my spine and my legs turned to jelly. I set my jaw and pulled myself upright. No way could I show fear in front of Leah, but I'm not sure who was more frightened.

Leah eased the door open a few centimetres and peered out. The courtyard was dark and, on the far side, the outbuildings loomed up tall and threatening. The howls were louder now, interspersed with low level whimpers.

"What do you think?" Leah whispered.

"We go see," I replied.

Side by side, we crept across the yard. I could feel the heavy dew soaking into my slippers and I shivered in the chill wind which whipped around the corner and wrapped itself around my thin night clothes.

Peering along the side of the building we saw a shaft of light which seeped under the door of the farthest store room. The howls were much louder now. Taking a deep breath Leah marched forward and flung open the door and advanced inside knife at the ready.

I rushed forward to join her and dropped the rolling pin.

Sitting on a bale of straw, Belinda was cuddling a large ball of fluff on her lap, rocking backwards and forwards, trying to shush the animal which kept throwing its head back and howling, before she grabbed it and pushed its snout back into her lap to cut off the noise.

She looked up and gasped.

For a moment no one moved then Leah asked, "What's that? It's the dog you were not supposed to have, right?"

Belinda stared at us defiantly in the gloom. "I had to have him. The farmer was going to drown him. I've saved his life. So there, what you going to do about it?"

"You could have mentioned that earlier," Leah's voice was sharp. "How long have you had it?"

"It's a him, and his name is Monster. And I got him today. And I didn't know he'd make such a row and now you've found out."

"Have sense Belinda, you can't hide a dog indefinitely." Leah sighed. "Bring him into the kitchen, it's warmer there and give him some milk. Had you thought he might be hungry?"

"He's missing his mum." She wrapped her arms around him protectively. "I'm not giving him up."

"We'll talk about that tomorrow. Just bring him in for now."

Belinda scrambled to her feet, hugging the dog, which looked very large to me for a mere puppy.

"What breed is that?" I asked.

"No idea, but it's going to have a huge appetite, and did you see the size of its paws? I shall have to let her keep it, and pray it doesn't run away or cause too much damage," Leah flung over her shoulder as we scurried back inside to the warmth of the kitchen.

As the puppy wolfed down bowl after bowl of milk there was a heated discussion at the kitchen counter, with Leah flatly refusing to allow Monster to sleep on Belinda's bed.

"Have you seen the state of him? He's filthy. You'll need to get up an hour early tomorrow to give him a good bath before Madame arrives. He stinks."

She was right, the animal's fur was matted around several bald patches. It was probably flea and tick-ridden as well.

"Hold still," I commanded Belinda as I scooped a tick off the front of her nightdress.

"Oh yeuk," she cried, as I showed it to her before going to flush it down the toilet.

"Leave the dog in the laundry room with a couple of old blankets and go back to bed. It's three in the morning and I need my sleep even if you don't."

Leah went off upstairs and I gave Belinda a wry grin and made for my own bed. My slippers were wet through and I was cold and shivering.

Belinda did not get up an hour early as she'd promised. She was still in bed when Madame du Pont and Sophie arrived at 7.30 a.m. As Claudette let them in the front door, they were bowled over by the black bundle of fur which had escaped from the laundry room.

"*Mon Dieu*, what's that?" cried Madame, while Sophie tried to keep it at bay with her school bag.

"Get it off me," she shrieked. "Look what it's doing to my clothes."

"Oh sheeit," cried Belinda rushing down the stairs, her nightdress billowing out behind her. "How did Monster get out?"

"I don't expect Claudette knew there was a dog in the laundry." Leah appeared in the hallway.

The next few minutes were chaos. Belinda was trying to catch Monster who had no intentions of cooperating. He raced around the furniture, skidding on the tiled floor and knocked over a side table which sent the glass vase on top smashing to smithereens on the floor.

Leah was frantic he would get glass in his paws as he ran round and round.

Madame was shrieking about her teaching plans being disrupted and shouting about Belinda delaying her lessons.

Claudette was running around with Belinda trying to catch the animal and doing more harm than good by flicking a tea towel and scaring it witless.

I refused to join in the chaos and wandered off into the kitchen to turn on the coffee maker. The sooner the dog was caught and we could get it to the vet to be checked over and have it washed and deloused the better. Watching the hound having a great time avoiding capture I guessed we were in for a difficult time. Not Belinda's finest choice. If she couldn't even get out of bed on the first morning to see how it was, I suspected her devotion wasn't going to last too long.

At last, peace was restored. Leah found some rope to use as a collar and lead and I helped her bundle Monster into the SUV and after breakfast we drove off to the vet.

Two hours and a very hefty bill later we drove home, with a sweet-smelling Monster wearing his new collar and lead.

I hoisted the bags from the car. We had bought bowls, puppy food, a dog bed, worming tablets, toys and chews, his prescription medicines and everything a dog could ask for.

As we turned into the drive Belinda came rushing out of the front door, ignoring Madame's angry cries.

"How is he? Is he OK?"

Leah handed her the lead. "The vet says he'll live but he needs tablets twice a day and worming, and we've to take him back in a couple of weeks."

Belinda flung her arms around Monster holding him

tightly, but he wriggled out of her grasp and took off towards the road.

"Don't run after him!" Leah called out. "He'll think it's a game and you'll never catch him."

It was too late. They turned the corner and disappeared from view. Now it was time to calm Madame down. Did no one but her take these exams seriously?

The next few days were spent racing after the most ungrateful animal I'd ever met. If Belinda thought she had rescued a gentle, loving dog from the jaws of death who would shower her with affection, she was wrong.

Monster had more energy than a kennel full of mutts. The vet had suggested it was a cross between a Pyrenean Mountain dog and a Newfoundland. Leah googled the breeds and nearly had a fit. They were possibly the largest breed of dogs on earth.

We consoled ourselves that he might turn out to be a great guard dog and a blessing in disguise, if we could get him to stop chewing the cushions, the furniture, shoes and anything else he could get his teeth into.

Belinda came close to taking him back to be drowned when she discovered he had crunched her iPod earphones and then got the cord stuck in his throat. That necessitated another visit to the vet.

Claudette complained bitterly that it was impossible to keep the house clean and I thought she was on the point of walking out before Leah had a long talk with her and doubled her wages.

Apart from the chaos caused by our new family member, the first half of the month passed quietly. The next milestone was Sophie's twelfth birthday party. We were all invited to the day-long celebration at the chateau, to be followed by dinner in the evening. This time we knew what to expect.

I noticed Belinda trying to play it cool, but this was a big event and once again she dragged Leah off into Nice to find suitable attire for the grand occasion.

I wasn't sure what to expect as we drove up the long approach to the chateau. There was a large marquee on the front lawn, and a stage to one side. The engineering crew were putting the finishing touches to the sound system and I could see other entertainers in fancy costumes strolling around the pathways.

We were directed round to the back of the mansion into a courtyard area surrounded on three sides by stables. I saw Madame's little Fiat Uno parked in the far corner.

Walking back to the front lawn we were met by waiters bearing trays of champagne and finger bites.

"A bit over the top for a twelve-year old," Leah murmured as she accepted a glass in one hand and took a sausage roll in the other.

"How the other half live, I expect. Do you know anyone here?"

"I don't think so. Oh, there's Geraldine, come let me introduce you properly."

Geraldine Morrison wore a bright yellow sundress with matching shoes and bag. Her hair was piled high on her head and I unkindly decided she had plastered her makeup on with a trowel.

"Leah, darling," she gushed as we drew close. They went through the usual 'air kissing on both cheeks' routine.

I stood stock still and stared at her. Round her neck she wore a pretty chain in an intricate design of yellow, white and rose gold. I had an identical necklace, given to me by my father on my twenty-first birthday. Perhaps it wasn't a unique design but he'd told me before he died that he'd instructed the jeweller himself. My father never lied. I couldn't wait to go home and check to see if it was still in my jewellery box. In the meantime, I couldn't take my eyes off it and Leah had to nudge me to say hello.

While I was glad Leah had found a friend, I didn't feel the same warmth. Call it a sixth sense, or my intuition, but I had a strong instinct that the Morrisons were bad news. Daniel knew Mason, and that could not be good news for Leah. We had been so distracted with Monster's antics the last couple of weeks that we'd made little progress on the files in the attic. Tomorrow, I promised myself, it was time to delve further and see just how close they had been.

Margaret Fenton, the other English guest from that disastrous night, wandered over. "Such a relief to chat in English," she said. "My French is improving, but it's hard work and so often they get the wrong end of the stick and misunderstand me completely."

We strolled over to a range of market stalls similar to those held in the village every Friday morning. The difference today: you could help yourself to anything and no payment was expected, except for the sign over the stalls which said: '*Les Gros Dons s'il vous plaît*'.

"They are asking for donations to charities," Geraldine whispered. "Large ones. Can you imagine the chaos if they tried this at home? Here, everyone is too well-bred to take advantage of such generosity."

I ran my hand over a cashmere pashmina and had to agree with her. These cost a fortune in the shops.

"There's an auction later on, after dinner." Geraldine was well informed. I still couldn't take my eyes off her necklace.

Browsing the jewellery stall next to me, Leah gasped. She came over and tugged on my arm. "Deidre, come, look."

The stall was beautifully arranged with what at first, I thought of as bling, but on closer inspection, the gems looked real. Fake stones didn't sparkle quite so brightly in the sunlight.

"See the pendant?" Leah hissed in my ear. "The silver chain and the emerald?"

"Yes. What about it?"

"It's identical to one I have at home. Mason bought it for me just before we got married. It's the most expensive piece of jewellery I have."

"Could it be an identical piece?"

She shook her head then leaned over and picked it up and turned it over. On the back was a small inscription, M & L.

"See, it is mine!"

I peered at it. I was difficult to make out the tiny letters but I could see it was engraved.

"What are you going to do? Buy it back?"

"I don't know." Leah stood there stunned.

"Problem?" Margaret came up behind her then stretched out her hand to take the pendant. "Oh, this is pretty. I love emeralds, don't you? I have a green dress and this would go so well. Excuse me," she called to get the attention of the lady manning the stall.

"You can't have it," Leah snapped and grabbed the pendant back. "It's mine."

There was an uncomfortable silence, then Leah said. "Sorry, that sounded rude. I mean it's mine, it really belongs to me, see the engraving on the back?"

Margaret and Geraldine looked closely at the tiny letters.

Watching them I wanted to grab the necklace off Geraldine's neck and make a similar claim, but I had no way of proving it belonged to me. I'd never had it engraved nor were there any dents or scratches. I'd taken great care of it. I could only suspect and only until I got home. If it wasn't in my room what was I going to do? I couldn't accuse Geraldine of theft, now could I?

I whipped out my mobile phone and grabbed Leah by the arm and manhandled her next to Geraldine.

"What are you doing?" she asked.

"Just cooperate, will you?" I hissed. "Photo," I cried, "to remember this day." I lined up Leah and Geraldine in the view finder and pressed the button. "Wait, one more." For the second picture I zoomed in tight on the necklace round Geraldine's neck. I was just in time as another lady came over and engaged her in conversation.

Leah looked down at the pendant still in her hand. "What am I going to do, Deidre?"

"I think you'll have to talk to the Marquise. Ask who donated the jewellery for the stall, and show her the engraving on the back, that proves it's yours."

"That's not going to make us very popular in the area is it?" She looked close to tears. "For the sake of one pendant?"

"And Geraldine is wearing my necklace. Not only is it the most expensive piece I owned, it's got a lot of sentimental value as well."

Leah gasped. "Really? Are you serious?"

"It's identical to mine and I was told the design was unique."

It wasn't going to be possible to talk to Sophie's mother today. In her long flowing, chiffon dress she fluttered like a butterfly from one group of guests to another. There must have been over six hundred people milling around in the tented area. For us the day was spoiled but we had no option but to put on a brave face.

"What shall I do with this?" Leah was still clutching the pendant.

"I'd hang on to it. It's yours and, if you put it back on the stall, I guarantee you'll never see it again. Unless you want to watch Margaret wearing it next time you have coffee together."

She slipped it into her pocket.

"And don't look so guilty," I whispered. "If by some amazing coincidence you find it at home. You can easily return it."

She nodded.

I caught occasional glimpses of Belinda and Sophie who appeared to be enjoying themselves. The last time I saw them they were walking into the chateau. I wondered if Belinda had persuaded Sophie to give her the full guided tour yet.

Marchioness Lampierre used a bullhorn to summon all the guests to walk with her to the stables to view the racehorse that was Sophie's birthday present. She looked around for her daughter but she was nowhere to be seen. After hovering on the lawn, calling out her name several times, she shrugged her shoulders and we all trooped after her to stand and admire the magnificent beast they had purchased for their twelve-year-old daughter.

I caught Leah's look and we had to supress a fit of the giggles. We didn't need to say a word; we could read each other's thoughts on this subject. For a while I felt like Alice down the rabbit hole, in a surreal world where nothing was quite as it should be and nothing made any sense.

The afternoon dragged on but the French eat early and, by 6 p.m., those with invites for dinner were ushered into the large banqueting hall and seated.

The chandeliers suspended overhead were stunning, the metres-long polished table was set with crystal glasses, bone china plates resting on gold underlays, and each place sitting had a frightening array of cutlery.

"If Belinda and Sophie weren't studying together, I know for sure we'd not be on the guest list." Leah grinned at me.

"Let's enjoy it while we can."

Waiters dressed in formal attire lined the walls ready to serve but, just as we were expected to start, there was a pause. Sophie was missing. The chair, covered with gold cloth and a fake crown balanced on the back, was empty.

"*Où se trouve* Sophie?" Veronique Lampierre's voice trembled.

Everyone looked around as if she was hiding behind the drapes on the windows or under the table. Madame instructed several of the staff to go and search for her.

Leah slid her phone out of her bag to send a text to

Belinda. "They will be together and lost track of the time." She stared at the screen for several seconds then sent a WhatsApp. One little green tick appeared in the corner to show the message had gone, but no second tick to show it had been seen and read.

"That's strange," she murmured, "Belinda is welded to her phone, I wonder why she's not answering?"

"Bad reception?" I suggested. "These stone walls are thick enough to absorb radio waves?"

My adopted niece shook her head. "No, in that case it would not have registered as sent." She rested the phone in her lap glancing at it every now and again.

The guests around the table began to get restless. The waiting staff started to fidget and whisper, and a man in a chef's outfit slipped into the room presumably to find out what the hold-up was.

I couldn't help feeling sorry for Veronique. She was embarrassed but put on a brave face. I hoped she would not blame Belinda for her daughter's rude behaviour. From her look of amazement this was not a normal occurrence.

The door off the hallway opened and everyone turned to look, but it was Marquis Jules Lampierre who entered. He paused, his face puzzled as he looked at the nervous guests and then at his wife who rushed over. She indicated the vacant chair waiting for the birthday girl.

The Marquis was not amused, but brushed his wife aside and went around shaking hands and greeting the guests as if nothing was wrong. When he reached Leah, he took her hand and said "I hope we don't have reason to blame your daughter for this lack of politeness?" He didn't give her time to reply before he moved on to the next guest.

She squirmed in her seat and fixed her eyes on her lap while her cheeks turned bright red. If I could, I would have given her a cuddle, I could only mutter words of sympathy and tell her we would laugh about this tomorrow. "Something to write about in your memoirs," I added, but she was too ashamed to respond.

Every person of any importance was seated around the table that night, and the Marquis' statement had not gone unnoticed.

Veronique gave up and ordered the food to be served. While guests chattered and glasses clinked, you could feel the uncomfortable atmosphere. There were frequent glances towards the empty chair at the head of the table, and although everyone tried to pretend everything was normal, none succeeded.

The entrée was served, followed by the main course and the dessert. I couldn't tell you what any of it was, I ate mechanically while my heart ached for Leah, and the guest on my right ignored me.

There was a fanfare and the head butler, or he may have been a head waiter, entered carrying an enormous cake in the shape of a horse, the twelve candles burning brightly on the top.

The Marquise jumped to her feet and ordered the man to take it away immediately, but at that moment Sophie made her grand entrance.

She was wreathed in smiles, ran over to her mother, and kissed her on both cheeks before seating herself at the head of the table.

"*Chere invités, je suis vraiment désolé, je suie en retard.*"

The guests responded with platitudes, but Leah was asking where Belinda was. The table was too long for Sophie to hear her unless Leah shouted very loudly, but if she was worried before, she was now trying hard not to panic.

"Where is the bloody child?" she asked no one in particular.

Sophie was oblivious to either the guests' discomfort or Leah's distress, but waved the cake over and made a big performance blowing out the candles while everyone sang Happy Birthday. Taking an enormous knife from the waiter, she lopped off the horse's tail, placing it on her plate then indicated they should slice up the rest of it for the guests.

There were a few toasts. The local Mayor stood and made a small speech, of which I only caught a few words; he spoke so fast. He was followed by other local dignitaries who had something to say. It all dragged on interminably.

Now that Sophie was back, it was as if she had been there from the start. Her parents were all smiles, the diners relaxed, chatting and laughing, all except Leah and myself. Several times I caught Geraldine staring at Leah, but I couldn't guess what she was thinking.

To my great relief, at long last, the dinner was over. Guests stood and, in groups, began making for the hallway, calling for coats and wraps.

Leah leapt off her chair and rushed over to Sophie but it was impossible to get close to her; she was surrounded by well-wishers congratulating her and she was smiling and laughing and not once looked in Leah's direction.

Leah waited patiently for several minutes then pushed

a couple of people aside and put her hand firmly on Sophie's shoulder. "Where is Belinda?"

Sophie looked up, her big blue eyes wide and innocent. "I have no idea, Madame. We were upstairs and then she disappeared. I have no idea where." She flung her hands wide and shrugged her shoulders before turning to greet another well-wisher.

Leah walked back to me. "Let's go home. She may have hitched a ride and is waiting back there."

"It's possible, but I think we should ask the Marquise first. She may be in the house somewhere, locked in, or fallen and hurt herself."

"Why didn't she answer her phone?"

I had no answer for her. We decided to hang around to talk to Sophie's parents, ignoring the pointed looks from the straggling guests. We were not the flavour of the month. After the fuss tonight I wasn't sure we would ever fit into this community. It was a depressing thought.

At last Veronique noticed Leah hovering and walked over. She was angry. "I do not think your daughter is good for my Sophie," she said.

"I'm not sure that's fair," Leah protested. "What has Belinda done? Where is she?"

"I have no idea." Veronique was about to turn away when Leah stopped her.

"I want every inch of this place searched until my daughter is found. Last time we saw Belinda she was going inside with Sophie. It's ridiculous for her to say now she doesn't know where Belinda is."

"I will speak to her." The Marquise turned away just in time to catch her daughter as she was about to leave the room.

We watched as they had a heated discussion, Sophie brushed her mother off at last and bolted from the room.

Veronique walked over. "All Sophie knows is that they were in one of the hallways upstairs and when she turned around, Belinda was not behind her. I can tell you no more than that."

"We must search for her!" Leah reached out and took the Marquise's arm.

"But of course. I will tell the staff to look everywhere." With that she walked off, leaving us standing alone in the dining room.

I did my best to keep Leah calm.

"It's one thing after another," she moaned.

"I agree, a lot of unpleasant incidents, but nothing life threatening."

"Not so far, but what if one of us had been in the car when it exploded, or caught fire?"

She did have a point. The local gendarmes had never come back to us about that, or the break in at the villa. Had they even made enquiries in the village? We had no idea. I suspected if we went to ask them, they would shrug their shoulders and brush us off. So typically French this shoulder waggling habit, it could be very infuriating.

The time passed as we waited in the grand hallway perched on ancient, faded velvet spindly chairs. I had already counted all the black and white tiles on the floor several times, got up to peruse the family portraits on the walls, and traced my fingers round the gilt-covered scrolls on the bannisters.

Madame la Marquise had instructed us to wait. We were tempted to go searching but how can you go peeping and prying around someone else's house? Even one as large and impressive as this one?

"We'd have more freedom to wander if we'd bought entrance tickets." I tried to make Leah smile, but she sat rigid, her fists clenched, her feet pressed to the floor.

Sophie came past and consoled us. "I do not understand," she cried. "One moment Belinda was behind me in the top hallway and the next, poof, she was gone."

"Are there any secret passages, doors that might swing open and..." I paused. I sounded ridiculous.

Sophie's reply was more shoulder shrugging.

"How old is the chateau?"

"I am not certain. It is said that Pope Clement stopped here on his way to his new home in Avignon."

I thought for a moment. "Goodness, that was at the beginning of the fourteenth century. The chateau is old."

"But the family have added more parts," she replied.

"On the days when families were large and the staff even larger," I added.

After Sophie had consoled Leah, she wandered off muttering about feeling tired after a long day and it was time for her to go to bed.

I couldn't help wondering how a family of only three could live in a pile this size, and how many staff they had. They must rattle around like dried peas in a metal bath.

At 2 a.m. Jules and Veronique entered the hall together shaking their heads. "I am so sorry, but Belinda is nowhere. We have looked in every place. I think it is best you go home."

Leah stood up, brushing her hands over her long skirt. "Thank you for searching for her."

"We look everywhere." The Marquise repeated.

"Maybe she is back home." I took Leah's arm. The Marquis opened the front door for us and muttering our thanks we walked down the steps. Someone had thoughtfully brought our car around from the stable area and, bundling Leah into the passenger seat, I drove us back to the villa.

The house was in darkness as we drove in. I breathed more easily when I saw the front door was closed and, as we walked into the hallway and turned on the lights, we could see nothing had been disturbed. We had woken Monster who was dashing around the laundry room making a hell of a noise. His barks and howls bouncing off the tiled walls.

"Maybe getting a dog wasn't such a bad idea after all." Leah dropped her wrap and evening bag on the sofa before making for the coffee machine.

"Coffee? At this time of night, Leah?"

"I'm not going to sleep, I couldn't. Not that coffee has ever kept me awake. I can't relax while Belinda is missing."

I hurried up the stairs and checked to see she wasn't asleep in bed, but the room was undisturbed, if you ignored the clothes on the floor and the wet towels flung over the bath.

I went back downstairs. In the end neither of us went to bed that night. We agreed it would do no good to contact the police. It would be the same old story. At seventeen you still worry about them but at that age, they are not small children.

"There will be a simple answer," I told Leah. "She

skipped out of the dinner for some reason of her own, and then couldn't get back in time. You know what she's like, Leah. There will be a boy involved somewhere."

"I hope it's not the one that's bad news. He's in his twenties and…"

"We both know Belinda is no wilting violet, or virgin for that matter and, if I'm brutal Leah, she can take care of herself, probably better than you or me."

So that was a bit of an exaggeration, but I was beginning to get angry. I was tired; the warm glow from the drink earlier in the evening had worn off and I needed to sleep.

"I'll see you in a couple of hours." I went upstairs, undressed and fell into bed. If Leah had any sense, she would do the same.

I slept far longer than I intended and it was mid-morning before I opened my eyes. I could hear the faint sounds of Claudette sweeping the terrace below and her shouts for Monster to get out of her way. Puppy-like he loved to chase brooms and the vacuum cleaner making life extra difficult for our housekeeper.

Throwing on my robe, I found Leah downstairs, out cold on the sofa. She was frowning in her sleep, her hands fluttering, and her feet twitching. A dream or a nightmare? It was difficult to tell.

I crept into the kitchen to fix myself some breakfast but, before I could start, Claudette came in, dragging Monster behind her, his teeth firmly embedded in the broomstick attempting to pull it out of her hands. She let the brush go, and Monster slid backwards and bumped into the wall.

Claudette insisted I sit down. Like housekeepers the world over, this was now her kitchen, her house, and she was in charge. Madame and her friend were not supposed to lift a finger to help or to change anything.

A few minutes later, bleary-eyed and still in her long dress from yesterday, Leah shuffled in and joined me at the kitchen table. No sooner had she sat down when she jumped up again.

"In all the trauma I quite forgot!" She raced out of the room and ran up the stairs, coming down a few moments later.

"It wasn't there," she announced.

"What wasn't…?" Then I remembered. "Your pendant?"

"Yes. But the one I took off the stall is still in my pocket." She pulled it out and laid it on the table.

"And I was going to check my necklace. I was too tired last night."

My frantic searching in the box in my bedroom showed me my necklace was not there either. I sat on the bed and wiped away a tear. It wasn't the price of the gold, but the sentimental value. My father was long dead, but I'd always treasured the gift he'd given me on my twenty-first birthday. I was devastated at the loss, but resolved to chat to Geraldine at some point and ask her where she got it.

The day passed slowly. We didn't feel like leaving the house, just in case Belinda returned. Leah rang her phone over and over, but it was switched off. She fretted about that; like most teenagers, half Belinda's day was spent with her ear to her mobile. Who she was talking to we had no idea, and casual questions only elicited a toss of the head, or comments like 'Mind your own'.

I shuddered. When had young people taken to ignoring their elders, even if they were not their betters?

The only positive result of the day was we returned to the attic room and sifted through more paperwork.

Sneezing in the dust, we piled up anything that might be useful, only replacing the files of the successful cases of the clients Mason had defended. The pile we had left was daunting. To our surprise we discovered that at one time Humphrey Fenton had also been up on fraud and money laundering charges. Now we had two local families with ties to Leah's almost-ex and imprisoned husband.

We discussed how friendly they might be, and if they might be working together.

"Often people move somewhere overseas if they already have contacts in an area," Leah observed, pushing a stray lock of hair behind her ear.

"So, one criminal family will choose to settle near another? Yes, that makes sense. We need to make a list of anyone who might be tempted to harm us." I said 'us', but Leah, and possibly Belinda, would be the real targets, and my blood ran cold as it occurred to me she might have been abducted.

"If Belinda is not back today, we go to the police and we make a fuss, a huge fuss. If necessary, we tell them something of the family history."

"Mason in jail, and all the stuff that happened in the past?"

"Yes."

"Deidre, I really don't want to do that. I feel so ashamed."

"You can get that out of your head right now. None of

this, not one thing, is your fault. Who could ever have guessed you were landing in a hornet's nest when you married Mason? You didn't have a clue."

She sighed. "No, I didn't. He was charming, charismatic, swept me off that supermarket floor and wined and dined me. I couldn't believe my luck."

"Yes, we all know now what he was after, but you are a great catch for any man, and Bill loves you to bits."

"I wish he was here." Leah, trailed her fingers in the dusty floor. "But I am so lucky to have you here," she added immediately, and smiled at me.

"You're stuck with me," I smiled back. "I'm not going anywhere. Well, not before Bill returns. Have you told him how things are?"

"No. Deidre! How can I bother him when he has his daughter's divorce to deal with? It must be so painful when your child's marriage breaks up. I've told him everything is fine and we're loving it here, and I miss him of course."

Typical Leah. I should have guessed. "What shall we do with the files we're going to go through? It's too hot to work up here and we need to compile a spreadsheet for cross referencing from your notes and list possible people with a grudge?"

After some discussion it was decided that Leah would order a large safe online. We could also use it to house the remaining jewellery, as both of us were missing more than one pendant and a necklace.

"And they told us this was a crime-free area," grumbled Leah, as we stacked the papers into two of the boxes.

While Leah went down to order express delivery on

the safe, I finished up in the attic and went for a shower. There was still no sign of Belinda but, having made a decision to pursue her disappearance tomorrow, there was nothing more to do today.

Late in the afternoon Veronique phoned to ask if she was back home, but didn't seem phased when we said no. "She's a big girl now," was her last remark before disconnecting the call.

SEPTEMBER LEAH

I am worried sick about Belinda. Where is she? My imagination is running wild. I have her lying in a ditch, or bleeding to death in a car that has crashed. I also have her trapped in an *oubliette*, one of those forgotten holes in old piles like the chateau; they were fond of building those in medieval times. I can feel her suffering, hear her calling out for help, taste the stale air as she's deprived of oxygen with the sounds of her cries echoing in her ears. I can see her nails bleeding as she scrabbles for purchase at the bottom of a deep stone pit. And like a coward, I'm sitting here in my room scribbling in my diary.

Should I have insisted I go search the mansion? I'm too meek, too scared. It would take me weeks, especially if I stopped to tap walls and panelling looking for secret passageways. I've seen examples of them on the television, so I know they exist and that pile of stone has been there for centuries.

It was almost a relief to get out of there and return to a normal-sized villa. That sort of life is not for me. But, try as I might, I can't stop thinking about Belinda. It's possible she took the opportunity to go off with some unsuitable boy; her hormones are raging, but can't she see the dangers? I'm beginning to think the whole family is wild if not mad.

September has been a horrible month, and only the amusing antics from our newest arrival made us smile. We are becoming very fond of Monster. If it wasn't unkind, I'd be tempted to send him to a new home in retribution for Belinda's behaviour, if she has just run off and not had an accident. Doesn't the wretched girl realise how upset we'd be? Can she only think of herself?

Maybe I'm being too hard on her; it may not be her fault.

No Leah, don't even think of taking your anger out on an innocent animal. He's an excellent watchdog, barks the house down the moment any stranger comes through the gate posts. That's quite reassuring. You never feel quite as safe in your home after it's been breached by person or persons unknown as the police describe them.

I could kick myself that I didn't check my jewellery after the break in. In the panic, we saw that only one of Belinda's electronics had been taken and, if I'm honest, I'm not sure I believe her about that. But the television, the sound system, and even the money left on the table were all undisturbed, so we didn't check anything else.

I feel so bad Deidre has lost her necklace. All as a result of staying here with us. I attract bad luck wherever I go. It's one thing after another.

What began as a safe haven is fast becoming a house of nightmares. The villagers were so friendly before, but now all I receive are sullen looks. They still serve us in the shops, but I've noticed on a couple of occasions they will ask the person who came in after me what they want as if I wasn't even there.

Sophie's party is one I won't forget in a hurry.

I can only hope Belinda will be back tomorrow and that October will be a better month. It can't get worse, can it?

OCTOBER   DEIDRE

I sat on the terrace and listened to the church bells ring, calling people for morning mass. Gazing out over the beach below, where the waves washed gently on the stones and over to the headland, I thought for a moment I saw Belinda walking next to a taller boy, their arms around each other, stopping to kiss and cuddle every few steps. When I closed my eyes and opened them again, the vision was gone. The beach was empty except for a few sea gulls pecking at the flotsam.

It's going to be difficult to keep my hands off her if she did deliberately run off with some guy. I know it's not my place, but I'm going to have a serious talk with her. I think underneath she's a good kid. So what if she has family members in prison? Lots of people of all ages don't take to a life outside the law because their relatives do. She has her good moments, though they are few and far between, and I'm sure the experts would tell me she is hurting inside, but it doesn't make it any easier to be patient with her, or not to continually correct her.

I am determined to help Leah all I can. A comedy of

errors has nothing on our lives. I'd be more worried about Belinda's absence if I felt she was in trouble, but my radar doesn't tell me anything. Not yet.

Claudette came bustling out onto the terrace. Her face told me something was wrong. I reminded her to speak slowly. My French was improving but I couldn't cope with the speed most of them spilled the words out. She nodded.

She wanted to know if Monster had been home all day. On a couple of occasions, he'd run off but then returned a couple of hours later. At night he slept in the laundry room, an extra warning device we all appreciated.

Monster had stuck to Leah or myself like glue. He seemed to sense we were upset and worried, and his big floppy puppy feet padded between the pair of us, resting his head on our laps and gazing at us.

I told Claudette he'd not been out of sight since we'd returned from the party. I didn't mention we'd spent time in the attic, but I remember him sitting at the bottom of the extending ladder, whining occasionally after failing to climb up the rungs and join us.

"Why?" I asked Claudette. "What has happened?"

I think I got the family relationships correct, but a cousin to Old Giles who lived two kilometres from us had a chicken coup. Last night, something had broken in and killed every single bird. She handed over her phone and showed me pictures of the carnage.

I'm no expert, but it looked as if they had had their throats cut. There was blood everywhere. It had sprayed all over the nesting boxes, on the door, and there were pools of it on the floor.

I swallowed, and handed the phone back just as Leah

came down the stairs. I'd been waiting to accompany her to the police station to report Belinda's disappearance.

"We didn't think to check," she cried, breathless, and clutching an empty glass in one hand.

"Check what?"

She flung herself onto the couch opposite. "Check if Belinda was back. She is. She's in bed, and out cold. I couldn't even rouse her."

I breathed a sigh of relief. That was one problem solved. "Is she in one piece?"

Leah rearranged her skirt and grabbed the wine bottle off the table and filled up her glass. She took several large gulps. "As far as I can tell, without whipping the sheet off and poking and prodding her." She put the glass down and was silent for a moment. "I'm a bit alarmed. She has twigs and bits of leaves in her hair, as if she'd been dragged through the undergrowth."

"Best to leave her to sleep for now," I said. "Claudette came over to tell us that her cousin's chickens have all been slaughtered."

Claudette pushed her mobile into Leah's hand. Tapping the screen and making sliding motions.

Leah's face turned from relief to horror as the gruesome images slid into view. "How awful! A fox?"

"I don't think so, wouldn't it have killed a couple and either eaten them or taken one off to feed the cubs?"

"Deidre, I don't know too much about fox habits, but that makes sense." She turned to Claudette. "I am so sorry."

"*N'est pas Monster?*" She pronounced it 'Moensteer'.

Leah shook her head. "He has been with us all the

time, and locked in the laundry last night. I do hope you can find the culprit soon. I am so sorry."

Claudette stood and, shoulders drooped, she said goodbye and walked off through the back yard to the short cut across the field to her cottage, muttering about being late for the parade.

"It's never ending," Leah sighed. "One thing after another. But I'm so relieved it wasn't our dog, and I hope Claudette believes us."

"She's no reason not to. We have always been open and honest with her. Back to Belinda. Any speculation as to where she's been?"

"No. she's still wearing the dress she had on for the party. It looks as if she has staggered up the stairs and fallen into bed. She's still wearing one shoe."

We sat there for a moment each lost in our own thoughts. I watched a kite swoop across the sky. Had it been attracted by the smell of the blood from the massacred chickens? I shuddered, then felt my eyelids droop and the sounds of the waves and the cry of the birds faded away.

I was woken by a loud crash. The couch where Leah had been sitting was empty, so I scrambled to my feet and went to investigate. Monster wasn't barking his head off so there weren't any strangers around.

As I walked into the kitchen, I saw Belinda standing by the fridge. Broken china lay at her feet and the milk from the jug she was holding was slopping over the sides. I stepped forward, sliding the broken crockery to one side with my feet, relieved her of the jug, and guided her to a chair.

"Tell me what you want to eat," I spoke softly.

She looked at me. Her pupils were huge and she was disorientated. She waved her head from side to side and mumbled, "Anything."

I poured her a glass of milk and held her hand as she drank it. Leah was right; there were still bits of dried leaf and grass in her hair and I couldn't resist removing a few as she sat slumped over the kitchen table.

I made her a cottage cheese sandwich, slicing off the crusts and cutting it into triangles. While I was desperate to find out where she'd been, now was not the time for that serious talk.

Leah came in, about to rush over to her stepdaughter, but I waved her off, pointing to the state of the child. She nodded and noticing the broken china on the tiles went to get the brush and dustpan.

It was silent in the kitchen, a rare time with just the three of us. Madame du Pont, Sophie, Claudette and the outside staff were celebrating a local Saint's Day. We had planned to go to watch the procession – until Belinda went missing. Everyone in the village was involved of course, and I'd been too preoccupied with the pictures on her phone to notice her costume.

A starving man could not have devoured the sandwich more quickly than the teenager. I cut more bread to make a second one.

Monster nuzzled her legs and her hand shook as she reached down to stroke his head.

"He was worried about you," Leah said quietly. "He missed you. He was so lonely he stuck to Deidre and me like glue." There was no response to her attempt at humour. Belinda reminded me of a puppet with the strings cut off. She was half sprawled over the table, just lifting her head up far enough to cram in the second sandwich.

We had a quiet evening all together in the lounge. Leah found a comedy on Netflix but kept the sound manageable. We put no pressure on Belinda to talk, just cuddled her and murmured soothing words when we noticed the tears running down her cheeks. This was a different human to the sassy teen we were used to. This was a childlike young girl in pain. It broke my heart, and was having the same effect on Leah too. None of us had anyone else in the world, well, no family close enough to care about us.

I helped Belinda up to her room, while Leah ran her a bath and left her to clean up and crawl back into bed. There would be time enough tomorrow, or the day after, to connect.

Leah phoned Madame and told her not to come the next day as Belinda was not well.

"Ah, so the *pauvre enfant* has returned?" Her voice blared down the phone before Leah could hold it at arm's length.

"Yes. She is home."

"Where was she?" The voice boomed out.

"Maybe not on the phone," Leah deflected her. "I'll phone you again tomorrow to let you know if she will be well enough." She disconnected the call.

Leah switched off the television and we sat in silence for a moment.

"Madame was not pleased, of course," she remarked, breaking the silence. "I think she now realises that tutoring anyone from this family is not going to be an easy ride."

"I'm still trying to get my head around all the awful things that have happened in such a short time."

"Trouble follows me everywhere," Leah sighed.

"It's not fair. It's not as if you ever made any deliberately bad choices, or broke the law, or even hurt anyone. Life's not fair Leah, but it's going overboard with you."

"I've been thinking about making a will."

Leah's words made me sit upright in the chair. "What put that idea into your head?"

Leah's laugh was forced. "No, not a premonition, but I'm in my forties, and time I thought long term, but it's a big problem."

"Why?"

"Deidre, who do I leave all my new found wealth to?"

"I'll take it all darling." I smiled and clapped my hands. "But then, at my age I don't need it. I have enough to see me through."

"I'd be only too happy to give you the lot, and I'd want to leave some to Belinda as well, and possibly Bill. But I'm scared to do that."

"Why?" I couldn't see the problem.

"I might put them in danger. If whoever is targeting me for the money, and then bumps me off, the inheritor is next in line and…"

"Ah, I see. How about tying it up in a trust or something for years, so even if something awful happens they still can't get their paws on it?"

"I've thought about that too. But how would they know – they being whoever is behind all these bad things. Remember, there were plenty of unpleasant incidents in

Weston-super-Mare as well. Now it's followed me to the south of France."

I sat back. Leah was right. Ever since Mason's dog, Zeus, had died there had been a constant stream of, what could you call them, 'happenings'? One bad and upsetting thing after another. She'd discovered who was behind them before, but now they had started again, and the original culprits were locked away. Maybe they had not been the only perpetrators all along? Who out there wanted to hurt Leah, and possibly Belinda as well? Was it anyone we knew?

"I'm just so worried that anyone I choose I'll be putting in the firing line. Oh, dear, Deidre, does that sound hysterical and stupid?"

"From many people yes, but not from you Leah. You have every right to be suspicious and afraid. I won't sugar-coat it. I'd prefer to be honest with you. At first, I was going to keep anything I found in those files in the attic to myself. But I'm going to be open with you in the future. I think we both need to be on our guard. No more secrets to hide the truth."

"I'm not sure the chickens or the baby was aimed at us. I think that's just chance."

I thought about that. "While no one could possibly think we were responsible for either killing, the locals are not as friendly. Is it just a coincidence it's happened since we moved here?"

"From a crime free area to one that now has the police running in all directions?" Leah stood and paced back and forward. She fought to keep her hands still, while I made for the drinks cabinet and poured her a large brandy.

She took it from me with a smile. "I'll have to be careful. It would be too easy to start relying on this stuff every time I had the jitters. Soon be a lush and out of it. Tempting."

"You're far too sensible and strong for that. If only we knew what the next bad thing was going to be, we could protect ourselves."

Leah sat next to me and squeezed my arm. "You are so sweet, Deidre. You said 'we', and really you should walk away from all of this nonsense."

"Not a chance dear. You're stuck with me, at least for now. Before, I couldn't possibly move back into my place while the painters were still there, even if I'd wanted to, but I'm here now and staying put. In fact, I've been thinking. When you and Bill start looking for a place, I'd be more than happy if it had a granny flat or outbuildings we could convert."

"What a brilliant idea!" Leah's eyes were shining.

"There, does that make you feel better? What's in it for me? Now you know."

We both laughed.

I wasn't certain I wanted a granny flat just yet but, if it put Leah's mind at rest now, once Bill was back, she would not be as vulnerable and I could change my mind.

"I'm almost afraid to go to bed." Leah stood and began tidying away the glasses and snack plates, carrying them into the kitchen. I could hear her washing them in the sink. Even with a full-time housekeeper, she liked to leave the rooms tidy. I too was beginning to get nervous late at night. We humans feel more vulnerable in our night clothes, in the dark, and horizontal. Monster at least was a comfort and I heard Leah call to him to let him out for a last pee. He was already an excellent guard dog, even barking his head off when Claudette arrived in the morning and she was a regular visitor.

He flumped into the lounge, trying so hard to control his large floppy paws. As usual he was reluctant to go to his bed in the laundry. He nuzzled my feet, then heaved himself up to rest his front paws on my knees. He was one large ball of black, fluffy hair, and he'd wormed his way into all our hearts. He might be a mongrel of indeterminate parentage but he was a delight, and would cost a fortune to feed once he reached full size. Even in the short time we'd had him, he'd grown.

For once, we all had a good night's sleep or, more accurately, nothing happened to send us flying out of our beds.

The morning sun streamed through my window, warming my face and lighting up the dust particles dancing in the air. I looked forward to a quiet day. Was there such a thing in the Brand household?

Leah and I were having breakfast in the sun lounge when Belinda joined us. She was quiet, and just nodded as she sat down and helped herself to a croissant which she swathed in butter and strawberry jam.

I felt the slight tension in the air as neither Leah nor I were eager to break the silence. She was the first.

"Coffee?" She picked up the coffee pot, pulled a mug towards her and looked at Belinda.

The child nodded and Leah poured, then pushed the milk jug and sugar across the table. Belinda gulped it down without saying a word.

I deliberately started chatting about trips we could take inland, maybe go see the Camargue horses. I'd always wanted to see wild horses.

Leah was tapping away on her iPad. "Maybe not, seven hundred kilometres?"

"France is larger than we realise."

"The roads are good, but the tolls are horrendous."

We chattered on about possible places to visit, maybe on Sundays, while deliberately avoiding the questions we were both dying to ask: *Belinda where were you for almost 48 hours? Talk to us, tell us what happened?*

But the child was not saying anything. Not explaining the leaf mould in her hair, the fingernails I noticed were scraped right down to the quick, the ragged cuticles. And she was still shaky. We could only guess she'd been through some harrowing experience, but she was not sharing it with us.

We finally ran out of silence-filling conversation and I breathed a sigh of relief when Claudette bustled in to clear away the dishes. I tried to console myself with the thought that the only habit Belinda's experience had not shattered was her appetite. While Leah and I waffled on about nonsense the child had devoured four heavily laden croissants and three breakfast biscuits.

It took all my self-control to swallow the other questions which kept threatening to break out; to ask if Belinda wanted to see a doctor? Was she hurt? Did she need medicine?

The moment she finished eating and drained her coffee mug, she slipped away from the table and disappeared upstairs. She moved like a wraith, tiptoeing up each step as if treading on thin ice.

I raised my eyebrows and looked at Leah who shrugged in return.

"I need to pick up some things in the village," she said, "then get stuck into those files."

"Want some company?"

She hesitated for a moment, then shook her head. "Yes, I do, but I think it best one of us be here for..." She tilted her head towards the stairs.

"Of course. I wasn't thinking."

She sighed. "Though, if it goes on like this, I'll probably need you to ride shotgun each time I drive out of the gate."

We laughed, but it sounded hollow, even to our ears.

With no Madame here and no Sophie, I lugged the first box into the study area and picked up a file, marked *D A Morrison*. I'd deliberately left it on the top. We might find the answers without having to study all the dusty piles we'd dragged out to check.

It took a lot of concentration to plough my way through the legalese but, as far as I could tell, Daniel, our dinner guest, had been accused of fraud on a grand scale, and money laundering. From what I could understand, he was as guilty as hell; the police had masses of evidence. His co-conspirators were London based, in the clubland areas, and involved strip joints and private gambling clubs. Not on the scale of Monte Carlo but smart enough to attract the high rollers. Mason had indeed defended him, and there were pages and pages of counter claims against the police for missing details in procedures and lack of proper reading of rights, and the whole case collapsed as a result of slipshod police procedures. I can only imagine how mad they must have been after all those hours and hours of work to have some smartass lawyer defeat them on a legal technicality. The man walked away scot-free, and there was a newspaper clipping at the back showing him on the court steps, microphones pointing towards him, as the media screamed questions at him with Daniel beaming ear to ear. I held it closer and peered at the detail, wondering if that was Mason just behind him. He looked similar to the odd photo I had seen of him.

I did know the lady standing to the other side: Geraldine Morrison, and she was smiling, not at her husband, but at Mason. One of those 'we are intimate' kind of smiles. Pure conjecture on my part, but my fey feelings filled in the gaps.

I was interrupted by Monster's 'a stranger is on my territory' bark. Claudette was already on her way to open the front door, but I waved her away when I saw it was UPS delivering the safe. It took both men to drag it out of the van, and place it on the front step. Using my schoolgirl French, I hinted that I would be happy to pay a tip if they could put it in place for me?

The elderly man in charge looked me up and down and quickly came to the conclusion that a little old, fragile lady like me would never be able to shift it off the front step into the house. I pushed my luck even further and they were kind enough to take it upstairs and into Leah's bedroom. As they clattered back down the stairs, sweating profusely and wiping brows with overlarge kerchiefs, I was obliged to give them all the Euros I had in my purse. It was worth it.

As I walked back into the study area, I caught Claudette staring at the newspaper clipping I'd left open on the desk. The moment she saw me, she froze, and I waited for her to ask me about it. Instead, she scurried away, but not before she cast me a look that was full of questions.

When Leah returned from the village we played with the safe, setting a combination and practising spinning the dials to lock and unlock it, harder than I imagined; the door was solid and needed a hefty pull to open it. There was only just enough space inside for the files of interest, and we decided to store what was left of our jewellery.

"We'll only keep relevant files in here," Leah announced, pushing the door to and twirling the dial. "Only you and I know the code and let's keep to that."

"Agreed. No one else needs to know."

We made good progress that afternoon. While I made a pile of 'won and lost' cases, Leah logged down the different names in each, with the idea of following up where these previous defendants might be. Was Daniel Alexander Morrison the only neighbour who had past secrets?

He wasn't, but we knew that. It was almost supper time when I picked up the case folder for Humphrey Fenton. More fraud and money laundering, plus receiving stolen property. He'd been operating import and export, mostly garments, but there was a suspicion of arms dealings too. One witness had accused him of selling weapons to the IRA.

Leah leaned back and groaned. "Trust Mason to go for the high profile, really dangerous crooks. He's not bothered with the odd speeding fine or shoplifting offences."

"No, he was after the big bucks, right? And who else has all the money today but the wheelers and dealers?"

"I wonder if anyone ever made an honest fortune?" Leah stared at the ceiling.

"You did."

She laughed. "A few millions, enough for the rest of my life, but not the mega fortunes these guys have. Mason's fees were astronomical. I couldn't believe it when he told me how much he charged by the hour. And that's not the time he was in court. It was also for reading the paperwork, researching past cases, and writing up strategies."

"And a few extra hours thrown in for good measure?"

"For sure. Who could challenge him on that? And he'd take a slice of the billable time worked by his colleagues."

Leah looked over my shoulder. "So, Mason got Humphrey Fenton off?"

I flicked through the file. "No. Off most of the charges, but not this one. He was caught with stolen property, jewellery, in his car and more in his house. The judge sentenced him to five years. So, I guess he might have had a previous record?"

"Five years does sound a lot for a first offence."

"And a long time for possession of stolen goods, doesn't it? It doesn't mention any violence or harm to anyone."

"Yes. So, Humphrey Fenton has a record and maybe he's still on probation? He wouldn't serve a whole five years unless he was a problem prisoner."

"Don't you get a third remission for good behaviour?" Leah sighed. "Why bother to sentence offenders for five years and let them out early? Unless it's to stop them fighting in prison. So, Mr Humphrey Fenton is an ex-con. I wonder if the Lampierres know?"

"It's good to know others have secrets. You're not the only one Leah and, in your case, you're completely innocent. He isn't." I had a thought. "Geraldine Morrison wearing my necklace makes a bit more sense now, don't you think?"

"You're not suggesting those two broke in here, stole jewellery and spray painted the villa, are you?" Leah got up from the floor – she was amazing how she handled her prosthesis now – and leaned against the desk. She brushed the dust off her skirt before she replied. "It's possible, if unlikely. The Mob bosses get others to do their dirty work so they have clean hands. He could have hired somebody else."

I sighed. "We may never find out. The police have hardly been active, have they?"

"No," Leah agreed, before her mobile rang. She paced to and fro as she listened and pulled faces at me. "Yes, yes, thank you," she said. "See you Friday." She rang off.

"Who was that?"

"Geraldine. We've been invited to supper on Friday. I accepted, of course."

"A trip into the lion's den?" I chuckled.

"I'm curious to see how the conversation will go. Wonder if he's itching to find out more about Mason?"

It was getting late so we began to pack the files back into the boxes.

"You know, life might be quite unpleasant for Mason. There must be some crooks in there he didn't get off, or who hold a grudge because they were fingered to protect the client he was defending."

"Fingered! Deidre, I've not heard that term in years."

"Ah, you don't watch many old movies, do you? Prisoners aside, I'm sure Mason isn't flavour of the month with the police either."

"Negating all their hard work on such things as technicalities?" Leah paused. Clutching an armful of files she wiped her brow with her arm.

"Yes. We'd better put these in the attic until we have separated out the important ones."

"Put the Fenton and Morrison stuff in the safe. I wouldn't be surprised to learn that's what the intruders were after."

"Now why didn't I think of that sooner?"

"Well they failed and, now we have Monster, no one is sneaking back in quietly."

The moment we sat down for supper, Monster began his frantic barking, which was quite deep and mature for his size. Often Belinda would leap up to go and check out visitors, but she sat quietly demolishing the food on her plate.

Leah returned to the dining room with Francois Ecole trailing behind her.

"Police," she announced. "Gendarme Ecole wants to discuss the chicken slaughter."

Leah asked him to sit down and offered him a drink. I disappeared into the kitchen to fetch the coffee. When I returned, he was trying to push Monster away without success. The dog was intent on climbing onto his lap and making a total nuisance of himself. Leah told Belinda to take him into the other room and look after him.

Before Francois could say a word, Leah spoke firmly, assuring him that Monster had nothing to do with the dead chickens. He'd been with us in the house and then shut in the laundry room where he slept every night. There was no possible way he could have escaped. No one had let him out.

From the look in the gendarme's face I didn't think he was convinced. "You will swear to this in the court?" He asked in heavily accented English.

"Yes, of course, and so will Deidre, I'm sure."

I nodded. "Monster was in all night. And I doubt he would have attacked the hens. A couple of cats wander into the garden sometimes and he's never taken any notice of them."

Pen poised over his notebook Francois indicated the chair where Belinda had been sitting. "And the girl? She was here?"

There was a brief, uncomfortable silence before Leah replied. "No, she was out."

"Where?"

Another brief pause before Leah added, "with friends."

I found I was holding my breath. If he asked which friends and where they lived, things could get awkward.

"Any news on the break in here at the villa?" Leah rushed to change the subject.

Francois drained the last of his coffee. "Good coffee. No, I am sorry, no." He stood up to leave.

"There have been many incidents lately," I said to him. "The baby, the chickens, our car burning and the dead dog…"

He whirled around to face me. "Dead dog?"

A cold shiver ran down my spine. I'd spoken without thinking.

"It was a long time ago," Leah added hastily. "Some of the young boys, it was a joke."

He stood for a moment rocking on his heels, but he probably decided he had enough problems to solve without adding another one. "This," he said, finger in the air, "has always been the village quiet and safe. Now happen many things. It is not good."

With a brief nod to us both he marched out of the room and we felt the rush of air as he opened the front door and slammed it behind him.

We both fell back into our chairs like limp puppets.

"Life gets more complicated by the day," Leah moaned, leaning forward on the table. "I think I lied to a policeman just now. That's probably some kind of punishable offence. Perjury I think."

"Belinda must have been with friends of some sort, but then it turned nasty? It was just as well you didn't tell him we had no idea where she was and, now, she's not telling us. And Leah, be sensible, is Belinda going to break into a hen house and cut the birds' throats? From Claudette's photos it was some wild animal."

"Yes, you're right. And Monster is not the only dog around, and there must be foxes too. Exactly. I'm getting worked up for nothing." She jumped up and began clearing the table. "Can you go and release Belinda from her exile? Maybe if you mention why he called in she might let something slip about the other night?"

"I'll do my best."

My best wasn't enough. Belinda just nodded, hugged Monster, and nuzzled the top of his head. She wasn't saying anything and we were none the wiser.

OCTOBER LEAH

Dear Dairy,

I had a nightmare. They were marching me off to prison for lying to the police. It's a huge sin in France, this hollow, disembodied voice kept telling me. It carries a life sentence. I was screaming, thrashing around trying to break free from the two huge men on either side of me. They were dragging me towards the execution chamber. Through a narrow doorway I could see the rope hanging down and a tall shadowy figure, dressed all in black, was standing legs askew on the platform. He lifted his arm and was beckoning to me. I could feel rather than hear his words.

"Come closer. This is where it all ends. Come. Leah. Come."

The more I struggled, the tighter they held me. There was no escape. My breaths became shorter and shorter. Every lungful of air was a battle to suck in. I felt my legs give way, both of them. When did that happen? When did I last have two legs? Now I was dangling puppet-like between my two captors as they dragged me closer and closer to the gallows.

At the bottom of the steps it became even more confused. The steps were too narrow for three of us to mount. One man let go, and I twisted around and wriggled and slipped out of the grasp of the other jailor, and then I was running, blindly, out of the chamber, across the prison yard. I could hear them coming behind me, their booted feet thundering over the concrete. They were getting closer. I ran faster. Not fast enough. I flew straight into a solid brick wall, the prison boundary. It reached far above me to the sky, topped by razor wire which glistened in the sun.

By now the other prisoners behind the narrow, barred windows were screaming and yelling. Were they for me or for the guards?

My captors grabbed me again and threw ropes around my body. Trussed me up like a chicken. They hoisted me up and carried me horizontally back towards the death chamber. This time I knew I wasn't going to escape, yet my fists fought against the restraints. I wasn't giving up.

The scene faded and I was dancing wildly, a puppet being manipulated by someone far above my head. I twisted my head back, looking up to see who was in control. But it was impossible to see and then the strings were suddenly jerked and cut and I collapsed on the floor, breathless and gasping for air.

Where was the dog I could hear barking? I'd not seen a dog in prison. My arms and leg flailed against the restraints, the sheets on my own bed. I lay back exhausted, covered in sweat, shaking, thirsty and defeated.

As much as I tried to be brave, calm and rational

inside, I was a seething mass of uncertainty and fear. I needed a time of calm, order and peace, but one disaster followed another.

Chickens? Why would anyone in this household go and mangle domestic fowl? What kind of mind does something like that? It has to be a wild animal, but Claudette tells us that the padlock on the gate had been sliced open with bolt cutters. Beyond the ability of any wild animal, so it has to be human. What must the villagers think of us? And the baby, I still can't get that mental picture out of my head. It was asleep in its pushchair. The mother buying pastries in the bakery and then to return and see… It makes me shudder.

I'm so tempted to move away. Go to another country maybe but, I suspect until these crimes are solved, that would not be a good idea, even if the police would let us. Francois Ecole's last words were that he wanted to talk to us again. If we ran away now, we'd look guilty.

It's taking me all my will power not to grab Belinda and shake the truth out of her. I might feel sorry for her, she's obviously had a bad experience, but can't she see what she's putting us through, the worry she's causing? The suspicion that's hanging over our house like those umbrellas they show in the insurance commercials. Except this is an umbrella of doom, not comfort.

I tried, several times, to talk to her, to find out where she'd been and what happened. She either sat in stubborn silence, or blew up and ranted and raved about me being cruel, nosy or controlling.

Deidre tried too, she stayed calm and conversational but that didn't elicit any answers either. Belinda was not going to tell us, and we finally admitted defeat and let the subject rest.

Tomorrow it will be November, and Friday we're going to dinner with the Morrisons. Deidre is right, we'll be walking into the lion's den. Give me strength and courage.

OCTOBER BELINDA

Dear Journal,

Not sure why I'm writing in this sodding thing except it's something to do. It's a bloody nightmare living in this house. I can feel their thoughts, Leah and Deidre, each itching to know what happened, where I was, was I alone?

I'll never tell. Never!!!!! It was just too awful.

It was a great idea at the beginning and then it became a nightmare.

The old wrinklies would never understand, never. Please preserve me from living boring, uneventful lives like theirs.

I might make mistakes, but it's better than day to day drag stuff – isn't it?

The only one who truly understands is Monster. I just love him to the stars and back. I think they're bloody mean not letting him sleep on my bed. So what if he has the odd flea and tick? He's a dog and dogs get that stuff on them. Bet if Deidre crawled around in the grass, she'd get fleas on her too, and ticks.

That sodding policeman gives me the creeps. He looks

right through you, as if he could read your thoughts. Him and Madame frigging du Pont, her as well. What's with these French people, are they all mind readers?

She'll be back tomorrow. Leah did try and put her off, she really did try and I was so surprised, almost as if she was on my side. But, no, the old witch was insistent I missed no more days of tutoring. I could hear her voice blasting down the phone, the whole fricking village could have heard her.

"Belinda will have wasted all these days of hard work. We can't stop now." And on and on and on. So, Madame and Sophie arrive in the morning. I'm only admitting it in here, dear journal, but it will be something to do. The sooner I get to take these exams, the sooner I can duck out and go. I shall make a calendar and mark off my days to freedom.

NOVEMBER DEIDRE

I was in my bedroom, unloading my wardrobe, deciding what to wear to this dinner when the sound of loud, angry voices floated up the stairs. I paused to listen, then crossed the hallway and leaned over the bannister.

Leah and Belinda were having a huge row. Whatever had upset her, had snapped her out of her silent morose behaviour. She'd been gliding around the house like a wraith, with Monster in tow. He never left her side these days. He could sense she was upset, more than upset, unhappy. Unless she chose to share it with us, or anyone else, she was on her own to battle her demons.

She'd refused the offer of a doctor's appointment, or a check-up at the clinic, or a counsellor of some sort. There was nothing further we could do if she insisted on coping by herself.

I only heard a few exchanges to understand that Leah wanted to call in another adult to sit with Belinda while we were out at dinner. The teenager was incensed at the idea. She was too old for a babysitter. What if that got out? Everyone in the village would laugh at her.

As usual, Leah was keeping her cool. "It wouldn't be a babysitter, Belinda. Just a friend over for the evening. Company."

"I'm fine on my own, or hadn't you noticed? I never go anywhere."

"This would be a chance to ask one of the girls you like to come and spend some time together."

"On a Friday? You gotta be kidding. They'll all be at the night clubs in Nice. Living it up, not stuck at home with Netflix."

"I'm just worried about your safety, Belinda. I worry because I care. These are not normal times for any of us. Look at all the awful things that have happened. I've even booked an alarm company to come and give us a quote. Make us all feel safer."

"Yeah, and who dragged us all here? Who decided this was a great place to live? You, it was you. Yeah, and a great decision that was. Did you ask me? Was I consulted? Oh no! I just had to follow along like a ventriloquist's dummy."

Leah began to lose it. "That's not fair Belinda, and it's not true either! You were just as keen to leave England. I remember you saying what bad memories it had. And you liked the idea of living by the sea in a warmer climate. It's you who is being unfair."

"Yeah, yeah, Little Miss Perfect. Never makes a wrong decision. It's always me isn't it? Me. Me. Me."

Up on the balcony I shook my head. That was one unhappy, mixed up teenager. At seventeen she should have grown out of this behaviour by now, be more mature, more adult. It's as if she was stuck in a delayed maturity groove.

I'm not sure spending as much time with twelve- year-old Sophie was helping either.

I heard Leah's voice fade as she replied. "Be it on your own head then. We're at the other end of the phone, I'll keep it on my lap on silent so I'll feel it vibrate."

"Yeah go on, treat me like a baby. You'd like that wouldn't you? You can't replace the ones you lost, even if you wanted to."

Eavesdropping, I sucked in a breath. That was a low blow, even for Belinda. How I wanted to batter the kid at that moment. I didn't hear Leah's reply and went back to sorting out something suitable to wear for the evening.

Neither Leah nor I were looking forward to the dinner but, if we were ever going to settle here and make friends, it would be social suicide to refuse. Not only that, we were both desperate to find out more about their connections to Mason.

We left Belinda sitting on the sofa cuddling Monster, flicking through the Freeview channels on the television. Leah had bustled around double and triple checking the locks on all the windows and doors before she reluctantly climbed into the car and we set off.

"I don't know whether to feel happy Belinda has got all feisty again, or sad the quiet, peaceful girl has gone," Leah remarked as she shifted into second gear outside the gate.

"I know very little about psychology," I replied, "I can only go on my instincts."

"And what are they telling you?"

"She's suppressing her reactions to whatever happened to her. I'm not sure it's good to bury them."

Leah drove slowly along the main street in the village before turning at the T junction.

"I keep going over and over in my mind what could have happened. Rape, drugs, a brief kidnap to frighten us all?"

I sighed. "I have no idea, and I wish she'd talk to us. We need to stick together with this mystery hanging over us. I keep telling myself it's all a coincidence."

"What, Deidre? Setting my car on fire?"

"Well no, that was deliberate. Maybe vandalism. The Morrison boys maybe. We must find out, and tonight's a good opportunity to ask questions."

"Don't know about you, but I don't want to stay too long. I'm already fretting about leaving Belinda on her own."

"I agree. I'm surprised she insisted on it."

"That's typical of her stubbornness. I did suggest she come with us. I was prepared to tell Geraldine we had to bring her, but Belinda refused, quite vehemently."

"You did your best, Leah. Let's keep our wits about us tonight."

I saw her nod in the darkened car and felt sad that the only friend she had made since arriving in France was now under deep suspicion.

By now we knew the area well, and it was less than a ten-minute drive. The Morrisons lived on a quiet, tree-lined country road at the top of a very steep hill. The house was set back behind a high hedge with a short drive to a two storey, stone built, square, solid looking building of no particular architectural significance. It only just escaped in my imagination from emanating a disturbing atmosphere.

We were the first to arrive; there were no other cars in the gravelled driveway that wound around a waterless fountain in the middle of the front lawn. I also noticed several stone statues, the usual fake Greek gods and goddesses, which looked out of place in such a small establishment. OK, so it was bitchy of me, but typical of the mobster making good overseas on his nefarious earnings at the expense of those less ruthless.

Leah parked up but, before we got out, the front door was flung open spilling light onto the steps. Daniel Morrison welcomed us in and, if I was going to behave myself this evening, then my performance would be worthy of an Academy Award – move over Dame Judy Dench. I harboured a deep mistrust of this man. His business dealings, what I knew of them, went against every principle I held dear.

Geraldine hurried up the hallway to greet us. I blinked from all the sparkly bits that glistened off her bright pink cashmere sweater over cream tailored trousers that failed to reach her ankles. Her feet were crushed into matching pink high heels. Mobster's moll sprang to mind, before I squashed the unkind thought and did my best not to giggle.

We were ushered into an elegant lounge, filled with a variety of chairs, a chaise longue, sofas, and footstools in matching chintz covers. Long drapes beneath deep pelmets hid the floor to ceiling windows, and to one side was a long wooden cabinet sporting a huge variety of bottles and glasses.

While Geraldine shepherded us to seats near the fake, gas-fed, log fire occupying the old stone fireplace, Daniel offered us drinks.

No sooner had he handed them over when the doorbell rang again. He rushed off to answer it and returned leading the Fentons.

I could almost hear Leah groan. If I was fanciful, I'd have imagined myself as Daniel in the lion's den, surrounded not by two felines but by four wild animals. I wondered if they knew what we knew about their past lives?

I was horrified when I realised that, once again, Margaret was wearing what I was convinced was my necklace. I wracked my brains to remember if I had ever damaged it and could identify it as mine. I found it difficult to take my eyes off it. It stood out prominently against the sparkly black jump suit; sequins must be in fashion at the moment. It crossed my mind she was 'mutton dressed as lamb' as my mother used to say. For a woman who must be pushing sixty, her outfit was more suitable for a night in a rave disco. Her black patent high heels must have been at least four inches high. She crossed the Persian carpet, stumbling a little, and greeted Geraldine with air kisses aimed at both cheeks, then she turned to us. I suspected she might have had a few drinks before leaving the house.

"Oh hello." She looked at Geraldine. "Just the six of us then?"

Geraldine nodded and took a sip of her sherry. I observed them both, sensing there were unspoken words flying between them.

The atmosphere was a little strained, as the conversation bounced over the latest happenings in the village. Daniel and Humphrey stood over by the drinks cabinet talking in lowered voices, leaving us women perched on chintz chairs with spindly legs grouped around the fake logs. The couches would have been far more comfortable, but were set back from the heat and there was a chill in the air together with the frosty atmosphere.

Leah and I sat nursing our drinks in tiny, crystal glass schooners, saying very little.

Margaret startled us both. Her hand flew up to her mouth as she turned to Leah. "Oh, my goodness, I quite forgot. Tell me, how is Belinda? I heard she was home."

"Yes. She's fine, thank you."

"So where was the poor girl? It was so strange her disappearing like that, in the middle of little Sophie's birthday party."

"Yes, we were surprised too." Leah's voice was steady but she took another large slurp of her sherry, draining the glass. She glanced over to the men in the hope of asking for more, but neither of them was looking in our direction.

The ladies were not going to let go as easily. "So, tell us, where was she? What was she doing?"

I jumped in, eager to take the pressure off Leah. "She's always been a bit of an enigma, and very secretive. We're sure she'll tell us in her own time. When she's had a chance to think it through."

"She's given us a few hints though, but we'll not pressure her."

Why had Leah said that? We had no idea, but I wondered if she'd also caught the looks that were flying between the two women. Just the occasional eye movement, the odd flick of a finger, but both knew more than they were saying. I was itching to jump up, drag Geraldine or Margaret by the hair, I didn't mind which, and shake them until we had the truth. But I sat quietly, a well-behaved guest.

The door opened and a small woman, dressed in a French maid's outfit, black dress with a white frilled pinafore and a small white cap perched on her head, took two steps into the room. She nodded at Geraldine who gracefully rose to her feet.

"Thank you, Marcella. Dinner is served everyone. Come, follow me."

She marched out and we followed behind like newly-hatched ducklings. The hallway was a miniature version of the chateau, black and white tiled floors, a fake suit of armour at the bottom of the single staircase, and large landscaped oil paintings hung over every square inch of the wall space.

The dining room was smaller and cosier than the lounge, and I noticed another gas fire battled to cope with the chilled air. I'd not seen one radiator so far and wondered why they had not installed central heating. I clutched my pashmina close to my chest as Geraldine directed us to our places. Leah and I were placed on opposite sides of the table, at a diagonal with Humphrey next to me and Margaret next to Leah. Daniel and Geraldine sat at the top and bottom of the table.

When we first walked in, I pretended I didn't see where Geraldine was asking us to sit, and moved to go next to Leah, but our hostess gave a tinkly laugh and, taking my arm, placed me exactly where she wanted me. Humphrey placed his ample rump on the adjoining chair and tapped my leg.

"You'll love Geraldine's cooking," he leered at me. "Her dinner parties are always the best."

Our hostess simpered as she sat down and fluffed out her napkin. "You are far too kind, Humphrey. The French are famous for their food, we British are way behind their culinary achievements."

Daniel prowled around behind us, pouring wine into each glass. When he reached Leah, she smiled up at him and put her hand out.

"Just a half glass please, Daniel. I'm driving."

"Nonsense! No need to bother about that!" Humphrey boomed in my ear. "Constables around here are decent chaps. Never pick up the locals, do they Daniel? More than their life's worth."

There were a few embarrassed titters, before Daniel fixed his eyes on Leah and said, "But of course you have met the local gendarmes, haven't you?" His eyes lingered on her face, observing the pink that flooded into her cheeks.

"Yes, a couple of times."

Marcella approached with a tray and placed the soup in front of us. No one said a word until she had left and closed the door behind her.

"In fact," Daniel paused, his soup spoon halfway to his mouth, "you have met them several times I believe?"

Geraldine gave him a hard stare. "Daniel, no. Later please."

"As you wish my dear."

Silence fell, the only sounds were the quiet slurping of the soup off the spoons. As soon as we had all finished, Geraldine reached for the small bell, and the tinkling sound brought Marcella who, I guessed, must have been hovering outside the door with her ear to the keyhole to appear so quickly. She returned with a platter of meat which she placed in front of Daniel. He stood to begin carving as the maid hurried in several times with dishes of vegetables and gravy.

"Ooh, Yorkshire Pudding! What a treat," cooed Margaret. "They are so hard to find here. There was an English supermarket, but recently—"

"Homemade," boasted Geraldine. "Very easy to make, I'll be happy to show you."

"Don't. I'm hopeless in the kitchen. Our housekeeper does most of the basic stuff for us."

"Aye, queen of the ready-made foods aren't you, my love?" Humphrey chuckled, while Margaret shot daggers at him.

"I'm not that bad," she snapped back.

Geraldine rushed in to fill the uncomfortable gap, wittering on about treating us all to a good, old-fashioned British Sunday lunch just like we had at home.

"Do you miss England?" Leah asked.

Daniel began passing the plates around as he placed the meat on them.

Our hostess thought for a moment. "No, I don't. I don't miss the weather, who would? I love being so close to the sea. The language is a pain of course. Too old to pick it up now."

"We've met a few people in and around the village, but are there many more British expats in the area?" Leah asked.

I took a deep breath, willing my memory into gear to remember names. We would be looking for them in the files tomorrow.

"I think maybe three other couples we know well, the Lesters, the Campbells and the Reynolds. Can you think of any others, Margaret?"

"I've heard of a couple in Tresomme, and a new family over the back, near the forest. Not met them yet, but I heard they were enquiring about schooling, so they must have young kids."

"Where is the nearest school?" Leah asked.

"They would have to travel into Nice for high school, otherwise the local village school."

"Must be convenient for you with Belinda studying at home with Sophie and Madame du Pont," Margaret said.

They didn't miss much that was going on in the village, why should I be surprised?

Margaret added, "I hear Madame is quite a slave driver."

"She's very enthusiastic," was Leah's response.

"But then your boys, being younger must be a help? With the language, I mean." I forced a smile as I brought the subject back to the boys.

"Bart and Toby? Well they do chatter on to the locals in French when they are here of course. But they never stay still enough to help much."

"But they don't live here with you?" Leah asked.

"Goodness no. Boarding school, thank God. Hate to have them round my feet all day."

"But you're close enough to have them out for half term and holidays?" Leah persisted.

"They do go on school trips out of term time; skiing, adventure camps, water sports, and the like," Daniel cut in. "Not a lot for them to do here, too rural for much fun."

I recalled some of the 'fun' they had had, and the antics they had got up to, if we were to believe the village gossip and Madame du Pont.

"When were they last out?" Now, this is the question both Leah and I were desperate to know.

"Oh, a few weeks ago." Geraldine was decidedly vague.

"Which boarding school do they go to?"

"Sheraton in Wiltshire. They have such a good reputation and most of their students aim for Oxbridge, of course. Their pass rates are through the roof."

"And so are the fees," Daniel added with a scowl. "But hey, you do the best you can for your sons, don't you?"

"Do you have children?" I focused my gaze on Margaret, while I removed her husband's hand off my knee. What was he thinking? At my age. He must be at least a decade younger than me. I couldn't wait to tell Leah on the way home.

"No, we have never been blessed." Margaret's voice was so low I almost missed her reply.

"Mixed blessing, eh?" Humphrey turned to me, breathing wine fumes in my face. "Sorrow mixed with joy. What do you say, Dan?"

"Must say I'm proud of my boys. Credit to me." Daniel pushed his dessert plate away and rose to rescue another bottle of wine. He circled the table filling each glass to the brim, until he got to Leah, who held her hand firmly over the rim of hers. "No thank you." Her voice was firm.

"It's bloody good wine, cost a packet." Daniel's response was almost a snarl.

"Driving, remember?" She smiled sweetly at him. "But I would love a glass of water."

Geraldine sighed as she rang the bell again and Marcella tumbled into the room. "Jug of water and a glass please," she commanded.

Marcella cleared away the remaining plates and dishes, placed a large pitcher of water and a glass on the table and left us alone.

So far, Leah and I had begun to sound like a KGB interrogation team, and there were a couple of moments of silence before Daniel raised a toast to absent friends.

I had no ideas who we were toasting, but raised my glass anyway. I was about to find out.

"To Mason," he announced.

Leah's hand shook, her water glass halfway to her lips. She gasped.

Daniel pinned her with his eyes. "Not going to toast the old man, Leah? You are still married to him, aren't you?"

She placed the tumbler back on the table. "Only until the final divorce papers come through, and they are well overdue."

"Maybe they'll never arrive?" suggested our host.

I squirmed on my chair, hoping no one would notice. I knew what it felt to be caught on the end of a fisherman's hook.

Daniel played out the line further. "Tell me…" He rose from his seat and began to pace around the table, wine glass in hand, which he topped up at frequent intervals. The rest of us followed him with our eyes. "Where were you living before you came over to France?"

"Leah and Belinda were living near me in Weston-super-Mare. They needed to get away from London."

"With the press breathing down your neck, I'm not surprised." Daniel took a breath. "But Mason's house in London? Why not stay there, once the story died down? Seems a shame to leave it empty."

"I needed a fresh start." Leah sat up straight and stared back at Daniel. "I... we, all needed some peace and quiet."

"Seems you came to the wrong place," our host smirked. "There's been plenty of activity since you arrived. Or am I mistaken?"

"Not as peaceful as I'd hoped." I admired Leah's bravery.

Daniel leaned over her, invading her personal space, threatening, his voice full of menace.

Geraldine intervened. "Daniel, that's enough."

"Enough what dear? I think we all want an answer to the same question, don't we?"

"What are you talking about?" Leah snapped back at him. She dropped all pretence of politeness. "You'll have to be a little clearer, Daniel."

He reached past her for the wine bottle and topped up his glass yet again. I could see he was less than steady on his feet; the odd word was slurred and his face had an unhealthy pink glow.

"I want to know what you removed from the London house Leah, my dear."

"Nothing!" She almost shouted the word. "Not a thing that did not belong to me. I've left all Mason's possessions intact. Not, that it is any business of yours."

I felt the tips of my fingernails dig into my palms. I

was way ahead of Daniel. He must know about the files. Didn't clients talk confidentially to their lawyers, and weren't those confidences written up and filed away? It made sense he wanted to get his hands on them and probably destroy them.

All of a sudden, the files in the safe and the attic resembled a time bomb. We needed to get rid of them, and fast. Or, hand them over or return them to Mason's house in London.

I tried to catch Leah's eye, but she didn't look at me.

I waited to see what Daniel would say but he stumbled slightly and fell back into his chair.

"I hope you will excuse my husband, Leah. A little too much to drink." Geraldine's laugh was forced and insincere. Margaret and Humphrey were also uncomfortable, so I rushed in.

"Geraldine, I have been admiring your necklace all evening. Where did you get it? I'd love one like that. I've never seen one quite like it."

"Oh, this old thing?" Margaret put her hand up and stroked it. "I've had it for ages, and I can't remember where I got it. Can you, Humphrey?"

"Thought it quite recent. Only seen it on you a couple of times." His hand began to wander again under the table and this time I dug my nails into the back of his hand as hard as I dared. He gave a start and swiftly withdrew it.

Seeing his wife's face filled with fury he added, "But then the old girl's got so many trinkets I often get her pieces mixed up."

No, you bloody don't, I thought, but kept my face neutral. I probed further. "It looks so valuable Margaret.

You can always tell quality and you must have listed it for insurance? Would you have the details there? Humour me, it's the nicest piece of jewellery I've seen in years."

Margaret was uncomfortable. I saw her wriggle on her chair and she confirmed my suspicions. It was mine, and somehow, she had acquired it illegally. I planned to get it back.

Daniel slumped down a little in his chair, but he wasn't about to let me change the subject.

"So, tell me my dear, why did you order a large, heavy duty safe?" He fixed his eyes on Leah, ignoring the frantic looks coming from Geraldine and the grunting noises made by Humphrey.

"I don't think it's any business of yours." Leah rose to her feet. She turned to Geraldine. "Thank you for your hospitality, the food was excellent. But, if you'll excuse us, I don't want to leave Belinda on her own for too long."

"She's a big girl now. Hell, at that age I was fending for myself down the East End." Daniel slurred his words. "Don't go running off, the evening is only just beginning to get interesting."

I began to stand up, but Humphrey grabbed my arm and stopped me from moving away. He wasn't drunk, but I could feel the waves of anger as he hissed. "We know what you have over there, and we'd like it back."

I was more than tempted to tell him to come and collect every scrap of paper that Leah had carted over to France on Mason's instructions. Did we need to know what crimes they had committed in the past? Was it any of our business? No, to both. But it wasn't my decision to make, and I could only advise Leah. I pulled away from him, thanked Geraldine, and the two of us left the room after nodding briefly and murmuring a good night as we escaped into the hall and retrieved our hats and scarves. I heard Daniel call after us but I didn't hear what he said.

It wasn't until we were at the bottom of the driveway and Leah was turning onto the country road that I let out the breath I was holding. "I've had better evenings." I did my best to sound cheerful.

Leah laughed, but I detected more than a little hysteria in her voice. "So, they want the files back? That's what they're after, yes?"

"Yes. Are you going to hand them over?"

"I don't know. It's too dangerous to keep them in the villa, even in the safe."

As we approached the top of the hill leading to the main road into the village, Leah let out a shriek.

"What's the matter?"

"The brakes! The brakes have gone! Oh my God! Deidre, we're going too fast!"

The road dipped down sharply ending at the T junction at the bottom.

Leah frantically pumped her right foot on the brake pedal, but the car was not slowing. Always a careful driver, she kept her speed down, especially after dark, but the intersection was getting closer and the car was gathering speed on the downhill.

"Change down, get into a lower gear!" I used both hands to pull on the handbrake but it had little effect.

Leah depressed the clutch and rammed the gear stick into second and we slowed a little but not enough to halt at the stop sign.

I looked both ways. "You'll have to drive straight round the corner. I can't see any headlights so the road's clear."

The car picked up speed.

"No! No! No!" she cried as she attempted to slalom down the hill in an effort to slow us down. She wrenched the gear stick into first, and we shuddered at the crunching, grinding noise as the metal cogs in the gearbox refused to mesh.

We flew round the corner, far too fast. The trees whipped past us on either side, the hedges a blur. I braced myself with both hands against the dashboard and pulled my legs back as far as they would go. The car was out of control and we were flung to one side, as Leah attempted to steer it towards the high grass verge. The vehicle fishtailed from one side of the road to the other, then mounted the bank and bounced back onto the road again, throwing us up towards the roof, restrained only by our seat belts. The airbags inflated pinning us back in our seats.

I yanked again on the handbrake and we fishtailed, spinning round twice before coming to a stop resting diagonally across the road. Even stationary, we were in just as much danger now. If any traffic came along the road, they would slam right into us.

Leah took a deep breath, pushed past the airbag, and reached round to turn the wheel and slowly manoeuvre the car to the side of the road. We were still not safe, even this main road was barely wide enough for two cars.

We both tumbled out of the car, fighting past the collapsed airbags, scared and shaking. I leant back against the vehicle and took a deep breath, waiting for my heart to slow down. I was trembling all over and the vice-like feeling in my chest sent pains shooting through my body.

"Leah, are you all right?"

"Yeah, I think so. But dazed."

"Come over to the side. It's safer."

"Give me a second to stop wobbling all over the place." I could tell Leah was trying not to cry. She hobbled around the front of the car, leaning against it to steady herself, and practically fell into my arms.

We stood there for several moments, until I stepped back and leaned in and turned the engine off. The headlights died and the dark enveloped us.

"Not such a good idea," I muttered. "We'll have to leave some lights on so it can be seen."

"Add the cost of a battery to the damage. I'm not sure how long the lights will stay on."

I rummaged in the boot for the fluorescent jackets and then walked back a little way to set out the warning triangle while Leah grabbed the papers from the glove compartment and phoned the breakdown service. Not surprisingly there was no answer at this time of night. She shrugged as she put her mobile back in her pocket.

"I guess we can walk from here?"

She nodded. We leaned against the vehicle, still shaking and scared. I tried to make light of it. "It's easier for you, you've only got one leg to turn to jelly. I have two." I swayed as we both broke into hysterics. The tears ran down our faces, and we hugged each other.

"Thank you for being here, Deidre. Thank you."

"At your service, any time your brakes fail."

We retrieved our bags from the car and shivering in

the cold, night air we began to walk towards the village.

"We can see if the police station is open, and beg a lift?"

"More involvement with the police? Let's see how we feel when we get that far. I'd phone Old Giles and his taxi, but at one in the morning he won't be too pleased."

"That might be more dangerous than driving with no brakes if he's been in the bar all evening," I said. "He likes his drink."

We walked on. Ten minutes in a car is a long way walking and it was dark. The sliver of moon I'd seen earlier was well hidden behind clouds and we could only feel we had veered off the metalled road when our feet hit the grass verge at the side. I took a step too far and would have ended down in the ditch if Leah hadn't grabbed my arm.

It was easier when we reached the village; the three street lights looked like Blackpool illuminations. It showed us that the police station, a small building that housed one reception area, an office and a holding cell of sorts, was in complete darkness.

Leah tried knocking loudly on the door, but nothing stirred. Country folk in France go to bed early, and not one dwelling showed lights from behind drawn curtains.

We walked on past the stone cross, the church, and onto the road to the villa. We were both a lot warmer now, still shaky and beginning to sweat inside our winter coats.

"So much for the hot southern French Mediterranean climate," Leah spluttered, as we wearily put one foot in front of the other.

"They only made those old movies in summer time. It

fooled all of us. But look on the bright side Leah, we could have been wearing four-inch heels."

She giggled.

In the pitch dark, we almost missed the turning into our driveway and, had it not been for the clouds moving across the sliver of a moon, we would have walked right past. Leah put a hand out and rested it against the pillar. "Not far, can I make it?"

"Do you want to use my car to go and tow yours back?" I asked.

"A few years ago, I would have said yes," she replied, "but I don't know how to fix a tow rope, especially in the dark, and oh, what the hell. Worse case scenario, I'll claim on the insurance and buy another car." She giggled again.

"That's the spirit. I'm ready for a mug of soup, and I suppose you'll be making coffee?"

"Yup. It's never kept me awake yet, and I need something to calm my nerves."

The light shining through from the study window was bright enough for Leah to find her key and open the door and we almost fell into the hallway.

I poked my head around the door into the lounge to see Belinda fast asleep on the couch, arms wrapped firmly around Monster who only looked up at us and wagged his tail. I walked over and placed a blanket over her before joining Leah in the kitchen.

"Fat lot of good he was tonight as a guard dog." Leah turned on the coffee machine and selected a pod from the packet.

"He heard our voices in the driveway, he knew it was us."

Leah handed me the box of packet soup. "That was no accident tonight, Deidre."

"You drove brilliantly…"

"No, that's not what I mean. The brakes. They were working perfectly before I parked up at the Morrisons'. If I was a betting person, I'd lay odds they were tampered with."

I paused, empty mug in hand. "Oh no, Leah, I didn't think… but… who had the opportunity to do that? The most obvious was one of the men, but they never left the room – did they?"

"I'm trying to remember."

I checked there was water in the kettle and plugged it in. "But if one of them had nipped out and cut the brake line or whatever you need to do, they would have got all dirty, wouldn't they?"

"I don't know enough about these things." She paused. "But it's not impossible, if he wore plastic gloves and an apron."

I slumped onto the nearest stool. "I think that's a bit fanciful. "What would they have to gain from it, either couple?"

"Scare us, a warning. Don't you remember Daniel's last words?"

"No. I heard him call out but not what he said."

Leah added sugar and milk to her coffee. "He called out for us 'to take care, ladies take great care'."

"A threat or a warning?"

"What do you think?"

"I'm more familiar with historical novels and I don't watch all that much TV," I replied. "I'm the last person to ask."

We stayed in the kitchen talking for most of the night, trying to decide what to do about the files. Burn them? Take them over to our new friends who were not so friendly anymore? If we did, would the terrors stop? Were the British expats responsible for everything that had gone wrong? It was unlikely they had spray painted obscene words on the walls, even if they were in French. Nor did we think they left a dead, maggot-ridden dog on the doorstep. Such things would be beneath London mobsters from the underworld.

As much as we talked and reasoned and suggested, by the time we finally climbed the stairs to bed, we were no nearer an answer.

NOVEMBER LEAH

Dear Diary,

This will be short, I'm too tired and, even after a full night's sleep, it's hard to think straight. I feel as if the hounds of hell are snapping at my heels. I can't make sense of the happenings; it's one thing after another.

I'm rather relieved Bill isn't here. I'm not sure what he would make of it all and, if he had any sense, he'd stay a million miles away and I wouldn't blame him. I'm glad he's there for his daughter. Divorce can be hell, like a living death. Which reminds me, I must chase up those papers. I can't believe the post can be that slow. The sooner I'm officially parted from Mason the better.

I'm not sure how I can ever repay Deidre for the comfort and help she has given me. She's one in a million. I shall make a list of things to do; I can't keep a thought in my head for longer than two minutes these days. It's December soon, and that means Christmas and presents and house decorations, that's if we are still here to celebrate it. I can sense a heavy atmosphere, as though the air itself is threatening.

I know one thing. I'm going to fight this time. No more gentle, placid, accept everything Leah. I've grown tough and, if necessary, I'll fight to protect Belinda, Deidre, and myself. This, is a brand new Leah Brand.

NOVEMBER   BELINDA

Hi Journal,

You're the only one who doesn't shout at me these days, at least you keep your trap shut. Leah tries but sheesh can she see her face. Nice, kind words, soft, tiptoeing round me as if I was a large meringue. Yeah, sure but I can see it in her eyes. She just doesn't see it. Bet she was a real goody-two-shoes when she was at school. Bet she had her homework done on time. Yeah, and top of the class too. Miss Perfect. Well none of us are having a perfect life, are we? All this sodding stuff going wrong. So I only have you, and Monster of course. He's the greatest. Can't wait to see how big he's going to get. Enormous I bet. Sophie says that puppies with large paws will be huge and she said that his father is a Pyrenean Mountain dog and his mother a St Bernard, the kind that carts those barrels of brandy around on the ski slopes in Switzerland so stranded people can drink while they wait for help. Or he might be part Newfoundland. Not sure how she knows that, but then everyone here knows everyone else and exactly what they do and who they talk to and sleep with and then they tell everyone else. That sucks. No frigging privacy at all. Ah, but there is stuff they don't know. Who killed the dog and the chickens and that poor baby with its throat cut? If they know, no one is telling, so I bet they suspect us as we've not been here long. That sucks too. Leah might be a pain and Deidre of course agrees with everything she says, but she's an old wrinkly now, neither of them would do stuff like that. Irritating for sure, but not mad bloodthirsty killers like you see in the movies. Shit, Madame will be here tomorrow and I've not done either of those assignments. Yeah, right, wait for the screaming and shouting to start. As if I cared. All I want to do is take Monster and run away, somewhere quiet where life is normal.

DECEMBER DEIDRE

I sensed a change in Leah when she came down to breakfast the following morning. We were both still tired, having been up most of the night, but her mood was one of determination and purpose. She placed her mug on the coffee maker, her movements precise and measured. There was a new bounce in her step and her posture was straighter, her body language confident.

Before I could ask her why the changes, the deafening roar of Madame's green elderly and battered Uno came thundering through the gate. To my surprise, the elderly school teacher let herself into the hall without Sophie. She popped her head round the kitchen door.

"You tell Belinda I am here?"

I was tempted to say the whole village would know she had arrived, but nodded as I got up to go and call her. "No Sophie?"

"No, La *pauvre petite* has the bad stomach. She is to stay in bed."

"Oh shame," I heard Leah say as I went upstairs. "I hope it's not too…"

Belinda was still in bed. I knocked on the door and, when there was no reply, I opened it a little and looked in. As I suspected, both Belinda and Monster were cuddled up. He looked at me and I swear he grinned, and his tail thumped on the bedclothes.

I shook Belinda's shoulder. "If you get up now," I whispered, "I won't split on you about Monster in your bed. Deal?"

She pulled herself up, rubbing her eyes while she wriggled out from under the puppy. She grinned. "Deal," she said.

I took hold of Monster's collar, he was already the size of a small Alsatian, and led him out of the room, pressing my fingers to my lips.

I heard Belinda giggle as I closed the door before I sneaked down the stairs and let the dog out of the front door. There was one thing we never had to worry about; not once, since those first few days, had he ever tried to run away or even go far. He was devoted to Belinda, and she would be devastated if anything was to happen to him.

Once Madame and Belinda were settled in the study, Leah grabbed her mobile, pen and paper, and frogmarched me out onto the terrace. Claudette followed on behind carrying a tray with a coffee pot and mugs. She left us in peace.

"So, what's this all about?"

"I've been thinking, and I need your advice."

"Fire away." I settled back in my chair after pouring myself a coffee.

Leah began scribbling. "We said last night that we were the victims from two different sources. The vandals and the criminals."

"Agreed."

"The vandals we can put on the back burner for now, but the criminals are a different matter."

"I'll agree to that too."

"It's obvious that our new expat friends want to get their hands on the files Mason left behind. I've thought long and hard about that, and I don't owe Mason anything, certainly not my loyalty. On the other hand, it sucks that I might help any lawbreaker, and the more I get to know them the sleazier they appear."

I thought of Geraldine Morrison, brazenly wearing my necklace, knowing I would recognise it, not once but twice, and I felt my anger rise. "Sleazy is a good word for all of them."

"I've decided we go through the files for those two families and then return them."

"Where?"

"That's a good question Deidre. There are four possibilities. One, we put them back in the London house. Two, we drop them into Mason's old law firm. Three, we hand them over to the police."

"And four, we give them to our new neighbours. I think that makes sense. It should take the heat off us." I smiled. "I'm beginning to sound like a character in some cheap gangster movie!"

We both laughed, then Leah's face changed.

"I don't feel comfortable helping them to cover up their crimes, if that's why they want the papers. While they are not exactly lying low here, there's information they don't want revealed."

"So, strike."

"It's important that the Morissons and the Fentons learn that we don't have the files. That way, I hope they will leave us alone."

I sat for a few moments gazing over at the Mediterranean, blue as ever, the seagulls swooping over the gentle waves off shore.

"I don't think the police will want the files and, by handing them over, it might open a whole can of worms. 'Why do you have them? Do you know what's in them?' I just don't see that working Leah. I think you're right though, take them back to the London house."

"I think that's best. Give me a couple of days to go through them thoroughly, and then I'll fly over."

"No."

She looked up, startled at the sharp tone in my voice.

"But I thought we'd just agreed…"

"Yes. But you won't take them back, I will."

"Deidre, I can't ask you to do that. It could be dangerous."

"Nonsense. What danger? I'm just a little old lady flying back home to, what can I say, sign final papers on the sale of my apartment in Weston-super-Mare? Goodness, who could look more innocent?"

The mobile in Leah's pocket vibrated and she pulled it out to answer it. Watching her face, I knew it was bad news. She disconnected, her lower lip trembling, and sat silently for a moment.

"Who was that? You look as if you've seen a ghost."

"I phoned the towing truck early this morning and that was the garage. It was deliberate, Deidre. The brakes had been tampered with, the lines to the brake fluid cut through."

I felt a cold shiver start at my neck and run all the way down my back. The hairs on my arms stood up and I had to take a deep breath to steady myself. "My God Leah, we could have been killed."

She nodded. "It doesn't bear thinking about. That settles it. I'll go to England – get rid of these bloody files. I want nothing more to do with them. It's like holding a grenade with the pin taken out."

"You will not. You must stay here, protect Belinda. We still don't know where she was for all those hours and she's too frightened to tell us. That might have been a first warning. They don't know the child and I'm sure they thought she would tell us but, of course, she clammed up."

I stood up, brushing down my skirt. "There's no time to lose. I'll go book my tickets online and then we give ourselves two days to comb those papers so we have an idea what we are up against. Anything beyond that, it's probably best for us not to know."

It would take two flights back to Heathrow. From Nice to Paris and then on to London. December, the very worst time to fly, peak season, and I was lucky to get a seat, but it would mean flying to Orly airport and then I needed to take the shuttle bus across Paris to Charles de Gaulle. I was quite looking forward to it. I loved travelling, but I did ask myself if I honestly thought it was safer for Leah to be here on her own while I returned to the UK; the honest answer was yes.

The next two days passed quickly as we holed-up in Leah's bedroom with the door bolted as we shuffled through the large pile of papers. A lot of it was legal jargon, but the transcripts of the interviews were in plain

English. Both Daniel and Humphrey were as guilty as hell, and I remarked to Leah that I thought if an attorney knew his client was guilty then should he or she still defend them and attempt to have the charges dropped?

She wasn't sure. All we knew of the legal profession was what we picked up from re-runs of *Kavanagh QC*, and *Judge John Deed*. The rest were American programmes like *Law and Order* and they did things differently on the other side of the Atlantic.

Leah was convinced there was something else, implied but not recorded. Another crime lurking beneath the surface. I didn't argue with her, but fraud, money laundering and drug running were quite enough for me to want the pair of them behind bars.

"I'm surprised there is no mention of either of the wives," said Leah, closing one of the files and replacing it in the completed pile.

"It's not unusual is it? I mean all this gangland stuff, don't the wives just cash in and visit beauty parlours and go shopping?"

"So the films tell us. But I thought they were often called as witnesses – you know, 'I was home all last night constable, and my wife can confirm it'."

"You have a point. I don't think we need to worry about that."

Leah had made copious notes on her tablet of all the major accusations and rebuttals and then we carefully removed all the treasury tags, those little green laces with metal ends, just in case they activated any alarms in the airport. We had a long discussion about whether to pack them in a main suitcase, or cram them into an overnight bag I could keep with me all the time. Both had pros and cons but, in the end, there was no contest. The bundles of papers were too large to fit in my cabin bag, however hard we tried to squeeze them in. I'd have to take a large suitcase and be patient and wait at the carousel in both airports.

I lied to Leah when I promised her that I would fly straight there and back. I'd made one extra appointment in London I didn't mention to her. She urged me to take my time, but I wouldn't agree. I told her I'd not have a moment's peace until I got back, which was true.

For either of us, returning the papers in person was a decision we were reluctant to take. It would have been easier to send the lot by courier. There were two reasons we regretfully decided against this. There was no one in the London house to receive the parcel and, while we combed the internet and online directories, we could find no address for Mason's old firm. We could only assume they had changed their name or their location. It would be my first port of call to track them down.

Leah wracked her brains for even one name of the other lawyers who worked with Mason, but she couldn't help. Mason had never taken her into his confidence, and the only time she'd seen them was at the Christmas bash, and then it was meet Jim, or Henry, or other given names which told us nothing. She also had a vague memory of a quick turnaround of staff at the office. If she ever enquired about any of the people she had met at the once a year get together, it was to hear they had moved on to another practice.

At that time we were not thinking too clearly, and

blindly following instinct, which screamed 'get rid of these papers'. In retrospect, we should have been more organised and used our brains, not our emotions. I can only explain it as a knee-jerk reaction, knowing that someone wanted us injured, or even dead.

Two days later, Leah drove me to the airport in Nice and I hugged her tight before I went through to Departures. We'd stood together at the check-in, and we couldn't take our eyes off the suitcase as it was weighed-in, and we watched it disappear along the conveyor belt and out of sight. I had opted to collect it at Orly. I'd have a five-hour wait, not counting the transfer from one airport to the other, and I didn't want to arrive in London to discover it had been routed elsewhere.

The pretty young airline employee in her smart blue uniform thought it a little strange, but then she shrugged and marked it for Paris pick-up.

I hated leaving Leah but, if my trip made life safer, it was for the best. I made her promise to stay at home, to use my car only to drive to and from the airport, since hers had been attacked twice while they had left mine in one piece. I didn't use it that often and hoped 'they', whoever they might be, would not connect it with our family.

It took ages to crawl through the security checks. These days you practically had to strip naked, and I was called through the metal detector three times before they swept me off into a curtained cubicle and patted me down. I was tempted to make small talk and lighten the atmosphere but, with my poor French, it was best to say nothing.

The one hour and twenty-minute flight to Paris passed without incident. I peered out of the window, straining to see my suitcase loaded onto the plane. We'd attached an orange ribbon to the handle so I could grab it quickly, but the baggage handlers were too quick and the wing partially blocked my view.

At Orly the noise, bustle and rush was a shock to my system after weeks spent in the peaceful, rural countryside.

I retrieved the suitcase, dragged it out to take the shuttle and, at Charles de Gaulle, wheeled it over the shiny, tiled floor to check-in at the British Airways desk. The contents made it heavy, and it needed two hands to lift it onto the scales.

The guy at the check-in desk frowned when he noticed I was a few kilos overweight and I held my breath. I was ready to hand over excess luggage fees but, after a brief pause, he let it go.

Once again, my eyes followed the orange ribbon as it vanished round the junction and onto the belt into the waiting hands of the luggage handlers below.

I wandered around the duty free, not seeing anything I fancied, but reminded myself to pick stuff up on the way back for Leah, Belinda and Claudette, and maybe Madame too. We'd given them all the same story about signing legal documents as the reason for my trip. The only signature I wanted was from Mason's old firm – if I could find it. Worst case scenario, from the police.

I think I began to suspect I was being followed as I bought a coffee and took it to the plastic table overlooking the departure concourse. I'd not noticed anyone in particular up until then and I could not have pointed out a specific man or woman. It was just an uneasy feeling, and I began to peer at individuals hoping I might spot one of them on the same flight to London. Now I wished I had taken more notice of the passengers on the plane from Nice.

My connection took off on time and I was pleased to see I had an aisle seat for this leg of the journey. As soon as the seat belt lights were switched off, I got up and walked slowly up the plane to the toilets. Coming back down the aisle I took careful note of the passengers, would I recognise any of them again? Probably not; there were just too many of them.

To double-check, I visited the toilets a second time, pretending to walk slowly as if I was in pain. I was so convincing the flight attendant asked me if I needed help, and had I requested airport assistance when we landed in Heathrow? I assured her I was fine, just a little stiff.

I didn't hurry to disembark when they opened the doors at Heathrow. I'd still arrive at the luggage carousel long before my suitcase and I wanted to see who else dawdled.

The problem with large airports is the distance to get from one point to another. Miles of long, glass lined corridors with brightly-coloured, industrial-strength carpets lay between the plane and baggage claim. I checked the information board and lined up with my fellow passengers to wait. The twinkling electronic lights indicated that the baggage from two flights would be spitting out luggage on belt number four, and now I didn't recognise a single fellow traveller in the dense crowd. So much for my detective work.

At last the angular rubber slats shuddered and began moving as the first case rose clumsily out of the chute at the far end and dropped down to begin the circuit. It was followed by a whole stream of assorted bags, boxes, rucksacks, cases and sporting equipment. There were flurries as passengers bumped into each other racing forward to retrieve their possessions. After a frenzied couple of minutes, the crowd thinned out, and fewer cases dropped onto the moving belt until at last the machine stopped.

I looked around, dismayed to see I was the only person left, and I had no case. I waited a little longer, but then the flashing lights on the board announced that the next flight number for this carousel was for baggage from Vienna.

I walked down to the chute in the hope my case was somehow wedged in the tunnel, but no, it was a wide, gaping, empty hole. I made my way to the Lost Luggage counter, clutching my baggage claim ticket.

I stood at the end of a long queue and wondered how many pieces of luggage were lost every day. I suspected a lot more than we realised.

After a lengthy wait, I reached the counter and the young lady, smartly dressed in airport uniform, was smiling and friendly. I thought it was an act as she looked quite frazzled. It's not a job I'd like, dealing with complaints all day. I was keeping my own feelings of panic under wraps. If they didn't find my case, I wasn't sure what I was going to do. I knew Leah wouldn't blame me, but it could put us all in danger. I was handed a form to fill in and shunted to one side while the assistant dealt with the next angry passenger.

The form asked for my UK address and that was a

problem. I'd not booked anywhere, depending on where I had to go. I needed to sleep over, but I'd planned to book into an airport hotel. My pen hovered over the vacant box on the form, unsure what to do. Whatever I filled in, that's where they would deliver the lost case and, in the meantime, I'd be unable to do anything but sit and wait. I wanted to scream.

I checked out the leaflets on a rack near the information desk and chose one of the popular hotel chains near the airport, phoned, booked a room and copied down their address.

I had no option but to take a taxi there, sign in and take a lift to the third floor where, once inside my room, I collapsed on the bed, sick with worry. I thought about phoning Leah to tell her what had happened, but decided not to upset her.

I'd been so occupied with the missing case I'd forgotten about my stalker, if he or she had ever existed. I hadn't planned to fall asleep, but I was woken suddenly when my mobile jangled. I sat up, rubbed my eyes and lunged across the room to take it out of my coat pocket. My heart sank when I saw the number. It was Leah.

"Hi."

"Deidre, your phone rang and rang and rang and I was beginning to worry you hadn't answered."

"I was asleep," I replied without thinking, then wanted to kick myself.

"Oh." There was a long pause.

I could read her mind. I've never been good at storytelling so I told her the truth. I heard her gasp on the other end of the connection.

"Lost? Oh no!"

"I'm sure it's just a mix up. I don't think they lose many cases, I mean not completely, for ever and ever." I was babbling.

"I'm sure no one would want to steal what's inside, not just a load of old papers and files."

"I guess not. Anyway, I'll sit tight for today and then tomorrow, if they haven't delivered it, I'll go back to the airport and make a big fuss."

"As only you know how to do Deidre." Leah's laugh was forced.

"How are things your end?"

"Quiet so far, if you don't count Belinda having a meltdown over Madame banning Monster from the study. He was trying to climb on her lap during the lesson. I can't make up my mind if that child is just bloody-minded or on the spectrum. I'm thinking about having her tested for autism."

"If she'll cooperate."

"A big if. And don't worry, Deidre, things happen. I'll leave you to go back to sleep. I can imagine you're worn out after the flights."

"It wasn't that tiring, two short hops, and I'm wide awake now. I'll go get something to eat and phone the airport, just in case."

"Nice pun," she said, before she rang off.

I flopped back on the bed. I prayed it would not be too long before I could fly back to France.

The restaurant buffet was open twenty-four hours, so I helped myself to a very late breakfast, English style. One of the few things I missed in France.

There were not many people in the dining room, so I chose a small table over to one side where I could see the rest of the room. As casually as I could, I looked at each of the other diners. The feeling I was being watched had returned, stronger than before. I tried to remember if anyone I could see had been on the flight from Nice but, without coats and scarves to remind me, I was at a loss.

It was impossible to relax. I wished now I had booked the suitcase through to final destination, although common sense told me it had travelled safely as far as Paris. I wished too I had had it wrapped in that cling film stuff, but I'd not seen the facility at Nice airport, and not looked for it in Paris.

After I finished, I walked through to the reception area. If someone was following me, there was nowhere to hide, but no one looked suspicious or was hanging around, except for one man who sat over in the far corner. He was dressed conservatively in a business suit, and looked far too respectable. He put his briefcase on the floor and checked his watch at frequent intervals. The longer I observed him, the more convinced I was he was watching me, though every time I glanced over, he looked away.

The exterior doors opened and another smartly dressed man entered, turned and approached him. Handshakes, greetings, and they left the hotel together. I began to feel silly. I'd watched too many spy movies and real life wasn't like that.

I was the only one left in the reception area so I wandered back up to my room. As soon as I opened the door, I had a sense that someone had been in there. I can't explain the weird feeling, but chills ran down my spine.

Perhaps it was just the chambermaid checking things were in place? If it was, then she was nosy, as someone had rifled through my hand luggage. I am fussy where I put things in my carry-on, and stuff had been moved and replaced, but not exactly as I had packed it, and I'd not thought to lock it either. I went through each item but nothing was missing, and there was nothing I could do about it either.

I took my Kindle out of my bag and worked hard to concentrate on the book I had started when we took off from Nice. After reading the same page over and over again, I gave up. I couldn't concentrate and I couldn't stop worrying either.

Through the sound-proofed triple-glazed windows I could see the planes as they came in to land. The sun, completely hidden, was setting and the dusk creeping over the runway, and the landing lights shone more brightly. Soon it would be dark and, as I gazed out, the street lights came on one by one.

I turned on the television, flicking from one channel to the next, but it was all doom and gloom; riots, border warfare, politicians accused of lying and fraudulent activities, an earthquake in the Far East, drought in northern Africa, and on and on. Was anyone happy, anywhere?

I was too wired to sleep, so I took a shower and ordered a snack from room service. I wasn't hungry but it was something to do. I signed the bill, tipped the waiter, and sat by the window.

I must have dozed off as I was startled by a loud knocking on the door. For a moment I froze, then crept over to look through the peephole. Whoever it was, was wearing the hotel uniform so, putting the chain in place, I cautiously opened the door and peeped out.

Glancing down I saw an orange ribbon on the handle of my case. I flung the door wide open, and only just stopped myself from giving the porter a huge hug. He retreated, smiling at the size of the tip I pushed into his hand.

I closed the door and examined every angle of the case. It didn't look as if it had been opened or damaged. I twirled the combination lock and opened the lid. Everything looked fine. I picked up my mobile to phone Leah and reassure her we were back on track.

The next morning, I was up early and, after breakfast, I packed up my stuff and caught a taxi to the address Leah had given me for Mason's offices. It was a huge expense, but after the fright I'd had yesterday I was past worrying. It took ages to reach the end of the M4 and then cut south onto the M25. Often described as the largest car park in Britain, we were stationary more often than moving as the traffic inched forward, from one exit to the next.

The driver crawled along the street looking for the correct number.

"Here you are, Missus." He turned and smiled.

I paid then stepped out, heaving and dragging the suitcase behind me. It still weighed a ton, and long gone were the days when the London taxi drivers helped passengers with their luggage. I'd been a little alarmed to see the wire mesh between the front and back of the cab, presumably to protect the driver.

It was beginning to spit with rain as I stood on the pavement looking up at the Georgian house Mason had converted into very smart offices. It had a deserted look and, when I struggled up the few steps, lugging the suitcase behind me, I could see the letter box was held half open with an assortment of leaflets and mail. Not expecting an answer, I rang the bell and waited. The raindrops began to trickle down my neck and run down into my shoes. Cold blasts of wind reminded me why I hated the British winter. I stood there for several minutes, but there was no reply.

Neither Leah nor I had seen this coming. What now? I stood and dithered a while longer, getting wetter and wetter. Stumbling back down the steps, I walked to the small shop on the corner. Local people always know what's happening in the neighbourhood. A bell tinkled over the door as I pushed it open and twisted and turned the case past the narrow, cramped shelves to the cash desk. The man of Indian origin sported a turban and an unfriendly face.

"I wonder if you can help?"

He shrugged his shoulders.

"I'm looking for solicitors, a legal firm, Mason Brand and Associates? They operated from one of the old houses just along the road, on this side."

"And?"

"I can't seem to find them. Do you know if they have moved premises?"

He shrugged again. This was going nowhere. He either could not, or would not, help. I turned as the bell tinkled and a lady walked in dragging a screaming infant behind her. The child was demanding sweets and she was refusing to buy any for him. In response he flung himself on the floor beating his little fists on the tiles. She sighed, stepped over him and gathered goods from the shelves.

My hands itched to pick the brat up and march him outside and straight home to a naughty corner. But then, I reasoned, the poor, frazzled mother needed groceries, and at least she was not giving him the attention the child was demanding. I was dismayed to see her add sweets to the pile of goods she dropped on the small counter.

I hovered for a moment in the warm shop, hoping another customer would enter. Now was not the time to question the harassed woman paying for her goods at the till, and the child's screams continued to bounce off the walls. I backed out of the shop into the rain.

The farther I dragged the case, the heavier it got and then, waggling it around a raised paving stone, one of the wheels snapped off. I had to tilt it to one side to move it, and it overbalanced and swung around in my hand.

I remembered that Leah had told me there was a small shopping centre nearby and I hoped there was a luggage shop. I pulled the case upright and tried to balance it on the remaining three wheels, and followed the sign for the shops.

I stood in the open square and almost cheered when I noticed a *Bags Я Us* on the left. The case bumped over the cobbles, which might look cute and 'olde worlde', but are death to suitcases even when the wheels are in one piece.

I ducked in out of the rain which was now pouring down to find I was the only customer. The shop assistant looked delighted and rushed over to help.

"I'm not sure if we have that wheel in stock, but I'll go

look," and she hurried off into a back room. Moments later she returned beaming from ear to ear. "Success. It won't take that long to fit. Can you come back in half an hour?"

I was reluctant to allow the case out of my sight, but I couldn't see a way to insist I watched it all the time. She held her hand out to take the handle and stopped when she felt the weight of it.

"Would you like to empty it first?" she enquired.

"No. I mean I'd like to but I've forgotten the combination. Can't open it."

"No problem," she smiled, "we can cut off this lock and sell you a new one so…"

"No, really, don't do that. I will be home soon and I've got it written down." I added. "I'm a pensioner and so…"

She understood. Pensioners had to watch the pennies. "Of course. Why don't you go across the way and have a coffee while we get this sorted for you?"

As I took a seat by the window, coffee cup in one hand, sandwich in the other, I saw the irony in the food and drink costing more than a new lock for the case.

I asked at the counter in the café if anyone knew of Mason Brand the solicitors, but no one had even heard of them. Nor had the friendly assistant in *Bags Я Us* when I went to collect the suitcase. It didn't look as if it had been tampered with or opened, and I breathed a sigh of relief.

As I searched for suitable coins in my purse, I had a bright idea. "Is there a library around here?"

Counting out the coins before handing me my receipt, she shook her head. "There was one last year, but many of them have closed. Government cuts. The nearest one is in the main street in Croydon."

I thanked her and went back out into the pouring rain. I had no idea what to do next. I watched a passing pigeon beating its wings as it made for a sheltered ledge and a sign caught my eye: 'Citizens Advice Bureau'. Why hadn't I thought of that sooner? I was operating on quarter brain power. I scuttled over and dragged the case in behind me to be greeted by a friendly, grey-haired lady dressed in a twinset from an earlier age. As I suspected she was wearing a tweed skirt, thick stockings and sensible shoes.

"Can I help you? Please sit down." She waved to a desk and settled herself on the other side.

I slipped into the plastic bucket seat and flicked the wet hair out of my eyes. The sign on the desk in front of me read *Mrs Dalton*.

"I hope so, I'm looking for solicitors, a law firm."

"Local?"

"Yes."

She stood up and rummaged in one of the filing cabinets. "We can give basic legal advice, but it's always best to consult the experts," she prattled on. "We are often consulted about overhanging branches and disputes over property lines but we prefer to send clients in the right direction."

"Of course," I murmured.

She returned with a sheaf of papers stapled together. "Any particular kind of solicitor? Criminal, property, civil, accident and injury, consumer rights?"

"Uh, I'm not sure. I'm looking for one firm which appears to have moved premises. Mason Brand and Associates."

She turned the papers sideways and we looked down the list of names. Mason's firm was not there.

"If these are only the local companies, then where would I find their new address?"

"We don't have lists for companies outside the area, but I could check on the internet for you."

"That would be great."

For an elderly lady – as if I wasn't one myself – Mrs Dalton's skills were impressive as her fingers flew over the keys. Every now and then she paused to read the screen, and then she was off again tapping at speeds I could only dream of.

"No special spelling? M-A-S-O-N, B-R-A-N-D?"

"Yes, no quirks. They had premises in one of the Georgian houses not far away, over on the main street." I found myself holding my breath.

"They are not listed on the register for England and Wales. If the company is in business they should be registered with The Law Society but, to find one, we need to put in the postcode. Not too helpful. There are one hundred and eighty-four thousand of them," she said.

"Oh dear." My heart sank.

"Wait, maybe we can narrow that down. Do you know if they worked in any particular speciality?"

"Criminal, as far as I know."

"Wait, I have an idea." She picked up the handset on her desk phone. "This makes a change from the usual queries we get here. Wakes up the old grey cells." Her fingers flew just as quickly dialling the number.

I guessed the person she connected with was maybe her own solicitors and, even if I leaned forward, I couldn't hear the voice at the other end. I saw her eyebrows go up and her mouth fall open as she listened intently. She forced a smile as she replaced the receiver and turned back to her monitor.

"That explains it," she said. "They are no longer in practice. My uh, colleague, says they were struck off a year ago. No longer permitted to practice law, and he remembers that within a week they had cleared the offices and shut up shop."

My shoulders slumped. That was one dead end.

She seemed reluctant to let me go, even offered me a cup of coffee, which I declined.

"Silly me." She looked up and smiled. "The name should have clicked, it was a big thing around here at the time. If I remember rightly, the principal was up in court himself?" Her fingers flew over the keyboard again.

"Yes, he was," I replied.

"And it was for something serious?" She cocked her head to one side.

"Yes." I was not inclined to say any more. I heaved myself off the plastic chair, slung my carry-on over my shoulder, took firm hold of the case, and asked where I could find the nearest police station.

"They have closed many of them," she remarked sadly, "but if you…" She began to give me instructions before asking if I had a smartphone. I nodded and pulled it out of my pocket.

She took it, peered at the screen and once again rapidly pressed the keys before handing it back.

"There, I've installed Google maps and programmed in the route for you. All you have to do is follow it."

I looked in awe at this elderly lady in her twinset and tweeds. All that was missing were the pearls, but she was a whizz with modern technology.

She noticed my expression and laughed. "I've got techie grandkids and they teach me everything. I'm keeping right up to date. You have to these days, don't you?"

I was too ashamed to admit I'd stuck to the basics, but determined, when I got back to France, to sit Belinda down and blackmail her, if necessary, to show me how to get the best from my phone and tablet.

I thanked Mrs Dalton profusely as she opened the door for me and waved goodbye. I glanced back to see her disappear back inside and guessed she was sad to see a customer leave.

It was tricky keeping the phone dry, with one hand manhandling the suitcase and the other stopping my shoulder bag from slipping down my arm.

Once out on the main road, I considered hailing a taxi, but the police station wasn't very far, and the thought of heaving the case in and out of the vehicle too much effort. The rain had eased a little, but the dark, grey clouds threatened more as they hung just above my head.

I bumped the case up the steps and pushed open the main door that had not seen a lick of paint for many years.

It was warm and dry inside with a high counter in front of me and walls peppered with posters. There was a row of wanted criminal faces, plenty of advice on where to report AIDS, a list of emergency centres, the Citizens' Advice Bureau, Social Services. Later, I would read them all from top to bottom as I waited to see someone who could help. The desk sergeant on duty was flummoxed when I told him what I had and that I wanted to discuss handing over the files. He was way out of his comfort zone and I was to wait for a more senior officer, who was currently out of the office.

The time dragged as one hour passed, and then another. No offer of coffee here, only a water cooler in the corner with no cups. My stomach began to rumble and I needed the loo as well. That they could provide, but I wasn't able to drag the case into the cubicle as it was so small. I moved as quickly as I could and, as I washed my hands, I glared at the offending piece of luggage. I was growing to hate it.

A tall, officious looking man appeared just after lunchtime and, as he lifted the counter top to go to the back offices, the sergeant waved him over. He nodded towards me and I jumped to my feet.

"Inspector Lowden," he extended his hand.

"Deidre Flynn."

"And how can I help you?"

"I have evidence here that might be useful." I pointed to the case and his eyebrows shot up.

He turned and beckoned for me to follow him and we walked down a narrow, dingy corridor, painted cream from ceiling to waist height and green to floor level. One of the neon tubes was flickering casting an eerie glow as we passed a line of closed doors on either side.

He flung open the last one on the right and I followed him in as he settled himself on the far side of a desk, and I perched on the wooden chair opposite.

"Tell me what you have." He picked up a pen and

flicked and twirled it around his fingers. It was distracting, but I looked away and concentrated. I explained what was in the suitcase, how we came to have the files, and now we were anxious to get rid of them. I hesitated to add any information about the Morrisons and the Fentons. I didn't need for him to think I was unstable or spinning a tale. Even to my own ears, it sounded like a cheap novel.

I bent over and began to work the combination on the lock before he stopped me.

"I can't take them, and you can't leave them here."

He couldn't be serious. "But why? The information in here might solve dozens of cases!"

For a moment he stared at the case and then shook his head. "This is not a simple matter of handing over evidence to the police. I understand you have tried to return these, uh, files, to the company, but that's where they belong."

"The law firm has gone bust, or de-registered, or whatever happens to law firms when they are shut down," I reminded him.

"Yes, you said. But none of this belongs to you, the privacy laws forbid us to even open them, and it is also a crime for you to destroy what might be evidence in a future case. I'm afraid, Ms. Flynn, you have a problem. All I can suggest is that you rent a locker and leave the case inside, then walk away and forget about it."

"But the information inside might be so helpful." I could hear the whine in my voice.

"Nothing we could use in there would stand up in court, so it's no use to us, I'm afraid."

I was about to tell him about our expat neighbours, but I sensed he'd not be interested. Not his patch, no jurisdiction, and nothing that would improve his crime statistics from this office.

I accepted defeat and left. As I bumped the case back down the steps it began to take on the properties of a nuclear bomb about to explode.

I wandered down the street, squinting at the weak sunshine which was battling to break through the clouds. For the first time I was aware of all the Christmas decorations, except few mentioned the word Christmas, it was all Happy Holidays and Festive Season. Were they so afraid of upsetting the sensitive souls who had nothing better to complain about?

Santa Claus was out and about, several of them and, as I turned into the high street, I saw twinkly lights strung across the road. All the shop windows were decorated for the biggest spend of the year. I felt strangely out of step, not part of the excitement and anticipation.

I made for the nearest restaurant and ordered an early supper. I'd missed lunch altogether. It was time to decide what to do next.

As I munched my way through a piece of tasty quiche, I thought about the suggestion of hiring a left luggage locker. Then I could, I suppose, try and return the case to Mason. Or, I could leave the files in Leah's old house.

I wasn't keen on the first as I doubted the prison would allow him to have them. I'd never visited a prison in my life and had no idea how things worked there. Perhaps the best plan was the house. If I took photos of them to show where they were, then it was up to our aggressors to do as they saw best. I hated the thought they might get away with further crimes, or hide what they had done in the past. But, if it kept Leah and Belinda safe, it was the lesser of the two evils.

There was a problem with my decision. I didn't have a key to Mason's old house. Would I have to break in?

Somebody bumped my chair and I turned round to see who it was and came eye to eye with a man I was positive had been on the flight from Nice. How much of a coincidence could that be?

The moment we made visual contact he dropped his gaze, murmured an apology, and squeezed his way between the tables to the other side of the room.

The hairs on the back of my neck were standing up, the fork shook in my hand, and my foot felt for the case on the floor beside me.

He'd positioned himself at such an angle that he could see me, but I had to twist round to look at him. I made a snap decision. I finished up my meal as quickly as I could, shrugged on my coat and pushed and squirmed my way between the tables and raced out of the door.

I had only gone a few steps when I heard a voice. "*Hé, arrét!*"

I walked on, not turning round, but the shouts persisted and a heavy hand landed on my shoulder, pulling me to a halt. I looked around. It was my stalker and in his other hand he was holding the handle of the damned suitcase.

"*Votre valise, Madame.*"

"Merci." I took the case from him, nodded, and walked briskly away down the street. I didn't look round to see if he was behind me, but I lost that creepy feeling and heard no footsteps.

It was getting dark, already late afternoon, so I booked into a nearby hotel for the night, horrified at the cost of the accommodation.

It wasn't until I had taken my coat off and ordered a light meal from room service that I realised the man, my stalker, had spoken to me in French. So, I wasn't paranoid. I was being followed. He hadn't attacked me, nor had he run off with the case, so what did he want? I was too tired to tax my brain solving riddles, so I had a shower and an early night.

The following morning, I left the case in the luggage room at the hotel. The longer this albatross hung round my neck, the less I cared what happened to it. The receptionist gave me a strange look. Most people would have left luggage in their rooms, and I had booked in for two more nights. I smiled and said nothing to answer her unspoken question.

I checked out the directions to Leah's old house and took a taxi which dropped me off on the corner of her road and sped away.

It was an elegant, two-storey house, exactly as I had imagined. The gate creaked when I opened it, I saw signs of rust on the hinges, and there were weeds growing up among the paving slabs and the lawn cried out for a good cut.

I rang the front door bell but, as expected, there was no reply. The whole place had an air of neglect, the blank windows an empty, deserted look. I followed the path along the side of the house, stepping over fallen branches, pine cones and layers of dead leaves. As I expected the back door was locked and when I tried to lever up the sash windows, they didn't move.

I stood back and stared. Why had Mason not tried to sell it? If he was leaving it for his wayward son Leo when he came out of jail, it would be in a worse state by then. It would cost a bit to get it back into good order.

Did it hold any other secrets? Leah told me she had only taken her personal belongings before moving down to Weston, and visited once more to collect the files on Mason's orders.

I needed to talk to him. They were his bloody files after all. Before I left, I retraced my steps along the side of the house, lifting up the plant pots one at a time. I remembered Leah had left a key under one of them when she lived here. I had just drawn a blank by the last one near the front door when a passer-by called out "Looking for something?"

I straightened up so quickly I felt a sharp pain shoot up my back. "Looking for the spare key," I called back hoping they thought I lived here.

"Place been empty for many months. Going on sale is it?"

I didn't need a nosy neighbour asking questions. "Just checking for a friend." I called out, hoping she would go away. I stared at her, willing her to move on, but she shuffled from one foot to the other. Did she suspect I was going to break in? She'd probably call the police and I didn't need that. I shrugged and, swinging my carry-on onto my shoulder, walked back up the path. She hovered for a moment then walked on, looking back over her shoulder to see if I went back into the garden.

There wasn't much point. I could see the house next to Mason's was even more dilapidated and run down. Leah had said it had been unoccupied for years, but the house on the other side of that had a 'for sale' board outside; Andrea's old house. While I stood there a car drew up outside and a smart lady, keys jangling in one hand, escorted a couple from her car and into Andrea's garden. For a second, I was tempted to gate-crash the viewing, but then I'd never met Andrea and it wasn't going to solve any problems.

I went in search of a taxi to take me back to my hotel. It was time to connect with Mason.

I sat on the bed and googled the Prisoners' Aid Society on my tablet. They showed lots of helpful information and I was directed to the Offenders' Families Helpline. I phoned them. I lied, said I was Mason's older sister, recently returned from overseas. We had lost touch and I had urgent and important family news for him. I didn't need to visit him, but if they could tell me how I could speak to him on the phone?

I must have been convincing. When they rang me back a few hours later they gave me the number for the prison governor where Mason was being held. I dialled again, giving the same story and was put on hold.

I sat on the bed, taking deep breaths, wiping the sweat off my hands on my trousers. The central heating radiator under the window creaked, I heard the murmur of voices as people walked past in the corridor outside. Each second felt an hour, each minute a week. There was no sound on the other end of the phone, no musak to entertain me, no voice telling me how important my call was and I began to wonder if I'd been cut off when a voice said:

"Hello. Who is this?"

"Mason Brand?" I said, keeping my voice as low and steady as I could while I twisted the fringe on my scarf around my fingers with my free hand.

"Yes. Who is calling?"

For a moment my brain went blank, and then I told him.

DECEMBER LEAH

Dear Diary,

We planned for Deidre's visit to England to last a couple of days and she's been gone over two weeks. She called in a few times and then nothing. She didn't answer her phone, and I've tried not to panic. The only information I have is her name and her location: London. I wouldn't know where to start. I can't believe anything has happened to her. She's probably had her phone stolen and I put all our numbers in for her, I knew she wouldn't remember them. Why anyone would want to grab an old, out of date model such as hers I have no idea. If she's not back soon, I'm going to take Belinda and go look for her.

All my new-found confidence is beginning to ebb away at a rapid rate. I can feel the panic setting in. Those tablets in the bathroom cabinet are so tempting, but I'll hold out as long as I can.

DECEMBER BELINDA

To my Journal.

Same old, same old. Nothing ever changes. Madame is a slave driver. No one should have to work as hard as this, no one, and what for? Just to pass some sodding exam no one cares about. I sure don't. Of course, clever Miss Sophie is way ahead, answers every sodding question before the words are out of Madame's mouth. But I can't help liking her. She's so sweet and so mature for twelve. It's hard to remember she's so much younger than me, we are on the same wavelength. So glad she's a friend. With her contacts, even some in Paris, she tells me I won't need any old exams to get on in life. And Monster of course. He's just the best dog in the whole, wide world. I love him to bits.

JANUARY DEIDRE

I stared at Leah over the kitchen counter lost in thought. Christmas had been very low key in France, nothing like the fuss they make on the other side of the Channel and across the Atlantic. Food, it seems, was the primary focus and the main meal, *le Réveillon,* was roast turkey followed by the French traditional chocolate log or *bûche de Noël*, which I have to admit, was delicious. Presents were simple, but expensive, and Madame was thrilled with her perfume and chocolates.

Leah gave Belinda a television for her room, together with a subscription package for programmes and films in English, so for once she was happy. Even Monster received a new collar and lead and lots of chewy toys.

Despite it being the festive season, all of us were subdued. It was our first Christmas in France, there were no invites to drinks, or parties. We only went out once together and that was to a local market. Fairy lights dangled between the stalls and small wooden cabins, offered a huge variety of food and speciality drinks. A few had an array of gifts, but there was no sign of a Santa

Claus. One pine tree towered over the old, central water pump across the square from a magnificent model of the Nativity, complete with tiny figures of the Holy Family, the animals by the manger, wise men, shepherds and all their sheep. It was cold enough to see our breath in the chill night air, but that didn't stop us from buying. We struggled home with bulging bags. Then I took that trip to England and what a difference, commercialism everywhere, spend, spend, spend – even if you don't have the money, and will still be paying for it next June.

It was strange that the day after Christmas in France is just another day here, no Boxing Day respite, everything back to normal. The holiday came and went so quickly, in the blink of an eye it was over.

The guilt weighed heavily over me for not contacting Leah from London, not thinking she would be so worried. The charging lead for my phone went missing, I have no idea where I lost it, and despite visiting several shops one supercilious assistant after another promptly told me they didn't stock accessories for such ancient models. What is it these days, with obsolescence? It's only ten years old and was working perfectly well. I'm sure it's a smart phone and the whizz granny in the Advice Bureau had installed the maps programme on it. I hesitated to buy another, but was forced to in the end, but with the Christmas rush, customers queuing six abreast, no one had the time to transfer my data and I couldn't remember Leah's number, except it was speed dial #1 on my keypad.

I'd taken a taxi back from Nice airport on Christmas Eve, and it was such a relief to find Leah safe, but not as well as I'd hoped. Her nervous mannerisms have returned.

I've noticed her swinging her good leg, and occasionally I've caught her rocking. But she assures me she's not on Prozac and is coping. I like to think my return to the villa has helped.

Her car is back from the garage and good as new, but it had been sabotaged and that has put us on the alert for the next attack. It's nerve-wracking wondering how and when and what.

With Belinda upstairs, headphones on, bingeing on Netflix, and Claudette across the field tending to her sick mother, it was time to talk.

I replenished our coffee mugs and perched on a kitchen stool, and took a deep breath.

I made light of being followed. I'd hesitated telling Leah about the stalker, but it was best she was fully in the picture. I'd not seen the Frenchman again, but I sensed him on the odd occasion. After he handed back the case, I wasn't afraid of him. On a couple of occasions, I walked towards him, determined to ask who he was and what he wanted, but he always melted away into the dense crowds. I do know he was not on either of the return flights.

"You have no idea who he was?" Leah juggled the sugar cubes in the bowl, then began piling them up in towers on the counter top. She was unable to keep still.

"No. Not the thuggish type, well-dressed and it might be a coincidence he spoke French. Perhaps he thought it was my native language? If his instructions were to follow this woman who lived in France on a visit to England, he could have presumed."

Leah shuddered. "You were so brave, Deidre."

"Nonsense. I'm too old to scare easily. Now, this is the

part I've not told you. I didn't want to ruin the Christmas season."

"It was hardly a joyful celebration, was it?"

"No. But next year will be different, I promise. We'll get this all sorted, find out who is behind all this nonsense, and make new friends. And, Bill will be back by then."

"You are such a comfort, I don't know what I'd do without you."

"Leah, anyone experiencing the traumas you've had would be in a mental home by now." I paused, realizing what I'd just said. "Whoops, I mean really, really mad, not just shoved out of the way."

Leah gave a slight smile and began to build another tower block of sugar.

"Now, this is the difficult part..."

She looked up, brow furrowed and her hand trembled.

"I managed to contact Mason."

The towers tumbled onto the counter, scattering grains in all directions.

"You saw Mason?"

"No. I only spoke to him over the phone. Don't look so scared. I had a lot of help from the Prisoners' Aid Society. They are amazing, have lots of advice for families of those locked up. I can't praise them enough. It was a little weird as I've never even spoken to a felon before. They helped me track him down to the prison that was feeding and housing him, and then I got through to the prison governor."

Leah gave a little giggle and began collecting the cubes and crushing them with her thumb nail. "What did he say? Is he well?"

I slapped my hand on the counter making her jump. "Darling, I wasn't there to make polite enquiries about his health, I loathe the man. I needed to know what to do with the, to use Belinda's words, the effing files."

She shuddered. "Oh, of course not."

"But it was a little strange, talking to someone who is locked up. Those imposing walls and barbed wire are strangely hypnotic, don't you think? I get a sense of awe just looking at them."

And…?"

"He said under no circumstances was I to destroy any papers as they are his insurance policy. Without them he was as good as dead."

"What nonsense!" Leah stood and collected a cloth to wipe up the sugar now scattered over the counter top.

"No, it's not. I thought that at first, then I realised he's in constant danger. Think, Leah, of all those guilty felons he got off, how the warders must hate his guts, and there must be other inmates who want payback too. I think he's in a more precarious position in jail than out of it."

Her hand on the cloth froze and she looked at me. "I'd no idea."

"Believe me, it's true. At the start, he was very cagey, reluctant to speak to me. He gave me the third degree about you, asked personal questions only you could have told me before he let his guard down. Then, he couldn't get it all out fast enough."

"Did you mention the Fentons and the Morrisons?"

"Yes." I paused. "That is apparently not good news. He said there were records on paper about other crimes which hadn't yet come to light. Leah, he was remarkably frank about it all. So, these two families at least would love to get their paws on the papers and destroy them."

"Get their paws on? I can't imagine Mason saying that."

I laughed. "No darling, my words. He spoke faster and faster, I guessed they were not allowing him to stay on the phone for too long. There was more. He had no idea his firm had folded and not heard once from any of his own company's lawyers."

"Not surprising; they would want to put as much distance between them and their convicted ex-boss as possible." Leah rinsed out the cloth at the sink. She had calmed down a little, but as soon as she settled back on her stool, she began to play with the sugar cubes again.

I continued. "If you were wondering why Mason was not flush with cash, it's because the Morissons and the Fentons were paying him in kind."

"I don't understand."

"I didn't to begin with, but the 'kind' I learned are antiques."

"Have I got this right?" Leah frowned. "They paid Mason to defend them not in money but in antiques?"

"Yes, weird isn't it? At this point Mason was whispering and I had to strain to hear him. Not sure how much privacy he had at that end."

"Well where are the bloody things, these artifacts? I've not seen any. They're not in the London house."

"Ah, he was not prepared to tell me that. But I was surprised at his reaction that we, plus his nefarious clients, are living close together in France. His voice went all funny and he gasped several times and asked me three times to confirm it."

Leah stood and began to pace up and down the kitchen, stopping to rearrange a plant pot, the dish cloth, the tea towel, anything that wasn't tied down. She suddenly swung round. "Do you think those antiques are stored here, in France?"

"I have no idea. I probed as much as I could, but he suddenly became very cagey. I'd hazard a guess that these valuables were not bought legally."

"Ha! I can just see Daniel and Humphrey receiving stolen property, it's just their style."

"I tend to agree. But that's nothing to do with us. They could have stashed away the Mona Lisa for all I care. No, our problem is the files."

"But you came back without them!" Leah sat down again and leaned over.

"Yes... and no."

She threw the kitchen towel at me. "You're not making sense, Deidre. Where are the files?"

Before I could tell her, Belinda made a noisy and theatrical entrance into the kitchen. "I'm going vegan!" she announced looking very smug, hands on hips, waiting for our reaction.

Leah put her hands over her face before she said, "Vegan? Are you sure?"

"Yes of course." Belinda walked over to the bread bin, and liberated half a baguette which she slapped on the counter top, then made a beeline for the fridge, grabbed the butter and cheese and began to make herself a sandwich.

"Hang on a minute," Leah shouted, "you can't do that!"

"Why not! It's my house, you're supposed to feed me. It's the law. What are you bitching about now?"

Leah pulled the butter and cheese away. "Vegans don't eat animal products."

"So?"

"So, where do you think butter and cheese come from?"

"Cows, I'm not that retarded." Belinda was not a fan of the pc brigade.

"It's still an animal product. Vegans don't eat anything that comes from livestock."

"But the cows don't need this anymore, do they? No one killed them for it?" Her hand shot out and snatched back the cheese.

"OK, so you're a vegetarian then?"

"Yeah, one of them. I don't want any animals killed just so I can eat. I'm a vegetarian now." She plastered on the butter and hacked thick chunks of cheese off the block.

I couldn't resist it. I took the remains of the Christmas ham out of the fridge and sliced it onto plates for lunch. Belinda gave me a death stare, and I smiled sweetly back.

"Tell me, have you been watching *Charlotte's Web*, or *Shaun the Sheep*?"

"What?" She paused, sandwich halfway to her mouth.

"Oh, you know, a film about soft, cuddly, fluffy, talking animals on the way to the abattoir, sacrificed to feed the ravenous, ungrateful humans."

"You're too much, Deidre. Very funny, I don't think." Belinda watched in disgust as I flung a piece of fat to Monster who caught it neatly in his jaws and gulped it down.

"I see Monster's not following in your footsteps then? Mind, I've never heard of a vegan dog."

Behind me I could hear Leah stifling her giggles.

"You're both impossible! Nobody cares about me, you're all so selfish," she screamed and, grabbing the remains of her sandwich, she marched off, Monster at her heels.

"It's so good…" Leah gulped between fits of laughter, "to see her back to normal."

I agreed, but wondered how deep Belinda's trauma reached into her psyche. The teenager needed some serious counselling, and soon.

It was good to see Leah laugh. The moment we heard the upstairs bedroom door slam we both burst out laughing, hugging each other as the tears rolled down our cheeks.

"Did you see her face?" Leah spluttered. "The horror, she adores cheese."

"We should take bets on how long she stays vegetarian," I giggled.

"Well she was only vegan for ten minutes." Leah wiped her eyes with the tea towel. "She might be a nightmare but she does cheer me up sometimes."

Claudette bustled in through the back door, sweeping the empty coffee mugs off the counter and running water into the sink.

"Come. Let's take a walk on the beach, not too far, we'll keep the house in sight."

Those old filmmakers spun unrealistic dreams about the south French coast. It's not always summer dresses and open sports cars. Leah and I pulled on our coats, scarves and gloves and made our way down the steps and onto the coarse sand. Leah turned her face into the chill wind and took in a deep breath. "Damn and blast Mason," she shouted, "I wish I'd never met him. From the first day in that wretched supermarket everything has gone wrong. What did I do to deserve this?"

I put my arm around her. "Darling you don't deserve it, you are the sweetest, most gentle person I know, and life has not been fair to you."

Leah kicked out at a small rock with her prosthesis and sent it flying towards the small waves lapping onto the shore. "So, you were about to tell me where the files are now."

"Are you sure you want to know?"

"Do you have visions of Daniel Morrison torturing me for information?" She lowered her voice. "'Tell me where they are, or else'."

I chuckled at her very bad impression. "Not exactly, but if you don't know…?"

Leah sighed. "I think it safer if I did know. I could use it as a bargaining chip."

"Well, if you're sure. They're in a left luggage locker at Nice Airport."

"Oh."

"A visit to England and all it has achieved is moving the time bomb from the villa a few kilometres down the road. But I'm not going to tell you where I've put the key. That can be my secret for now."

Leah turned and put her arms around me. "You are the best friend anyone can ever have. I'm sorry I'm so down and jittery. It's also the anniversary of…" she trailed off.

"The accident?"

"Yes."

We strolled on in silence.

The following morning, we decided to walk into the

market. I'm not sure if Leah was nervous about leaving her car anywhere, and I didn't ask. After the explosion and fire on the first one, and cut brake lines on the second, I could imagine her reluctance and how she was feeling. Not, she assured me, that we would stop using the car altogether; in practice the village was the only place we could reach on foot and that was a couple of kilometres. But we couldn't buy everything we needed there.

We wrapped up warmly; there was still a chill wind, but after twenty minutes we were both warm. I asked Leah if walking a long distance hurt, wearing a prosthesis. She told me that some days were better than others. If she overdid it, then the stump would get sore and inflamed even after all this time. We both agreed the exercise was good for us, though I've never been an outdoor freak, nor followed the current fitness trends.

The market was buzzing as always. Stalls were set up in the main street, traffic was diverted on market days. Each one was piled with local, fresh produce, vegetables – larger than I had ever seen in the supermarkets in Britain, even the eggs were big. The stalls were laden with an enormous variety of fruits, cheeses, pastries, cakes, and tubs of olives. A couple of vans sold meat and sausages and brewed fresh coffee and churros. The atmosphere was lively and festive and we even received a few smiles from the stallholders.

"Do you think they have forgiven us?" whispered Leah.

"They're not local people; they travel around from one village to the next." I saw her shoulders slump and squeezed her arm.

We wandered from stall to stall, stocking up on fruit

and vegetables and, with bulging baskets, we sauntered over to the café. Determined to ignore any hostile glances I ordered coffee and Leah's favourite doughnuts. I had only just taken my seat when I felt a tentative hand on my shoulder. I turned and looked up to see Margaret Fenton hovering behind me. She hesitated for a few moments and then indicated a spare seat at our table.

"May I?"

"Uh, of course." Leah reached over and removed the basket of produce and set it on the floor.

Margaret arranged herself on the chair, unbuttoning her coat and fiddling with her gloves. She was nervous and she glanced from side to side observing the clientele. I wanted to burst out laughing, she reminded me of the spies in those old war movies, all shifty and shrinking into the woodwork.

"Have you ordered?" I asked, to put her at ease.

"No." She glanced around and the waiter sidled over. She ordered coffee in very passable French.

"I don't remember how long you told us you've lived here, your French is very good," I observed.

"Ah, a couple of years at art college in Paris in my youth. We pick up languages quickly when we're young."

"Yes. I have problems at my age, I'm relying on lessons from school." I stirred sugar into my coffee.

Leah startled us both by saying "I'm surprised you are talking to us. The rest of the villagers are avoiding us like the plague."

I was so busy trying to remember what Margaret had mentioned about her poor French at Sophie's birthday party, that for a moment Leah's words did not sink in.

"That's why I came over. I feel bad about everything that has happened to you, especially as a fellow Brit abroad."

"Never a dull moment," Leah's words sliced into the air.

If Margaret wasn't embarrassed before, she was now. "Look, I came to explain. I don't want you to think badly of me. We are friends with the Morrisons, well we would be, wouldn't we? There not being many English around."

"But you knew each other in London, didn't you?" Leah spoke sharply.

The waiter interrupted us with her coffee and nothing was said as we shifted the crockery around on the tiny table to make space for it. Margaret took her time unwrapping the sugar cubes and watching them dissolve in the hot, brown liquid. "We met a few times at charity events, fund raisers and the like, but I can't say we were ever friends. We were never invited to dinner or attended anything together. Abroad, it's different, you gravitate towards others from the home country. Don't you?"

"That's true," said Leah, "but I was not impressed by Daniel's outburst the other night. He was less than friendly, don't you agree?" She sliced savagely into her doughnut.

Margaret's hand flew to her throat. "I didn't know where to put myself," she replied. "I wanted to slide under the table, and I'm afraid Humphrey wasn't much better." She leaned in towards us confidentially, after glancing around to ensure no one was listening. It would be difficult to hear anything even from the next table through the general din and chatter. "I think our husbands had a few business dealings, but I never got involved and I never enquired. Man stuff, you know, of no interest to me at all."

I didn't believe her for a moment, but now was not the time to disagree.

"What I wanted to tell you," she reached out to pat Leah's hand, "they have two boys, you see. And they are a little on the wild side. No," she corrected herself, "a lot on the wild side."

"We heard, their pranks are legendary around here." I didn't take my eyes off her for one second.

She stared at her teaspoon, twirling it over and over between her fingers. "Yes, and I guess, from the little Geraldine has told me, they are getting bolder."

"But they're in boarding school in England in term time, aren't they?" Leah asked.

"In theory yes, but they've both been expelled, though they use another word nowadays."

"Excluded." Leah knew; she'd been through that with Belinda.

"Excluded, yes." Margaret sipped her coffee while I wanted to shake her and tell her to get on with it. She lowered her voice even further. "What you might not know is that they've been here, in the village. I'm sure they are behind all these nasty little accidents."

I wanted to scream that setting fire to a car and vandalising our villa were hardly 'nasty little accidents', but I managed to control myself.

"No, not all surely," Leah protested. "What about those poor chickens…?"

"And the baby in the pushchair." I added.

Margaret sat back in shock. "Oh, I wasn't referring to those, no not at all. Only the other pranks."

"Cutting the brake fluid line on my car could have killed us both." Leah's assertiveness warmed my heart. I applauded her guts and courage, despite being knocked down time and time again.

The shock on Margaret's face looked genuine. "That was deliberate? Are you sure?"

"Yes, we are." Leah was emphatic. "I'd only had the car a few weeks. That's what the garage reported and I've no reason to disbelieve them."

"But in French, another language—?"

"The mechanic in Nice is English, so I understood him perfectly."

Margaret looked genuinely shocked. She bit her lip and twisted her fingers around the handle of her cup. "I... I had no idea, I'm so sorry. This is serious, very serious. And you think...?"

"We have no idea what to think, but our car was parked outside their house and the brakes worked perfectly on the drive over. But then, we had no idea the boys were home."

"I only saw them racing around the lanes in their father's yellow sports car."

"It nearly ran us over soon after we arrived."

"It won't be long before the gendarmes pick them up."

"Not very likely. Francois Ecole is in Daniel's pocket."

"A corrupt policeman." I stated.

Alarmed, Margaret looked around at the other customers. "Not to be said aloud," she whispered so quietly we could only guess what she said. She stretched out her hand and patted Leah's. "I only came to reassure you. There are a few other families in the area and we'll introduce you and you can ignore the Morrisons. Not good people and, now you have a better idea who is up to mischief, I hope I've put your mind at rest." She threw back the remainder of her coffee and rose abruptly, buttoning her coat as she moved away. She nodded a goodbye and rushed out into the crowded market.

Leah leaned her elbows on the table and sighed. "Do you believe her?"

"Not sure. She may think she's telling the truth, but what does she really know?"

"I wished I'd asked her about your necklace, Deidre."

"We need to ask Geraldine about that. Let's keep an open mind for now."

The waiter came hurrying over with the bill.

"That adds insult to injury," I said, glancing at the slip of paper. "The damn woman didn't even pay for her drink." I slapped a handful of Euros on the table.

We made our way back to the villa. Leah said nothing, but I could see she was replaying the conversation, looking for loopholes and lies.

"How do you keep two tearaway boys under cover in a village this size?" she asked, as we approached our driveway.

"I'm not sure. If we could attribute all the, what did Margaret call them, 'nasty little accidents'? Well they were nasty, but they weren't little, and they most certainly weren't accidents."

"I wonder if she knows about the dead dog?" With her hands full, Leah struggled to open the front door. "It all started with the dog."

I was about to add the blue rabbit, but I swallowed the words just in time. How could the Morrison boys have any knowledge of the genuine fear Leah had of stuffed, blue, toy rabbits?

Claudette went into ecstasy over the market produce. Anyone would think we had presented her with the crown jewels.

Leaving her to unpack and wash the fruit and vegetables, we wandered out to relax in the sunroom. Occasionally Madame's words floated out from the study as she exhorted her pupils to work harder.

Leah sighed. "If it wasn't for Belinda's tuition and exams I'd pack up and move, Spain or Italy, or even farther along the coast."

"Not too many months to go," I reassured her, "and then you'll be free. Belinda will possibly take off to work or for college and then you and Bill can decide where you want to live."

"You are such a comfort Deidre, but I do wish he was here too."

"What's the latest news?"

"We had a long Whatsapp on the phone last night. He is trying to get his daughter into some sort of rehab. She went to pieces after the divorce. The ex found a younger model, some 'arm candy' he said. It's been left to him to care for the child and he's only two years old. Bill can't just walk out and leave him, or her; she keeps threatening to kill herself."

"Oh dear, that's so sad. Leah, you are not the only one with a dysfunctional family, isn't that comforting?"

She laughed. "Deidre, you're the one person I know

who has both feet on the ground and is sound, sensible and just reliable."

"I'm glad you think so. I had rather an eventful youth. Remind me to tell you sometime about my wild adventures in California in the time of Flower Power and 'make love not war'. Ah, those were the days."

Leah smiled and shook her head. "I just can't imagine that."

"I was a tearaway, but it's all so long ago now. I've led a good life." Thinking about it I had. I'd loved, lost, travelled and been my own person. What I didn't tell Leah, was my visit to the clinic while I was in London. The prognosis wasn't good. The cancer had spread and it was too late to operate. I just prayed there was enough time left for me to support my 'adopted niece' to sort out her problems before I was no longer here to help her.

JANUARY   LEAH

Dear Diary,

Deidre wasn't away for all that long, but it felt like a millennium. She is so brave, and does so much for me. I can never repay her. I felt bad allowing her to go to England, carrying a time bomb. Any moment I imagine thugs descending on the villa and torturing us to force us to hand them the files. That one experience in the flat last year freaked me out and I never want to go through all that again.

I'm wondering if I've done something silly, but I'm not putting it into words, and I'm not telling Deidre either. I know she won't keep any secrets from me, but this is different.

It creeps me out, a typical Belinda phrase, Deidre spoke to Mason. Meeting him in Australia was uncomfortable and, as I walked away that night, I knew I never wanted to see or speak to him again. It's over, I've no feelings left for him now.

Belinda is back to her sassy self, complete with swear words. I wish she wouldn't use them. They are not ladylike and she's had enough education to learn other adjectives besides the 'F' word.

Is there a deeper trauma lurking inside? I don't know enough about these things and I'm not about to play amateur psychologist. I might do more damage than good. It's enough to provide her with food, clothes, a roof over her head, and an education, and she knows I am there for her. The only one who is.

I wonder how long it will be before they let her brother out of jail? Not for several years, I guess. And her father? Well he's in for life – whatever that means these days. They don't keep them behind bars for life, not any more.

My moods swing like a pendulum. One day I can cope, I was quite feisty with Margaret, but I was boiling inside. How dare she? I'm very suspicious of her motives. I suspect her husband sent her. She sat there pretending her innocence, and a casual acquaintance with the Morrisons? I don't think so. You can't stay innocent if your husband is a criminal. Even I realised Mason was on the edge, and he was supposed to be this top, squeaky clean, hot shot lawyer. I'm a dummy, but I'm not that stupid, I had my suspicions after a couple years of marriage. And who do criminals socialise with? Other criminals. She knew, I'm sure. And now to blame a couple of teenagers? It doesn't add up.

Other days all I want to do is curl up in bed and refuse to come out. Then I get angry with myself because I must be strong, especially for Belinda and Bill. Poor thing, he must be out of his mind with worry. I'd love to share my problems with him, but I'm not saying a word. He has enough to cope with. It's quite a strain to sound cheerful and make out all is well here. He has promised to be back as soon as he can. I had to tell him everything was fine here and not to rush.

JANUARY BELINDA

Hi Journal

It's me again. It's bloody cold here in France. I need more clothes. I'm sick of Sophie arriving every morning in a different outfit. Yeah, so she's offered to give me half of them but I said no. Her mother would probably have a cadenza if she saw me in her daughter's clothes. And they're too small for me. I mean she's only ~~eleven~~, no twelve. For f's sake, I wasn't allowed all that stuff at her age. You should see her makeup. She has tons of the stuff. I said she should start a YouTube channel and charge to show it off. She'd rake it in. Mind, she's got pots of money without all that bother. But we could do it together and if she didn't need the money, I bloody well do. I got plans, big plans the moment I can get away from Madame slave driver. Pity she ain't a man then I could complain about her to Leah, say he felt me up like one of those #metoo brigade. Then she'd have to fire him. But that aint going to work with Madame now is it?

Sophie is pretty cool, though I wish she didn't chip in with all the answers before I even get to open my mouth.

Hey, I know the bloody answers, well sometimes, but I never get a chance. Then Madame goes all gooey and smiles and tells her how clever she is. Had a dream that I wrapped duct tape over Sophie's mouth and she couldn't answer one question. Yeah, I was killing myself laughing. I could see she was desperate to impress Madame, her eyes were bulging but she couldn't get a word out. Best dream I've had in ages.

Not sure about going out tonight. Beginning to have my doubts about Christian. He was all lovey-dovey at first, now he just grills me about what Leah is doing and what she's said. Who the f*** is he interested in, me or her? She's much too old for him. 'Course Leah thinks he's too old for me but what's six years then? Like nothing. Anyway, she doesn't know him like I do, she's never even met him. Hate to admit it, and only to you my secret journal, but he's beginning to creep me out. I'll toss a coin whether to meet him tonight. Best of three for definite, not five and then seven like last time. I'll have to wrap up warm, yeah, I need new clothes. I wonder if he's a vegetarian as well?

FEBRUARY   DEIDRE

We are into February, and the days are flying past faster than I want – even the wealthy can't buy time.

Leah caught me this morning. I didn't realise she had walked up behind me and saw what I was doing. It was too late to pretend I was using the binoculars looking out to sea, that's on the other side of the villa.

She made me jump so I blurted it out without thinking. "There's a man, loitering out there on the side of the road."

I could feel her tense up. "What's he look like?"

"I'm sure it's nothing to worry about but for a moment I thought it was my Frenchman from England."

"Here, let me see." Leah snatched the binoculars from me and peered through them. "I can't see anyone."

"I probably imagined it." I tried to brush it off.

"Oh no you didn't, I don't believe you." Leah glanced at me before focusing the glasses back on the road. "Well whoever was there is not there anymore." She handed them back. "Do you think we are being watched, Deidre?"

"I have no idea." I sighed. "I've been thinking. Should we go to the police here?"

"Francois Ecole! You must be joking, he's worse than useless and you heard what Margaret said, he's in Daniel's pocket, and that I do believe."

I followed Leah into the sun lounge.

"No, I was thinking of higher up the ladder, Interpol or even the police station in Nice or Cannes. Which town to you think is larger?"

"Nice, by far. But what can we tell them?" Leah pulled the blinds up to let in the dying sunlight.

"We could list all the events that have occurred since we moved in here, hand over the papers, and walk out. I think you have a good case. It's time we connected with some authority. We can't sit here and just wait for the next 'nasty little accident' to happen."

"Dump the files on the counter and run away?" We both laughed.

"Not exactly Leah. We can't leave them in Nice airport forever. I paid for a month and they charge by the day."

"I didn't realise. I must reimburse you." Leah reached for her bag.

"Don't be so daft. I don't need the money, but it might look suspicious if I keep returning and paying month after month, don't you think?"

She nodded. "Tomorrow, then we sit down and list everything. I know we've done this before, but we'll add detail. It's an idea worth considering. Let me sleep on it."

Any further discussion was interrupted by Belinda who flounced into the lounge in a filthy mood.

"I hate it here!" she screamed.

"Do you want to go back to England?" Leah asked.

"I hate it there too. I hate it everywhere." She flung herself down on the couch clutching a cushion to her chest. I saw her stepmother's face as she began to unravel the fringe, flicking the threads onto the floor.

"Must you, Belinda?"

"Oh yeah, everything I do is wrong." She continued to pick away at the fabric.

"What's upset you now?" I did my best to keep my tone even and non-confrontational.

"Sophie was asked to babysit tonight in the village and she said she would take me, but then the family said it was okay for her to go, but they didn't want me there. Charming! What's wrong with me? I'll tell you. Do you know what they call us in the village? *Les Miserables* – the Unfortunates. Everything happens to us. We're doomed."

As Belinda continued to rant, I tried to switch off. The poor kid had a point. Bad luck didn't follow us, it lived with us.

Leah walked over and gave her a cuddle and, to my surprise, Belinda burst into tears and cuddled her back. It was nice to see her bonding, but at what expense?

When things calmed down a little, I suggested a walk on the beach would do us all good. As usual Monster barked at the waves, daring them to come any farther on shore. Belinda threw sticks for him to fetch and he raced after them but never brought them back. In the last few months, he'd grown beyond belief. He was going to be large, even for a Newfoundland cross.

The next couple of weeks were quiet. To cheer her up,

Leah took Belinda on a trip into Nice to empty more boutiques. Madame was laid low with a tummy bug so Belinda couldn't wait to make the best possible use of her short freedom. I stayed home. I could feel my energy levels sink, slowly but surely. I was also reluctant to leave the villa undefended, although I know that sounds silly. Before settling down with a book, I scoured the perimeter of the property with the binoculars. I'd got into the habit, several times a day. On three sides our land was bordered by fields, with the farm road on the fourth. Claudette lived over the small field to one side, out of sight, shielded by our outbuildings. I'd taken to poking my nose into both of them at least once a day. I had no idea what I might find, but it put my mind at rest.

We still hadn't decided to visit the police. Each afternoon, Leah disappeared into her room for a couple of hours. She'd never done this before and I didn't like to ask her what she was doing, but I was curious. When I eventually did find out, I had a fit, but that was much later. I'm not sure now why we procrastinated, but there had been no further disruptions and maybe we both hoped it was all over.

While she was in the city, I'd asked Leah to drive the seven kilometres out to the airport and either collect the case, or pay for it to remain there for another month.

I had just dozed off in the warm sunlight when there was a loud knock on the front door.

Monster was in the back garden, barking his head off and running around in circles going ballistic.

I staggered to my feet, still half asleep, hoping Claudette would answer it, but she was on her siesta.

When I opened the door, it revealed Daniel Morrison on the doorstep.

"What do you want?" I was not in the mood to be polite.

He barged past me into the hall and I was forced to follow him as he peered into each room. Satisfied I was there alone he asked where Leah was.

"Out."

"Then you can pass on a message for me." He leaned in, violating my personal space and I could feel his sour breath on my cheeks. He'd been drinking, a lot. "Tell your niece, or whatever relation she is, that I want those papers, and I want them tonight or she will regret it."

I took a step back and glared at him. "Let me say this once only. We do not have any papers. We are not hiding any secrets. And frankly, we are not prepared to get involved with you or any of your activities. So, you can walk out that door right now." I drew myself up as tall as I could, but my head only reached up to his shoulder. He was a big man and solid. I pointed in the direction of the door, quaking inside, holding myself as still as I could.

He wavered, took a step forward and I was scared he was going to hit me, but I stood my ground. He froze, and then turned round and stalked out of the villa, shouting over his shoulder. "You tell her, or she will regret it."

I followed him, slammed the door shut, then stood back out of sight looking out of the window. I saw him weave unsteadily towards the bright yellow sports car we'd seen before, and fall into the bucket seat. He sat there fumbling with the keys before he finally got it to start and he roared off, sending showers of gravel into the air and narrowly missing the gate posts.

I found I was trembling all over and tottered over to the drinks cabinet and, hand shaking, poured myself a large brandy. I deserved it.

By the time they returned from the shopping expedition, Belinda in high spirits behind a mountain of paper carrier bags, I'd determined that we would be pro-active and stop procrastinating. Tomorrow we would take action.

Belinda was too hyped up to sit and have supper. She was bouncing up and down the stairs modelling the clothes she'd persuaded Leah to buy. I had to admit she had good taste, even if a couple of the outfits were a little revealing. I was about to remark on this when images of my wild youth flashed inside my head. You are only young once. So what if my skirts had brushed the ground, my frilly tops had shown plenty of cleavage.

I said nothing when she settled down to eat, devouring the sausages, mash and gravy without a word about her diet.

"It's OK," Leah whispered, "they're vegetarian sausages."

"We need to talk, right after supper," I replied firmly. I looked at Belinda. "When she goes upstairs."

With her earphones in, attached to her iPod, head nodding in time to the music, I thought Belinda couldn't hear me, but as it turned out, I was wrong.

With everything cleared away, and Belinda safely in her room, we settled in the front lounge and I told Leah about the visit.

Her hand flew to her mouth. "Oh Deidre, I'm so sorry.

I've brought nothing but trouble for you. You should go back to your own villa, yes tomorrow, and distance yourself from all this, this, mess."

"Don't talk such nonsense. I'm not leaving and that's final. You'll have to try a lot harder to get rid of me." I attempted to lighten the mood. "But my point is, we need to do something about those files. Either destroy them or take them to the police like we talked about days ago."

Leah twisted her fingers and plucked imaginary pieces of lint off her trousers. "I know you're right," she sighed. "I'll go back into Nice first thing tomorrow and get the case." She gave a hollow laugh. "They'll think I'm mad, paying for another month then asking for it back tomorrow. But who cares?"

"And then what do we do with them?"

"You're talking about Daddy's papers, aren't you?" said a voice from the doorway.

"Belinda!" Leah gasped.

She walked in and plonked herself down on the sofa. "You think I'm too stupid to know what's going on, but you're wrong. Remember, it was me that carted them all the way to Australia?" Seeing Leah was about to interrupt her she waved her down. "And I know they are so dangerous that other people, like the Morrison guy wants to get his hands on them."

"Oh!" We stared at her.

"I'm not so dumb. Easy problem to solve, why didn't you ask me?"

"What do you mean?" I asked.

"And how do you think you're going to solve it for us? For all of us," Leah added.

"It's easy, if you live in the modern world of course." Belinda looked so smug.

"Okay Miss Brilliant Idea, cut the sarcasm, what would you do?"

"Technology, that's the answer. First, we make a bonfire in the garden and, one by one, burn the lot."

"So, we destroy them. And what do we say when Daniel Morrison visits again?"

"He won't, he'll know we don't have them anymore."

"Oh, and how does that work? We invite him round to watch?"

Belinda sat up straight and rolled her eyes. "Duh! We film it, don't we? On the phone, and then we send it to him."

"By carrier pigeon?" I couldn't resist it.

"I don't have an email address for them," Leah said.

"I can get that for you from Sophie. Her mother has it on her laptop."

"And won't she be curious when Sophie asks for it?"

"Nah. Sophie won't ask. She'll just wait until her mother is out. Sophie often noses around in there. She finds all kinds of stuff her parents don't tell her about. You can leave that bit to me."

Leah and I looked at each other, eyebrows raised and, wisely, we made no comment.

I turned to our amateur Sherlock Holmes. "I think you might have solved our problem; that's a pretty good idea."

Belinda rewarded me with a huge smile. "Have to practice first of course, the filming bit – show each file in close up, and then fling it into the bonfire."

"Wait!" Leah startled both of us. "What do you know

about the files? You were eavesdropping just now, but before?"

"Well I didn't lug them all the way over to Australia without reading them first. 'Course I wanted to know why Daddy wanted us to take them to him."

"But they might not have been the same files. There were dozens in his home office in London."

"No, they were not the same. The ones we have here are about other clients."

"Wait!" I almost shouted. "How do you know that?"

Belinda sighed and gave me a look as if to say 'I'm talking to an idiot'. "OK then. I read the files I took to Perth and gave Daddy, right?"

"You've already told us that."

"So, then I read the files you brought over when we came to France. And they weren't the same."

"And when did you see the files, and have time to read them?" Leah was angry.

Belinda sighed again. "I'm not a dummy you know. I knew you kept them all in the attic, and every time you went out, I'd go read some more. I couldn't for a few days when you got that bloody big safe in."

"At least that kept them private," Leah said.

"Not for long. Remember, it's me you're dealing with and I know you, Leah. Took me a while to hunt down the code but I found it. And then I read most of the rest."

"You little…" Leah sprang to her feet and, for a moment, I thought she was going to hit her stepdaughter. "Have you no respect for privacy?"

Belinda was on her feet, hands on hips, she faced up to Leah. "It's my father, and this is all the family I've got left, so it's my right to know what's going on." Her face turned red with anger, she was shaking, and in turn I thought she was going to hit Leah. "Have you forgotten that all the things that have gone wrong affect me as well. Have you? What if you had been killed when the brakes failed? Who would look after me then? Did you think of that? No, you were only thinking of yourself and Deidre. But I'd have been left all alone in a foreign country to fend for myself."

Leah took a step back.

No, neither of us had given it a thought, but the angry teenager had and, at that moment, we both understood how scared she was. Her bravado, swearing and appalling behaviour was a front, a protection.

Leah suddenly moved forward and hugged her daughter. "Darling, I never even… we were just so grateful to be alive. Maybe it's best to go back to London, at least there—"

"Not bloody likely," Belinda snapped, pulling away. "It's cold, wet, damp and I've worked too frigging hard to learn the language and swot for those effing exams. I'm not letting Daniel Morrison and Co. chase me away just because he's a bloody criminal. And, I don't want to live in the same place where both my sodding father and wastrel brother are locked up in prison. It's just too humiliating." She ran out of steam and fell back onto the sofa, cuddling the cushion that she was slowly shredding to pieces.

There was a long, stunned silence. Leah hovered for a few minutes before collapsing into the nearest chair. She studied her hands, then pushed her hair back and looked at Belinda.

"I may have underestimated you," she said.

"Yeah, well, lots of people do." She clutched the cushion like a drowning man clings to a lifebelt at sea. Monster climbed up on her lap almost smothering her, as she wrapped her arms around him as well.

"So, you know as much as we do about your dad's dealings?"

"Dunno, don't know what you know."

"You really should follow in your father's footsteps, you'd make an excellent lawyer." I smiled at her.

"Not bloody likely. Not getting involved with all those crooks."

"Perhaps it's time we all put our cards on the table. Belinda, I'm elevating you to full adulthood for now, is that okay with you?"

She looked at me. "'Bout bloody time. I'm not a child."

I bit back the words. There were plenty of times Belinda acted even younger than Sophie, but for once we needed to be united.

"I think that's an excellent idea," Leah agreed. She explained what we had discovered so far, the records in the files revealing crimes not yet charged, and the payment in kind, in the form of antiques.

Belinda sat up straight and listened carefully, nodding every now and again.

"Pretty much what I sussed out. And I think Sophie's parents are involved too."

"What!" both Leah and I said together.

"Yeah, well I'm not sure, but she has sort of hinted that they sort of have dealings, and it would be bloody easy to hide a whole barn-full of antiques in that pile."

"Oh no, I'm not going up against Marquis Lampierre, no way." Leah was quite emphatic about that.

"So, simple. We burn the files, let them know, and that will be an end to it."

"Hang on a moment. There's a problem with that," I said.

They both turned to look at me. I noticed it was getting dark outside and went to draw the curtains. On my way back to my chair, I stopped by the drinks cabinet and poured all of us a large brandy.

Belinda accepted hers with a smile. "Only one," I told her, "no more. This is not dinner at the chateau." I grinned at her and winked.

Belinda had the grace to look slightly embarrassed, but took a large slurp.

"You were about to tell us what the problem is," Leah prompted me.

"Yes. If Mason had been paid in antiques, he would have been in possession of them before he skipped the country, so it's highly unlikely they are stored in some chateau in the south of France." That made sense to me, I hoped the others would agree.

"Good point," Leah agreed.

"It was only a suggestion," whined Belinda as she made a dive for the drinks cabinet but, before either of us could say a word, she held up the glass of tonic water she had just poured for herself. She grinned and we laughed.

"I don't think it's anything to do with us, the antiques I mean. That's solely between Mason and his nefarious clients."

"What's that mean?" Belinda chipped in.

"Just another word for criminal, or immoral."

I tossed off the rest of my brandy. "I agree. I think we can forget about the loot and follow Belinda's idea. Tomorrow we burn the files, record the bonfire and email both the Morrisons and the Fentons for good measure.

"We will have to be careful we don't appear on film." I sat and thought for a moment. "And we don't send the email from our service provider, but use an internet café to hide our tracks."

"Goodness I never thought of that." Leah was shocked.

"What, you think it might be illegal or something?" Belinda looked worried.

"I'm not sure," I replied. "On the plus side, your dad's law firm has been dissolved, he has no access to them, and they can't accuse us of destroying evidence because, while I was in London, I tried to hand them over to the police and they refused to take them. So, illegal or not, Daniel Morrison doesn't need to know who burned the evidence, just that it doesn't exist any more."

Belinda jumped to her feet, full of energy. "I'll try to make the old battle-axe leave early tomorrow, tell her I've got a headache or something and we can have a practice. There's an old oil drum cut in half in the end outbuilding. That'll do, eh?"

Leah nodded. "That sounds like a plan. I'll go rescue the case from the airport first thing."

Even Monster thought it was a good plan as he wagged his tail, thumping Belinda in the face. She shrieked at him and then hugged him tighter.

It was a good plan, but we didn't carry it out.

We were woken in the early hours by howls from Belinda's room. I almost fell out of bed, disorientated, as I struggled into my dressing gown and searched for my slippers.

Leah reached Belinda's room before I did. The light spilled out across the corridor as I blinked to get my eyes open.

Belinda was crouched down on the floor next to Monster lying on his side, his whole body convulsing. His eyes were glazed, and his paws were fluttering, trying to make traction in the air. His head was lying in a pool of yellow-green froth which was leaking from his mouth.

Leah flew back to her bedroom to grab her mobile and was flinging on her clothes as it rang. I put my finger on Monster's nose, it was red hot. He was panting for breath and then he went limp.

"Deidre, what's the matter with him? What's wrong?" cried Belinda, tears streaming down her cheeks.

"No idea, but Leah's calling the vet now." I'll throw a few clothes on and you do the same. I'm not sure they do house calls."

Leah came back into the room, pulling a jersey over her head. "It's the same vet as last time," she said. "We're to take him in straight away."

"It'll need all hands to lift him into the car."

"I'll bring it round to the front door," Leah called back as she hobbled quickly down the stairs.

The three of us heaved Monster into the back of the SUV and crammed Belinda in beside him, lying on the floor. She wrapped her arms firmly around the now comatose bundle of black fur. Her tears dripped onto his

252

face as she cradled him repeating over and over, 'Don't die on me, please don't die on me, Monster."

I stood in the doorway and watched as Leah raced off down the driveway. I wandered into the kitchen and plugged in the coffee machine. I wasn't even going to try and go back to sleep. Was this just another accident or was it deliberate?

I switched on the television and channel hopped but I couldn't concentrate. I tried to doze off on the sofa, but I kept coming to, as one noise after another had me sitting bolt upright, wide awake. There were creaks on the stairs, a thump on the back door, a branch scratching against an upstairs window. An owl hooted in the night and my nerves tingled and jangled at every little sound.

It was a couple of hours later that I heard the car return and rushed to open the front door.

Belinda was in tears, and Leah's face was white. They climbed out unsteadily and followed me into the kitchen. I waited until they were sitting at the kitchen table and poured coffee for both of them.

In fits and starts, Belinda blurted out that the vet was sure Monster had been poisoned.

"But he's still alive?" I asked, dreading the answer.

"Only just. If we'd waited…" Leah didn't finish the sentence.

"He doesn't think Monster will live. And he wouldn't let me stay with him. He was so cruel." Belinda's tears dripped onto the counter top.

Leah comforted her. "He'll need to rest. The vet pumped him with enough stuff to make him sleep. He's in the best hands."

"The cause?" I asked.

"He can't be sure," Leah replied, "but something he ate."

"I'd never feed him anything that would make him sick," whined Belinda.

"No, of course you wouldn't darling, we know that."

"Was Monster missing at any time today?" I asked.

"No. Not for a minute. He was with me all the time," Belinda sobbed.

"Even when he wanted to pee?" I pursued.

"We walked down to the post boxes early and he did all his stuff then. He's been next to me all day. You know he never leaves me."

"I've never known such a chewing gum dog," Leah said, then seeing the puzzled look on her stepdaughter's face added, "a description of a dog that never leaves its owner's side. I can even tell when you go to the loo, he sits outside the door."

"You don't think Claudette…?" Belinda asked.

"No." Leah and I answered in unison. "Not for a moment," Leah added. "I've seen her hug him more than once. She's fond of him, despite the extra work he gives her."

"I love him so much. I'll die if anything happened to him."

"Wait, I've had a thought." They both looked at me. "He was fine all evening, yes?"

Belinda nodded.

"Then you let him out last thing and waited by the back door?"

Belinda shrieked. "When he came back in, he was chewing something. I went to take it out of his mouth but he wouldn't let me, so I thought… Oh, you mean…"

254

"There's only one way to find out." Leah stood and hobbled stiffly to the back door.

As we all ventured out into the back garden, the sun was already peeping over the horizon making it light enough to see where we walked. We fanned out and scoured the ground. The gravel area extended from the house to a section of grass that ran all around the property. The ground close to the house was undisturbed, but hidden in the grass were several pieces of raw meat covered in a pale green powder.

"Look!" shrieked Belinda. "Come look!"

"There's more here," called Leah, over by the stone wall.

"I'll kill the bastard who tried to kill Monster," sobbed the teen.

Leah ran back into the kitchen to fetch rubber gloves and a plastic bag. She scooped up the evidence while Belinda and I checked the rest of the garden was clear.

"I'll take these straight back to the vet," she said, waving the plastic bag in the air. "It may help, if there's an antidote."

"I'm coming too." Belinda rushed over. "He might let me see Monster. I'll make him."

For the second time, the pair drove out through the stone pillared gateway at breakneck speed and I crossed my fingers that no one had tampered with the brakes a second time. At that rate, neither of them would stand a chance.

When Madame arrived shortly after 7.30 a.m. she was quite distraught when she heard the news. "*Le pauvre petit chien*," she murmured. "*La pauvre petite fille*."

I could think of one thing that would not be *le pauvre*

petit, and that would be the vet's bill. But worth every cent to save Monster. Even I had grown to love his fur dropping, wet tongue hanging, tail thumping, floppy paws, and soulful eyes.

When Leah and Belinda returned Belinda dragged herself off into the study, but I suspected that Madame would not succeed in pumping an iota of learning into her. Sophie put her arm around her elder friend and muttered something in rapid French that I failed to catch.

Leah found me in the garden a short time later.

"This has gone beyond a joke," she said, hands on hips, her face like thunder.

I sat back, trowel in hand. "It went beyond that when they tampered with the car. That was aimed at us, remember."

"What are we going to do?" Leah waved her hands before dropping them down by her side. "Oh yes, we could go to the police and then what? We're in a rural area. It's probably rat poison, that's the vet's best guess, and all the farmers probably use it."

"They might think it very strange that we now report an attempt on a dog's life and we neglected to go to them about our lives in danger."

"Goodness, I never thought of that. By the time the mechanic confirmed it and then you took off for the UK and with Christmas approaching…"

"And we suspected the Morrisons who are cosy with Francoise Ecole… "

"We had a mental block?"

"It's possible."

"We can't go on living in fear like this, Deidre."

I agreed with her. Maybe destroying the files would put an end to it all. It was the only thing we could do – prove we were no longer a threat to any of our criminal neighbours.

Leah drove into the police station later that morning, but when she returned, she was despondent. As I'd suspected they brushed her complaints aside and she was convinced they pretended to misunderstand most of what she said. There was lots of shoulder shrugging and arm waving, as only the French can express their feelings. She persevered and insisted on making a statement, but suspected the moment she climbed back into her car, it would be screwed up and lying in the waste paper basket.

Twice more that day, I thought I saw my stalker near the property but, by the time I had run indoors to grab the binoculars, he had disappeared. This time, I did not mention it to Leah; she had enough to worry about.

FEBRUARY LEAH

Dear Diary,

I've not prayed for years but I wanted to today. My heart aches for Belinda, for all of us. Poor, poor Monster. Who would be that cruel? It's more understandable they tried to kill us, but why a defenceless dog? He's been in the animal clinic for almost a week. Every day, Belinda and I have driven over to see how he is. He's awake now, the vet had to induce vomiting, I'm glad neither of us were there to see that. And the powder helped too, as they got that analysed so they could pump the best drugs into him. He is on the road to recovery but still weak and they want to monitor him for signs of internal damage, kidneys, liver and so on. It's thought we caught it early. Sometimes it takes a dog days to get sick after swallowing rat poison. We were lucky.

Next time, dear God if there is a next time, something happens, I'm not going anywhere near Francois bloody Ecole in his police shed in the village. It will be straight into Nice, to the main station, and I'll lay a complaint there, against him too. I've done a bit of googling and, here in France, it's not the same as back home. In Britain the police have to prove you're guilty. Here, you have to prove your innocence. You are presumed guilty from the start. I admit that thought sends shivers down my spine. If you don't have witnesses for the time of the crime, how do you prove you didn't do it? We need to tread carefully.

One piece of good news: Bill will be arriving next month. He's got his daughter sorted in a rehab place and he's found a relation to care for his grandson, who will take him to visit his mother every day. I can't wait to see him again. It will be such a comfort.

Hmmm, reading that back, I sound like one of those little women who must have a man in their lives. I'm not. I can manage without; I coped after James died, and I don't have to worry about money any longer, but when you're under attack, as we have been, there is safety in numbers.

Tomorrow it will be the first day of March and the Brand and Flynn family are going to have an early Guy Fawkes. We'll light the bonfire and burn every scrap of paper and maybe that will be the end of it. I can only hope, and pray too, just to be on the safe side.

FEBRUARY BELINDA

Journal, it's me, who else? I'm glad to see no one has tampered with the lock, and I've put an extra chain on it, no one can get in now so you are nice and private.

The French are really weird. I've been so worried about Monster and yet when I told Sophie, she patted my back and shrugged her shoulders. They do have dogs at the chateau, but they sleep in the outbuildings so I guess it's not the same. Vet says Monster can come home soon, and that's so, so cool. I won't let him out of my sight for a moment.

If I ever find out who harmed poor Monster, I'll kill them, I will. They are so beyond gross and sick. Leah was pretty cool though. Wow did she move fast on that false leg of hers. And she's run me over there every day. She's not so bad, I guess. Not real cool or awesome but for an old person she isn't so bad. Wow, she's over forty and still does most things. 'Course, old wrinklies live for decades now. I can't imagine ever getting that old, it must be gross. It's years and years off though, not worth thinking about. Though Deidre now is even older. She said she was seventy, wow! She's not as fast as Leah though, even with her gammy leg. I've watched her stand up, she's slow and takes her time. I think she's got a lot slower lately, but maybe her bones and things are sore. Body parts must wear out by that age.

I wish all these gross things would stop. Tomorrow should sort it though. Trust the young to think of destroying the files. I felt quite proud of myself and the oldies agreed with my idea. Yeah, we know how to do stuff. Just wait till my age are in charge, we'll put the world to rights. No more poverty, stop wars, all get on together. It's about time someone did the right stuff. And, it will be my generation, I know it. Youth forever, yeah!!!!!

MARCH DEIDRE

I hope I'm not becoming paranoid, but I saw my stalker again this morning when we went to the market. We drove into the village, rain was forecast, and we parked down by the river. The moment I stepped out of the car I saw him, watching, and this time I was determined to stop him and ask him why he was spying on us.

He saw me stare at him, turned away and disappeared around the corner. I walked after him as briskly as I could but he was nowhere to be seen in the side street.

"What are you doing? Wait for me," Leah called out, as she rescued the baskets from the back seat and hurried over to join me.

"Uh, just a cute kitten." My reason was rather lame, but I didn't want to frighten Leah.

She looked around. "Where?"

"Took off when it saw me coming."

Leah put both baskets in one hand and took hold of my arm in the other. "Don't lie, Deidre. You're a hopeless liar. What did you really see?" She tightened her grip.

I took one last look down the side street and admitted I'd seen my London stalker again.

"The same man you thought was watching the villa?"

"The same."

We began to walk to the central square. "Whoever he is I don't think he means any harm." I tried to reassure her.

"I've not been that close to him, but I don't get any nasty vibes. And you are fey, or so you tell me, and he doesn't scare you either, does he?"

"No," I admitted, "but I want to know who he is and what he wants. It is a bit creepy."

"Maybe he's your guardian angel?" Leah laughed and I shuddered. I didn't want to think about angels, in fact I didn't believe in them.

Later that day, after Madame du Pont – Sophie trailing behind her – had spluttered off down the drive, Leah went to give Claudette time off. She was a good worker, but always happy for an extra few hours to spend with her ailing mother. Leah packed her off across the field with a basket of fresh produce and went out to join Belinda who was already piling wood chippings and shredded paper into the half oil drum she'd dragged from the outbuildings onto the gravel path.

"Look what I found." She waved a box of firelighters and shoved six under the kindling.

"Not too many," Leah warned, gathering wood offcuts and a couple of larger logs.

"Are we burning all the files? There are boxes of them."

"Let's start with the ones that refer to the Morrisons and the Fentons. We could shred the rest we don't have time to burn."

Belinda nominated herself both producer and director of photography. She had positioned her mobile phone on a chair, piled high with books and she was fiddling to get the best angle.

"I need to see only your hands," she shouted. "Leah, take your ring off and Deidre, your bracelet too. We don't want them to see who it is, do we?"

Belinda stood up. "I should have painted your nails bright red or similar and then taken it off as soon as we finished. Then it wouldn't even look like your hands."

I went out to my car and brought back thin plastic gloves.

"What are those?" Belinda came over to look.

"I always carry some in my glove compartment in case of an accident."

"Were you a nurse too, like Leah?"

"No, but I've done first aid courses."

"Those would be handy too if you have to pick up a half dead dog off the road, or a cat or…" Trust Belinda to think of that.

"Will you two stop nattering!" Leah called. "We need to hurry or we'll run out of wood to burn."

Belinda took her new position very seriously, directing us to hold up a folder, while she recorded the name on the front, before it was consigned to the flames.

I was never so aware how slowly paper burned. As the ashes piled up, we had to rake them to one side to keep the flames going.

Leah went off to get more wood and reappeared with a bag of charcoal and, while that took time to burn, once the coals were red hot, we piled on one file after another.

As the sun sank lower in the sky we were forced to stop; there was not enough light to identify which folders we were burning. This was not the first time Belinda had put her camera to good use. The last time was in Weston-super-Mare, an occasion that changed all our lives.

Tired, dirty, smelling of smoke and ash, we threw a bucket of water over the dying embers and went back indoors.

I looked at the remaining pile of folders in dismay. "It's going to take a long time to burn them all."

"We'll have to do a few each night, but at least we've done the most important ones, for the people around here that is," Leah sighed.

Meanwhile Belinda was shrieking in delight as she downloaded the footage onto her laptop. "Wow, look at this, you can see it all so clearly. See, the name and… there it goes, into the drum."

She was right, we had then taken each piece of paper out and fed it to the flames. It was positive proof the evidence was gone.

Leah pushed her hair back behind her ears and washed her hands in the sink. "Who's up for scrambled eggs and bacon?"

"I could eat a horse." Belinda was glued to her screen.

"It's not vegan bacon, that macon stuff," Leah whispered.

"Maybe she won't notice," I whispered back. We smiled.

As she had promised, Belinda had got Sophie to check out her mother's phone and given her the email address we needed. I could hear the child – I mustn't call her that, there are days when she behaves like a mature adult. And we know that not all adults are mature, it's not an age thing at all. Anyhow I heard her chortling as she pressed the send button.

"Wait!" cried Leah. "I thought you said we'd go into Nice and use an internet café so they can't trace us?"

"Whoops! Bugger." Belinda's hands flew off the keyboard. "Shit," she added.

Leah dried her hands and came to peer over her shoulder. "Well it's too late now. We'll just have to hope there are no repercussions."

"What are those?" Belinda's shoulders slumped, and I felt sorry for her, she looked so miserable.

Leah explained and asked her to lay the table while she served up.

"Cheer up," she said. "Can't be helped. "There's one thing to look forward to."

Belinda smiled. "Yessss. The day after tomorrow we bring Monster home."

"Not letting him out of your sight doesn't mean he sleeps on your bed."

"Leah!"

"He'll be in the house of course. And it's not up for discussion, right?"

For once she nodded and attacked her bacon and scrambled eggs with her usual appetite.

From behind, Leah winked at me and I had a problem keeping a straight face.

We opted for an early night. Burning evidence is tiring work.

The next day was uneventful. We burned a few more papers and decided to go and celebrate with a meal out in town. Belinda insisted we go Italian and so we gorged on pasta and chianti at a red-checked table cloth under landscape pictures of the cinq towns and St Peter's Basilica. We returned happy and more relaxed than we'd been for weeks.

We were woken in the early hours of the morning by a tremendous crash from downstairs. In my dazed state it sounded as if a herd of elephants had broken through the front door.

I bumped into Leah on the top hallway. She was hopping and trying to strap on her prosthesis. We looked over the railing and were horrified to see at least five gendarmes in the hallway. Two of them disappeared into the lounge and the kitchen.

"What's going on!" I shrieked as I rushed down the stairs. I ignored Belinda's frightened cries as I looked to see who was in charge.

"Madame Brand?" asked the policeman wearing the most badges and stripes on his uniform.

"No, I'm Madame Flynn," I replied. "And why did you not ring the doorbell like civilised people?" I pointed to the broken latch on the front door which was hanging open at an odd angle.

"Eet ees for de surpreese," he replied with the usual Gallic shrug.

I could feel my blood boil as I watched several of his men methodically search every cupboard, drawer and shelf. They moved on from the kitchen into the laundry area.

"Just what are you looking for?" Leah was breathless. She'd hobbled down the stairs clutching the leg she was still trying to strap on securely. "If we knew," she added, "we could show you."

"If it is here, we will find it. Please sit."

Leah, Belinda and I sat huddled side by side on the sofa, shaken and scared. We both put our arms around the youngster who had begun to cry. We both murmured platitudes, but we had no idea what was going on.

Three of the gendarmes ran up the stairs, while boss man towered over us. When Leah went to get up, whispering she'd get us a drink he barked at her to stay where she was. She sank back against the cushions.

I glared at the senior policeman who I noticed was staring at Leah's false leg. He appeared quite fascinated, if not a little alarmed.

There was a shout and he left us and ran up the stairs, taking them two at a time. We heard a lot of excited chatter then they called down and the fourth man joined them on the landing.

From where we were sitting, we couldn't see what was happening, but a few moments later one of them reappeared carrying a painting. He hovered in the doorway, clutching the top of the frame in both hands.

A second man joined him cradling a box in his arms. They piled them next to the front door, and one stood guard while the other went back upstairs.

"What the f*** is that?" Belinda asked.

"I have no idea. But I don't have a good feeling about this."

Three more paintings were brought down and stacked against the wall and three more boxes.

"What do you know about...?" The chief gendarme pointed to the pictures.

We all stood up and went over to look. Belinda put her hand out but Leah hissed at her not to touch. "I have never seen any of these things before," she said loudly and clearly.

I peered into the boxes. One contained a porcelain Chinese vase, which looked old and valuable. The other was a jumble of silverware, I guessed a tea service, with milk and sugar bowl.

"I have no idea where all this came from," Leah repeated.

"I haven't seen any of this stuff either. Where was it?" I turned to look at the gendarme.

He pointed up the stairs and quick as a flash, Leah slipped past him and bounded up to the first floor. I followed.

The ladder from the attic was hanging down and we were in time to see the last gendarme descend. He brushed his hands and nodded. "That eees all," he said as he joined his fellow officers in the hallway below.

"Deidre, we've been set up." Leah said.

I could only nod. We'd not seen any of those items in the attic room. After we removed the boxes and files, the place had been empty.

"When did you last come up here?" I asked her.

"It must be a couple of weeks. I have a horrible gut feeling that those paintings are valuable..."

"The antiques linked to Mason?"

"Yes."

"So, we have a very good idea who planted them in our attic."

"And told the police."

The gendarme in charge called up the stairs wanting Leah to open the safe they had discovered in her bedroom.

To our relief, they found nothing of any interest in there, though the boss man rifled through the birth certificates, personal papers and held up the passports, which he slid into an evidence bag. "I need for you too," he pointed to me and I went off to fetch mine.

It took another hour for the gendarmes to minutely search every square inch of the villa before they climbed into their cars, lights blazing on the roof, and roared off. We'd been instructed to appear at the station in Nice promptly at 2 p.m. the following afternoon.

Belinda pushed and shoved the front door but it was impossible to close it.

Leah grabbed her mobile and phoned the insurance company. She wanted the front door fixed now. To our surprise they promised to have someone there within the hour.

Belinda was full of questions. Where? Why? What? But we had no answers to give her.

As we hung around the broken door, headlights appeared coming up the road outside.

Leah glanced at her watch. "Wow that was quick," she said.

But it wasn't the repairman, it was a taxi from Nice Airport. As it came to a stop Leah gave a cry of delight as Bill stepped out. He left the driver to rescue his cases from the boot as he wrapped his arms around Leah and hugged her tightly.

"Thank God you're here." Her voice against his coat was muffled. "You have no idea how happy I am to see you."

He pulled away, saw the damaged front door and his mouth fell open. "What the…?"

"Long, long story. Come inside."

There seemed little point in not recounting all the details of our trials and tribulations since last May. Belinda perched on the kitchen counter while Leah made the coffee and I watched as Bill's eyes opened wider and wider.

We were interrupted by the arrival of the bleary-eyed handyman who set about banging and hammering as he manoeuvred the door back into its proper place. He found time to drink two mugs of coffee and devour four of Leah's fairy cakes before he finally drove off and left us in peace.

The sun peeped over the hills to the east, glistening on the sea when we finally fell into bed. Belinda was all for staying up, but Leah insisted we get some sleep before we faced a barrage of questions later in the day.

Leah had a rather fraught conversation on the phone with Madame. I could hear wails of 'another day lost!' But Leah stood firm.

Bill drove us into Nice after brunch. He'd suggested he stay with us, but Leah gently declined his offer. Taking my arm, she strode into the police station as if advancing on the enemy, leaving Bill and Belinda to hit the shops.

"I wonder what Belinda will persuade him to buy for her," I muttered, hoping to make Leah smile, but she was deadly serious. "You can only push someone so far," she was mumbling to herself.

We were taken to separate rooms and faced a barrage of questions. I wasn't worried we would tell different stories; we had both agreed we would tell the truth, the whole truth, and so on. Looking back now, I was not aware that Leah had not been completely honest with either me or the police but, that day at the station, I must have sounded convincingly open and honest.

They kept us there for hours, asking the same questions over and over again. All we could do was repeat ourselves over and over again. When a new officer I'd not seen before walked into the bare, green painted room and sat on the opposite side of the plain steel table he threw me.

"I want you to tell me all the events starting from last night up until the day you moved into Madame Brand's villa." His English was flawless. He sat waiting, pen in hand, hovering over his notepad. I took a deep breath and began with the repairman fixing the door, all the way back to finding the dead dog on the front doorstep. It wasn't easy. I had to stop and think several times, intent on putting things in the right order. It's a lot more difficult to tell any story in reverse and I was careful not to leave anything out.

Every now and again he would nod, and scribble something, despite the camera up in the corner recording every word and movement.

He slammed his notebook on the desk, stood and told me I could go, but not to leave the place where I was currently residing. I assured him I had no intention of going anywhere.

I had to wait a further couple of hours in the outer

office before they released Leah with the same instructions.

Exhausted and drained we found Bill and Belinda in the closest Italian restaurant where, once again, the teenager was carbo boosting on pasta.

We ordered from the menu, and I mentioned I had been asked to recount all the events in reverse. Bill nodded. "It's an old technique. I think it was used to interrogate spies in the second World War. It's easier to trip up and contradict yourself."

"And prove you're lying?" Leah remarked. "They did the same to me. It took a lot longer, but I did not contradict myself once."

I asked Leah if she had told the police about our stalker and she had. Another piece of our story that matched up. I'd felt a bit of a fool recounting I had seen the same man on the plane to England, and I thought he had followed me around London, and then again hanging around the village. I was sure they didn't believe me.

"Do you think they're convinced we're innocent?" I asked her.

"It's impossible to tell. The guys I spoke to didn't give anything away. And who do they believe? Two rich, expat businessmen, who've been here several years with their families, or a couple of old fogies like us? Sorry Deidre, but that's how we must come across. New arrivals to a peaceful village, and then all hell breaks loose."

"Nope," Belinda chipped in. "There's been plenty going on before we got here."

We all turned and stared at her.

She grinned, and wound spaghetti around her fork.

"Go on, spit it out." Leah leaned forward.

"Madame told me lots about all the pranks the boys got up to. There were so many of them, and the gendarmes went around asking questions, loads of times. Sophie knew too, and she gave me all the gruesome details."

"I can't see them blaming us for the dog, the chickens, the dead baby, or poisoning Monster. So, someone is up to no good."

"What happens now?" asked Bill, taking a sip of his wine. "You should both get a good lawyer."

We agreed. We hadn't been charged with anything but if we were guilty until proved innocent we would need all the help we could get.

On the way home from Nice, we stopped off to collect a rather subdued Monster. Belinda sat in the rear compartment while he covered her from head to toe in wet, slobbery kisses.

"I'm glad we got our guard dog back," Leah said as we arrived at the villa. "If the police return, he'll bark and give us time to open the front door before they smash it in again."

"Monster's the best." Belinda nuzzled his fur. "You'll protect us from those nasty, horrible policemen, won't you?"

"Bath for him first thing in the morning," Leah told her. "He smells of vet and kennels. I've phoned and told Madame not to come tomorrow."

"Yay!" cried Belinda as she barrelled into the house.

"I'm actually past caring if she passes those exams or not," said Leah, taking her coat off and hanging it up. "What we've been through has changed my priorities."

I agreed.

We didn't hear from the police for several days and life carried on as normal.

Bill made himself useful pottering about clearing out the external buildings, I lost myself in frantic baking sessions – much to Claudette's disgust, Belinda began to study really hard, and Leah – well Leah disappeared into her bedroom for hours on end and I hesitated to ask her what she was doing in there. Once or twice I met her coming out and raised my eyebrows but she didn't take the hint, and only smiled back.

There was another attack on a chicken farm close by, this time definitely not a fox as, again, the chain link fencing had been severed with bolt cutters. As before, the chickens had been ripped apart but not eaten. We heard the whole place was covered in blood. Francois Ecole was seen questioning people in the village, but he didn't approach us.

Then, there was a second murder. This time a toddler playing in the street was abducted and his body found dismembered on the other side of the river.

The atmosphere of fear in the village was palpable. Now, we were not the only ones viewed with suspicion. No one smiled, no one laughed, and even the old boys who hung around outside the local bars were subdued and drank their pastis and wine while puffing on their roll-ups in silence.

Bill remarked that these incidents could not be linked to stolen art treasures and unsolved gangland misdemeanours in London. This was the work of some deranged individual who was out of control.

The culprit was labelled *Le Tueur au Clair de Lune* – The Moonlight Killer, and everyone was on the alert.

I was afraid Bill would give in to Belinda's nagging that they go out patrolling at night to catch the murderer. But he assured her that this was real life, not a TV series, and ordinary people just didn't do that. And, it would be very dangerous.

When I heard this, I breathed a sigh of relief and hoped she was not daft enough to go off on a vigilante expedition by herself.

Unfortunately, she found someone else.

MARCH   LEAH

Dear Diary,

I'm over the moon that Bill is here. I keep telling myself I'm not a shrinking Victorian violet who needs a man in her life, not in this day and age, but it is a comfort. And he's been amazing. Most men would have taken one look at the mess we're all in and run a mile, but not Bill. I love him to bits.

I'm getting to be an old hand with police interrogations. I wonder if they realised this was not my first time being grilled by police? I was curious to know if they had checked with London and got the story of my arrest before? I decided it was wiser to say nothing.

Of course, I had to mention Mason and all his dealings, so it won't take them long to tie up all the loose ends. I just hope they do investigate properly. Deidre and I are sitting ducks. You read about police forces having to solve cases and they just go for the easiest target to get their statistics up. It would be a simple matter for them to arrest us. They have the evidence we were storing stolen antiques. They probably don't need any more than that to charge us with something. They now have our photographs and fingerprints on record and, of course, hold our passports.

I am seriously worried, while trying to act normal and cheerful and get on with life. I've almost finished my project and tomorrow I'll type up the last bits and I'm hoping that will make a difference.

I've had to stop Bill taking the bed to pieces to find out why it's so uncomfortable, managed it so far.

I just need to take one day at a time. At worst, Bill will take care of Belinda if I am locked up and, if they arrest me, I hope they will believe that Deidre had nothing to do with any of it, except for the trip to London and burning the files. It does seem so very unfair that the English police refused to take them, and then they charge us with destroying evidence of criminal activities. We were sunk either way. I should have given Deidre the key to the London house to dump the papers in there, but I never thought. Too late now.

All we can do is sit and wait for the police to ignore us, or take us into custody. I can feel my nerves jangling, but it's one day at a time, that's all I can manage. I still have a lot to be thankful for, Deidre, Bill, and Belinda too. And the money to pay for a good lawyer. I have no idea who to ask for recommendations or where to start looking for one. That's my task for first thing tomorrow.

I can't even think of the threats from Morrison and Co right now; it's too much to cope with all at once.

MARCH BELINDA

Hiya Journal,

Our lives would make a blockbuster Hollywood movie, honestly. Stuff keeps happening all the time around here. This time, Leah and Deidre got arrested and for some reason they let them go, dunno why. Maybe the police are watching them to see if they smuggle more paintings in. Hell, I wouldn't even give that load of crap houseroom. Old, dull things, real faded. One had horses galloping across fields with a load of dogs, like booooooring!!! And some old biddy in a see-through dress sitting holding a glass of wine. Probably nicked that out of a brothel. And another one had those old-fashioned sailing ships in a battle, gunfire, and a huge black sky with hundreds of clouds. Real depressing to hang that on your wall. I read once that rich collectors keep stuff like that in underground rooms and sit and stare at them but they can't tell anyone they have them. Some people are really weird.

Best thing is Monster is back. Vet said not to get him too excited, no long walks for a while, and lots of love and meat. He's getting all that, I'm making sure. I've also managed to let him in my room most nights. He likes sleeping on my bed but I'm going to get it if Leah finds out. Monster won't tell on me though. (Smiley face and lots of kisses).

Had to hang around Nice for ages while Leah and Deidre were in the police station. Perfect shopping opportunity wasted. I'll work on Leah for next week.

Might as well put in a few hours for these effing exams. Madame will kill me if I don't pass. Can't get her to lighten up for a moment, not like our old teachers; if you could get them talking about themselves you could just sit back and listen, or not. She sticks to the subject like glue and there's no shifting her. Not sure why Sophie's bothering to have lessons. She knows it all. She wanted to go to the Sorbonne which she tells me is a lot of universities, not one. But then she decided on Oxford in England and was really pissed off when Madame informed her she would not be the youngest to attend. That was a black dude, Joshua Beckford, who went there when he was only 6 years old. She sulked for two whole days and wouldn't even pat Monster.

Guess the most exciting news is The Moonlight Killer is loose. More chickens, and a kid, can you imagine! Who'd do that? The body was all cut up and spread all over the park near the village. Some sick people out there. Sophie and I plan to go out and hunt him down. Well that's the talk, not sure I really want to, but Sophie is sooooo keen. Says it will be a big adventure. She's dared me, calls me a sop for ducking out. Bet she won't go. Good thing the locks on you, journal, are strong. Leah would have a real hissy fit if she read this.

Bill is back.

APRIL   DEIDRE

The beginning of April brought good news and bad news.

The good news was the delivery of the final divorce papers. Leah came rushing into the sun lounge waving the letter with the biggest smile on her face.

"It's through at last. I'm free!" She thrust the paper into my hands. "It's the Decree Absolute. I'm no longer married to Mason. What a relief."

"This deserves a toast." I made for the drinks cabinet.

"Deidre! At ten o'clock in the morning?"

I laughed. "Why not? This is a very special occasion. Just this once." I poured two rather large brandies and handed her a glass.

"What's all the fuss?" asked Bill, walking into the lounge.

"You are no longer living with a married woman. She's free and clear. Here, have a brandy, or would you prefer whiskey?"

He burst out laughing. "That's cleared my conscience. You've made an honest man out of me. Whiskey please."

"And tonight, we all go out to celebrate, if we're sober by then," Leah laughed.

It was a great night out and I think we all relaxed for the first time in weeks, although we weren't out of the woods yet.

Bill collected the post the next day, and this time the news did not have any of us dancing around the lounge.

The moment he walked back in the villa I could see something was wrong. He handed Leah an official letter – On Her Majesty's Service.

She stared at it while I wanted to scream 'open it, quickly'.

It was an official letter from the prison in England expressing their deep regret that Mason had suffered a fatal accident, and offering their sympathies to his family at this sad time.

Leah stood there in shock. "I don't believe it," she cried. "Oh, poor Mason, poor Belinda. How am I going to tell her? Oh God, how awful."

Bill put his arms around her.

She sobbed quietly for a moment and then pulled back. "It's so weird, am I widow or a divorcee? No, that sounds so selfish."

"No, it doesn't Leah. Do they give any details? Cause of death?"

"No, a fatal accident, whatever that means. I can't take it in. Mason, gone. He was so full of life, so successful, so vibrant…"

"So nasty," I added. "Also, criminal, ruthless and cruel."

"I know all that, but it's still a shock."

I shuddered. It was not all that long since I had spoken to him. None of us would ever hear that voice again. Had burning the files been his death warrant? It was difficult not to feel guilty.

After yesterday's ebullience, the mood in the villa was sombre. When Leah went to tell Belinda, she accepted the news in silence. She didn't cry, she didn't say a word, but walked out onto the beach, Monster at her heels. I saw her sitting by the sea, arms around her dog, face in his fur while he licked her hands.

I wanted to run down and sweep her up and hold her tight and tell her everything was going to be all right, but I couldn't guess the future and I wasn't sure what life was going to throw at us next.

It was a solemn meal that evening. No one said anything besides 'pass the salt' or 'do you want more potatoes?'.

Belinda was jittery, unsettled, but at the time I put that down to her recent loss. I wish I had taken more notice, or been pro-active, but twenty-twenty vision is a perfect science.

We settled down to watch an old film but I suspect no one was concentrating on the screen, each of us lost in our own thoughts. We climbed the stairs for an early night.

As you get older you sleep less soundly and, yet again, I was abruptly awakened by the sound of police sirens, and what I guessed were fire engines.

I shot out of bed and ran to the window. There was little moon but the night sky was lit by a huge red glow in the distance.

By now everyone else was up, peering out of the windows and the front door. Leah went back upstairs to check on Belinda. I heard her cries before she came rushing back down.

"Belinda's not there. Her bed has not been slept in." She was frantic with worry.

"We'll go search for her," Bill said.

"If we take both cars, we can cover more distance."

There was a loud hammering on the back door.

"Oh, thank goodness." Dressing gown flying and slippers flapping, Leah rushed to open it. Claudette stood on the step shaking, gabbling so fast in French that no one could understand her. In her panic, she lost every word of English she ever knew. The more she failed to make herself understood, the more frantic she became. Despite her panic, Claudette made it crystal clear. We needed to go and find Belinda. How she knew the teenager was not fast asleep upstairs in bed we had no idea.

Ten minutes later, Bill and Claudette left in one car. Leah and I were not far behind. While they turned left outside the gates, we turned right towards the village. The glow in the sky was larger now and Leah had to wrench the wheel hard over to the right to avoid the fire engine, blue lights flashing, as it roared past on the narrow country road.

"Do you think she is anywhere near the fire?" Leah asked, choking back a sob.

"I have no idea. I'm not sure where we should even start to look for her."

As we drove into the outskirts of the village, we could see several police cars parked up at odd angles on the pavements, the verges, and slewed across the road. We couldn't get through. Something big was going on.

Leah swung round, doubled back, parked on a side street and we jumped out. We kept close to the walls as we crept towards the plaza in the centre.

"We must be mad," Leah hissed, "but I have a feeling…"

I nodded. I had that sense too that somehow this involved Belinda. Yes, I know that sounds ridiculous, but true.

There were police everywhere, knocking on doors, rousing anyone who was able to sleep through the shrieking sirens. We had to duck back around several corners to avoid them. It seemed a sensible thing to do. We guessed they were speaking to the residents, telling them to stay indoors. Besides the gendarmes, Leah and I were the only people walking or, in our case, creeping along the streets.

We ducked and dived, often slipping into doorways to avoid the gendarmes, as we zigzagged our way towards the main square. We still couldn't see what the problem was, except for the fire. The wind changed and we were forced to cover our faces as the smoke and ash blew in our direction. There was the occasional bang and crash, which I guessed were parts of the burning building collapsing.

Overcome with fumes, we slid down the bank, landing next to the river to catch our breath and some fresh air.

"This is madness," said Leah. "What can we possibly do here? We have no idea if Belinda is around, or if she is mixed up in the fire."

I'd been studying the sky, lit up by the glow which had grown considerably larger. "I think that might be the Morrison house. It's over in that direction."

Leah looked up. "I don't think Belinda would be there, do you? She'd have no reason to... unless she got friendly with the sons."

"Last I heard she was lusting over that very unsuitable twenty-something surfer, Christian was it?"

"I hope she's more sensible than last time."

"What last time?" I hadn't a clue what Leah meant.

"Uh, old news, way back in Weston. Not my story to tell."

I was piqued and now very curious, but Belinda's past history was really none of my business.

There were shouts in the distance. We saw several police run down the road at the top of the bank, and then shots rang out.

"Was that gunfire?" gasped Leah, clutching my arm. I saw the fear in her large eyes reflecting in the light from the street lamp.

"Yes, yes, I think so." Instinctively we crouched lower, flattening ourselves against the cool, damp, green grass.

"Of course, the gendarmes are armed, aren't they?"

"Yes, this is not Britain, and I for one am scared. I have no idea what we're doing here Leah. Did we think we'd drive down the road and bump into Belinda? She could be anywhere. What were we thinking?"

Another barrage of shots rang out, more cries, shouts, and a scream.

"It was stupid, but then Claudette was so anxious for us to drive out to find her. I have no idea why, what does she know—?"

"That we don't," I finished for her.

"I should have worked harder on my French lessons," Leah groaned. "What are we going to do now? We can't lie here on the river bank all night."

I sat up and shaded my eyes. The police had disappeared and there was only the occasional gunshot. "Make for the car?"

"And then what?"

I had no idea. I also had no wish to meet up with the police and try to explain what Leah and I were doing here. It made us look so guilty.

"I'm not sure there is anything we can do. We are in the wrong place at the wrong time, and what if one of us gets shot by mistake?"

I could feel Leah's body shake and we briefly clutched each other for comfort.

"Let's go," she whispered.

We crept, keeping low, farther along the river bank, then raced up the slope and hugged the walls of the houses which fronted onto the narrow footpath. Every shadow made us jump. We slid from one doorway to the next, ducking out of view before peering to check the road was empty. On one occasion, I bounced off a door which flew open and only just managed to stay on my feet.

We had almost reached the top of the street, just around the corner from where Leah had left the car, when she bumped into an elderly gentleman who was looking up and down the street, craning his neck to see what was going on. Now that the police were several streets over, the villagers were coming out to find out what was causing all the commotion.

"*Hey! Attendez,*" cried the old man and Leah took fright and raced off down the road. He continued to shout and holler and I followed her, running as fast as I could. As I reached the corner, I clung to the brickwork, gasping for breath, battling to suck in lungfuls of oxygen, red clouds floating in front of my eyes.

I heard shouts from the next street, pushed myself off the wall and dived towards the car. Leah was already in the driving seat and turning the key. I grabbed the door handle and heaved myself onto the seat, my legs hanging out as the car began to move.

"Deidre..." Leah gasped.

"Just go!" I screamed back, as with one hand I held onto the door and, with the other, I grabbed the far edge of the seat to pull myself into the vehicle. It fishtailed as Leah slalomed around the parked cars, and the open door clipped a wing mirror before I was able to swing my legs in and slam it shut.

"They've seen us!" cried Leah.

I glanced back and saw two men in the street, one raising a weapon and aiming it towards us. Surely a bullet wouldn't reach us from there? We were saved by a little old lady who wandered out into the middle of the narrow village road, oblivious to the danger she was in.

Leah screeched around the corner, up a one way street in the wrong direction, and then we were on the road out of the village.

"Are you okay?" Her voice wobbled.

"Yes. Fine." I looked in the wing mirror and saw lights behind us. "But I think we're being followed."

"Oh shit!" Instinctively Leah put her foot down and we careered along the unlit, single width country road. She swerved to avoid a deer, eyes reflecting back in the headlights and frozen with fear. I think at one point we crushed a rabbit; the car lifted slightly as the left-hand wheel rose and fell. Veering too far over to the right, the wheels skidded briefly on the wet verge before bouncing back onto the road again.

"Slow down Leah! Slow down! We can't run from the police. This is crazy!"

In the dim interior of the car Leah's face was white, eyes wide open, a kind of madness in her expression. She glanced briefly at me, shook her head, and eased off on the accelerator. She slumped forward slightly and burst into loud sobs.

We could see the headlights from the police car getting closer. I thought for a moment Leah was going to race off down the road again, but we were now by the entrance to the villa and she turned into the driveway and came to a sliding stop on the gravel outside the front door.

Neither of us attempted to get out of the car. Leah lay her head on the steering wheel, shoulders heaving, while I was battling to stop myself from shaking. The car was stationary but my body was still moving.

A gendarme appeared at my window and yanked the door open. He leaned in, filling the car with tobacco fumes. He gabbled away in rapid French and I replied with a Gallic shrug. I was past caring. He grabbed my arm and levered me out of the car, and I stumbled when my feet hit the ground.

A second police car drove in and four more men got out. At least one of them spoke good English and he directed us all into the house.

As we assembled in the lounge and I turned to look I gasped and took several steps back. I was staring at my stalker from London, the same face I had seen watching the villa more than once. With my legs still wobbly, I sank into the closest chair but, before anyone could say anything, more vehicles drew up outside. Bill and Claudette had returned, followed by another police car.

As they all piled into the front lounge it was getting decidedly crowded. Claudette bounced forward and rattled off sentences in French to her captive audience, relieved that, at last, everyone understood what she was saying. She finally ran out of steam, perched next to Leah on the sofa, and gave her a huge hug.

My stalker turned to me. "We have met before?"

"In London?"

"Correct. I am Pierre Durand, *Inspecteur* at Interpol." He offered his hand to shake. "You think I am a spy, or a criminal, yes?" He smiled.

I could feel my cheeks turn red. It had never occurred to me that he was on the side of the angels.

He turned to the men leaning against the walls, and propping up the door frame. Whatever he said to them, all but two of them left the villa, climbed into their cars and drove off.

Inspecteur Durand then smiled at Claudette as she prised herself away from Leah and went off, presumably to make coffee for everyone.

Durand pulled forward a dining chair and settled down.

"I need to explain, and quickly, because I fear your daughter may be in danger."

Leah gave a cry and felt in her pockets for a tissue. Tears were running down her cheeks and she twisted her hands together, unable to sit still.

"Where is she? What danger?"

"That we have to find. First we must talk of the people who may want to hurt her."

"Like the Morrisons?" I asked.

"Yes, the Morrisons, and even the Fentons too," he agreed.

"So you know about them? You know about Mason and the connection with Leah and Mason and…"

As I spoke, he was nodding. "Yes, all this we know. I have been watching to learn and to keep you safe."

"Then you must know we have no part in any of this. Leah is divorced now and Mason is deceased and we burnt the papers. So, for us it's all over."

"No," Leah said out loud.

"No, what?"

"We burnt the papers, but I still have them. I made copies, before you took them to London, Deidre."

I jumped to my feet. "You did what! Leah, how could you, after all our work destroying them?"

"I've been reading them, making a case against the crooks."

"And then what were you going to do with them?"

"I hadn't decided, but either to blackmail them into leaving us alone or handing them over to the police." Her attitude was defiant, and I almost grinned.

"I hope you will give them to me?" The *Inspecteur* actually smiled at her.

"Of course."

I was still not convinced. "Leah, where were they? The police searched the villa from top to bottom when they came and found the pictures and other stuff."

"When you're brought up with a mother like mine, you become an expert at hiding stuff. I left them on the roof. No one ever thinks to look outside on the roof, do they? Not all the papers of course, just those about the two local families, and I think I've built up a complete case on them." She paused. "But what did you say about Belinda? Where is she? How is she in danger? Do they have her?"

"This we don't know," *Inspecteur* Durand replied, "but Madame here," he nodded at Claudette who entered carrying a tray of coffee cups and cakes, "she warned us that Belinda was lured away to go murderer hunting tonight, with her friend."

"The stupid child!" exclaimed Leah, running her fingers through her hair.

Claudette continued to hand round the cups and plates.

"What friend? Who did she go with? Christian?"

"Sophie Lampierre."

"Oh, that's all right then. What a relief." Leah smiled. "They are great friends. As long as they didn't go anywhere near those thugs and their boys."

"The men are looking for them now. They will find them soon, I am sure."

I suddenly remembered the fire, and asked him about it.

Over coffee and cake we got the whole story. The Metropolitan Police in London had been watching 'certain individuals' as the *Inspecteur* called them and, when the news got out about Mason's death, they came over and the result was the shoot-out in the village and setting fire to the Morrison's house. It was too early to report if there had been any casualties.

Monster came and laid his head on my knee, looking soulfully into my eyes. He'd been prowling round looking for Belinda.

Leah remarked that killing chickens, ransacking our villa and leaving a dead dog on the doorstep, seemed strange behaviour for a gang of London mobsters.

Inspecteur Durand shook his head. "It was nothing to do with them."

She gasped. "So there really is a kind of madman out there on the loose. And Belinda and Sophie have gone out to track him down?"

She stood and began pacing. "You have to find them. Why aren't you out there looking for them? We should all go. They may have teamed up with those awful Morrison boys." She began searching for her car keys.

Durand remained calm. "Madame, we have every gendarme from Nice and Cannes out there."

"But they won't know what they look like. I'll recognise them."

"Madame Claudette sent us pictures of both of them from her phone. My men will find them." He stood and wished us well and suggested we all go to bed, which I thought a ridiculous thing to say. He handed Leah his card, arranged to collect the papers next day, and left one man on duty to guard us.

In the silence, we sat and stared at each other. No one had anything to say. Leah kept glancing at her watch and Bill went outside to walk around the house, hoping to see Belinda walking home. It was eerie and uncomfortable. Everyone fidgeted, Claudette wandered through to the kitchen to brew up yet more coffee that no one wanted to drink, and Leah punished the cushion, pulling one thread after another out of the fabric. Between Belinda and her, that cushion didn't stand a chance.

I paced around for a while, even going upstairs to see if there were any clues that might tell us where Belinda was going tonight but, from the unmade bed to the tidy cupboards, there was nothing. I eyed the journal, criss-crossed with chains, in her bedside table drawer, and wondered if that would give us a clue. I took it downstairs.

It took moments to snap through the links and, though Leah remarked it was tempting to read it all, we only scanned the last two entries.

"Nothing," Leah sighed, throwing it back on the table. "Only that Sophie dared her to go after The Moonlight Killer, no information on when or where."

By now both of us were pacing the floor, backwards and forwards, we couldn't settle. Bill was still patrolling outside and the gendarme was sitting on an upturned flower pot by the front door, smoking.

Leah suggested that Claudette go home and maybe the gendarme would walk her over the field to her house. By now she had calmed down a little and understood, but assured us she could go alone. Already it was beginning to get light and she was worried about her elderly mother.

We watched her as she strode across the gravel and out through the gate in the back garden.

"I'm feeling dizzy," Leah said, "that feeling when you've been up all night."

Already the first rays of the sun were peeping over the headland, dark shapes morphing into trees, rocks, and boulders.

"I can't sit still." Leah scrambled to her feet. "I'm going to take Monster for a walk. I'll keep my phone on me."

We had kept Monster on the lead, even in the garden since his return from the vet, and when he saw her take it down off the hook, he bounced like a rubber ball, tail swishing from side to side.

"That dog will need some drastic training before too long," I told Leah, as he raced around in circles, all four feet in the air.

"I know." She made a dive for his collar. "You miss Belinda don't you?"

"Yes!" We both said it at the same time. "Why didn't we think of that before?"

Leah clipped the lead on. "Monster, where's Belinda?"

"Wait, I'll get one of her scarves, that's what they do in the movies, right?" I made for the stairs.

Leah looked doubtful for a moment. "She's a Newfoundland, not a bloodhound. Think it will work?"

"We can but try," I called back. "All dogs have a fantastic sense of smell, they can sense odours for miles and miles." I waved the scarf in front of Monster's nose. "Find Belinda. Find Belinda."

Bill appeared in the doorway. "I don't believe it," he said, "I just had the same idea."

"Let's all go. The gendarme can stay here."

"He's not guarding us, is he?"

Leah fished Durand's card out of her pocket. "I'll phone him and tell him what we're doing."

"And if you can't find your mistress, we'll replace you with a proper police bloodhound," I threatened Monster, who was now straining on the lead, anxious to go.

It was as well that Bill came with us, as the dog set off at speed and, even though he was still a puppy, he was strong and almost pulled the poor man over.

We set off down the drive, the gendarme loping behind us. Yes, it's us he's guarding, I decided, not the villa.

Once we reached the gate posts, Monster did not hesitate for a second. He turned left, away from the village and kept going.

"I didn't expect him to go this way," Leah frowned.

"The big problem is, we are going to run out of energy long before he does, and the vet said no extended exercise."

"If he finds Belinda, it's worth it."

"Pity we couldn't do this in the car." Bill was huffing and puffing, already out of breath.

Monster stopped so suddenly, we all piled up like dominoes.

"It's not going to work." Leah choked back a sob.

"Don't lose hope. He's not stopped at one tree, or the gatepost, and he always waters that."

Monster sniffed the grass verge, nosing among the cosmos, daisies and cowslips.

"Wave Belinda's scarf under his nose again, Deidre."

Monster pulled towards the low stone wall and leapt on top. Landing on the other side, he was raring to go as, one by one, we scrambled over after him.

"I'm thankful it's grass and not a ploughed field," Bill gasped, as the dog pulled even harder. With difficulty he changed hands, flexing the first one where the lead had cut into his flesh.

The land sloped down towards the river and, as we got lower, we zigzagged between the cherry trees, their pink petals carpeting the grass beneath.

Monster stopped when he reached the water. He put his head back and sniffed the air then set off along the bank.

I looked behind to see our pet gendarme was not letting us out of his sight, though he was struggling. He'd removed his hat, loosened his collar and was mopping his brow with a large, red spotted handkerchief.

There was a rustic bridge a little further down the river, and Monster bounded onto the wooden struts, defying all Bill's efforts to slow him down. He was making small squeaking sounds, his tongue lolling out, specks of foam on the edges, ears lifted a little as he strained to go faster.

I could feel the sweat trickling down my back. I opened my coat but it didn't help much and I wasn't going to carry it.

The undergrowth was thicker here, low lying bushes I had no name for, but Monster ploughed right through.

"If he's not taking us on a wild goose chase," Leah panted, wiping her forehead on her sleeve, "he's taking the most direct route."

The bushes were vicious. They scratched our skin, small thorns tugged at our clothes, and they exuded a strong smell I couldn't place.

When we were least expecting it, we broke into a small clearing. It reminded me of the pictures in children's books as, nestled in the middle, was a small log cabin.

Monster began to bark and, as Bill approached the

door, the dog darted in front of him, stood on his hind legs and scrabbled frantically with his claws, his nails scouring the soft wood.

"Belinda!" shrieked Leah as she pushed past to try and open the door. It was locked. We ran round, peering in through the two small windows but they were covered with years of dust and dirt.

The gendarme had caught up with us and rattled the large, shiny padlock.

"That's new," Bill pointed.

The gendarme drew his pistol as Bill handed Monster to Leah. He was now barking non-stop, turning in circles and tangling his lead.

"She must be in there," Leah cried.

Seeing the policeman about to shoot straight at the padlock, Bill rushed over and stopped him. The lock was new, but the wood attached to the rivet plates was old and rotten. Taking out his Swiss Army knife, Bill prised the lock away from its mounting. For some reason I couldn't guess, the gendarme discharged his gun and, as the shot rang out, it sent a screeching flock of birds skywards from the bushes.

The chain fell away and Bill kicked the door open. It was pitch dark inside and at first, as we all crowded in through the door, it looked empty. Then Leah rushed over and grabbed Belinda. She lay curled up on the dirt floor, unresponsive and her breathing was shallow. Leah attempted to pick her up but she was too heavy. Bill stepped forward to help, but we all froze at the shriek from behind us.

Sophie stood in the entrance, her face screwed in fury,

her eyes glistening. She yelled again, first in French and then in English.

"Keep away. She's mine. Leave her!"

"No!" Leah screamed back.

The child raised a gun and pointed it at us. "I may not be able to kill all of you, so who wants to be the first one to die?"

My eyes must have looked as manic as Sophie's. What was the child doing – here – with a gun. Was she...?

"You?" shouted Leah. "It was you, wasn't it? The children, the dog, the chickens, all of it?"

Sophie drew herself up, puffed out her chest and laughed. "You never even guessed, did you? No one did. I fooled everyone. The whole village running around like headless chickens. They even blamed the Morrison boys. And, I was doing fine, until," she pointed at Belinda's limp body in Leah's arms, "until she accused me of poisoning that mutt." She turned the gun towards Monster who growled at her and bared his teeth.

It happened so quickly that it took everyone by surprise, but the gendarme, who had remained outside, appeared behind Sophie and thrust his forearm across her throat. She tried to twist round but he held firm. Mad as she was, she was no match for his strength and, at the same time, Bill's hand shot out and he wrenched the gun out of her hand.

The pride of the French police force was none too gentle and I watched fascinated as he manhandled her and snapped on the handcuffs. She was raving mad, writhing on the ground, spitting, cursing, lashing out. It was a Sophie I'd never seen before and I wondered if she was on drugs.

Leah was already calling *Inspecteur* Durand, attempting to explain where we were, and that Belinda needed urgent medical attention.

We carried Belinda out into the fresh air, and laid her on the grass. Leah knelt beside her, cradling her as the tears streamed down her face and she murmured to her stepdaughter as Monster covered the face of his mistress with unhygienic slobbery kisses. Belinda made no response, but we'd found her, and she was alive.

MAY LEAH

Dear Diary,

It's taken me days to get my equilibrium back. I still find myself shaking, but both Deidre and Bill have been wonderful.

We spent days at the hospital, but Belinda pulled through quickly once they identified what drug Sophie had pumped into her.

The whole episode has rocked the village to the core. The only daughter of the local Lord of the Manor was responsible for killing and torturing not only animals but a baby and a toddler too. For sure she will be in an asylum for the rest of her life. She acted so sane, so charming, so normal and, of course, super bright. I can't imagine what was going on in that head of hers. I suppose they will test her and come up with some diagnosis or other.

Poor Madame du Pont was devastated when she heard the news. She sat at the dining room table, hands pulling at her grey hair and twirling it around her fingers. "*La pauvre petite*," she said over and over.

"*Pauvre*, bloody *petite,* my foot," was my response.

The little brat is plain evil. I felt very sorry for Madame, she'd lost the brightest and most promising pupil she'd ever had; Sophie was a teacher's dream.

Once Belinda was home again, life settled down on an even keel. I heard her swear yesterday and that suggests she is well on the way to recovery. And her appetite has returned to normal. Claudette's mournful voice floated out from the kitchen at lunch time bemoaning Belinda had finished off all the cheese. That made me smile. I am going to make enquiries to find a counsellor for her. She's lost her whole family in such a short space of time and, when it happened to me, I took months and months to come to terms with it.

I'm not sure we will even know the full extent of the mob's interference with our local criminal expat neighbours. Both Daniel Morrison and Humphrey Fenton have been taken into custody; both escaped the shoot-out in the village, but I heard a couple of hit men from London ended up pumped full of bullets.

The fire was indeed Daniel's home, and there is nothing left now but an empty shell. Sad, it was a nice house. Geraldine Morrison fled back to Britain making the excuse her boys needed her there. I suspect she took Deidre's necklace with her, we never got to the bottom of that, shame. Margaret is staying though. She was quick to assure me that she was not doing it to support her husband. She's popped round a couple of times and she's not so bad when you get to know her.

I cannot begin to imagine what the Marquis and Marquise can be feeling. It must be devastating for them. Sophie was their only child. It's not as if they can sell up and move, the chateau has been in the family for hundreds of years; now it was probably just a millstone around their necks.

One other mystery cleared up: the time Belinda went missing. That was Sophie again. She'd promised to show Belinda the secret passages in the chateau and, in one dark area, all Belinda remembers is falling asleep. She woke up hours later, and it took her 'like forever' (her words) to find her way out and then walk home. When she tackled Sophie about it the child denied all knowledge, and she got Belinda so confused she couldn't work out what had happened. So she said nothing. As she dramatically told me – her words again – 'how was I to know that a mere child of eleven could behave like that, I mean are you serious?'

Her lessons are going well. She and Madame are getting on a lot better, and both are convinced she will pass with flying colours.

Good news on the villa: the current owners are willing to sell, and we've drawn up plans to convert the outbuildings for Deidre. I'm so angry with her for not telling me sooner about her illness. I wouldn't hear of her going back to her place. She's staying here where we can care for her and be with her at the end. I threatened to set Monster on her if she didn't agree.

At last I'm looking forward to life again. No police charges to worry us now, all dropped. Bill is happy pottering about the place, he always finds something to do and the villagers have been very friendly too. Big plans are in hand for a Saint's Day celebration soon, and we'll be part of it. I just need to keep an eye out for Christian. He's making eyes at Belinda and that could spell trouble.

MAY BELINDA

Hiya Journal,

I'm effing glad I wrote stuff in here for a whole year or no one would believe what this family has been through. Make a brilliant movie. It's got all the Hollywood stuff, kidnapping, murder, a shoot-out and an off-the-wall child psycho. Yeah, the lot. And for the animal lovers throw in Monster too, he's the greatest.

Can't believe how I was taken in by that spoilt brat. What was she thinking? She had it all. Beautiful clothes, a huge, cool place to live, got everything she asked for. And, her parents allowed her to do anything she wanted. Wonder who will get all those beautiful clothes now?

Heck I told her everything and she used it all against us. She took old pictures from her place and brought them over, and she sent that blue toy rabbit to scare Leah, and she got the Morrison boys to help her trash our villa, promising them they could nick any jewellery they found. She couldn't help boasting to me after she stuck a needle in me, told me everything. Thought she was so clever, rotten bitch. Even that poor dead dog, it belonged to Claudette's niece and she was heartbroken when it went missing. Hope they lock her up forever, she's more than mental.

I'm gonna ace those exams. It isn't sooo bad learning and now that snotty Sophie isn't piping up all the time and I have Madame all to myself we get on a lot better.

Leah's okay I guess, for a stepmother that is. Shocked her yesterday. I called her mother. She turned and stared and then she gave me the biggest hug and said I should only call her that if I wanted to, but I was like a daughter to her. That was kinda cool. She even bought me some more chain to wrap round you, journal, and apologised for breaking you open and reading you. She only read the last bit and, as it was in a good cause, I've forgiven her. Anyway, she never mentioned Monster sleeping on my bed.

Summer coming soon, long, sunny days on the beach and Christian winked at me at the market last week. I think he likes me. Now that would be so radical.

MAY DEIDRE

I jumped when I felt a hand on my shoulder as Leah peered at the notebook.

"You're writing a book about us, aren't you?" she challenged me.

I had to admit I was. "The events of the last twelve months are so unbelievable I wanted to get them on paper before I forgot, and while I still could. I'd never publish our story of course, but we can keep it as a family record."

"I'm relieved to hear that," Leah told me. She needed a quiet life. She'd had enough excitement to last her several lifetimes.

If you are reading this today, I suspect a certain teenager upstairs might just have taken it upon herself to tell the rest of the world, but by then I may be with those angels I still don't believe in.

END
***

ACKNOWLEDGEMENTS

While a writer spends many hours in mental isolation committing words to paper, to bring a book into the public domain is always the result of teamwork.

My thanks to Cheryl Craig who advised on police procedure.

To my early readers – Tom Benson – Lesley Hayes – Frank Parker – Susan Wuthrich and Jodie Holloway (my comma specialist).

All errors are my responsibility.

Grateful thanks to my editor Andrew Holloway, Sharon Brownlie for the cover, Rod Craig for the formatting, and I cannot omit my long-suffering husband who has yet again given me the time and space to spend hours at the keyboard during our lockdown in Spain, surrounded in silence while we were isolated from the rest of the world.

ABOUT THE AUTHOR

Lucinda E Clarke has been a professional writer for almost 40 years, scripting for both radio and television. She's had numerous articles published in several national magazines, written mayoral speeches and advertisements. She currently writes a monthly column in a local publication in Spain. She once had her own newspaper column, until the newspaper closed down, but says this was not her fault!

Six of her books have been bestsellers in genre on Amazon on both sides of the Atlantic winning several medals and certificates. Lucinda has also received over 20 awards for scripting, directing, concept and producing, and had two educational text books traditionally published. Sadly, these did not make her the fortune she dreamed of to allow her to live in luxury.

Lucinda has also worked on radio – on one occasion with a bayonet at her throat – appeared on television, and met and interviewed some of the world's top leaders.

She set up and ran her own video production company, producing a variety of programmes, from advertisements to corporate and drama documentaries on a vast range of subjects.

In total she has lived in eight different countries, run the 'worst riding school in the world', and cleaned toilets to bring in the money.

When she handled her own divorce, Lucinda made legal history in South Africa.

Now, pretending to be retired, she gives occasional talks and lectures to special interest groups and finds retirement the most exhausting time of her life so far; but says there is still so much to see and do, she is worried she won't have time to fit it all in.

TO MY READERS

If you have enjoyed this book, or even if you didn't like it, please take a few minutes to write a review. Reviews are very important to authors and I would certainly value your feedback. Thank you.

Why not sign up for Lucinda's newsletter for special offers, competitions, news on other authors, new releases and interesting facts. http://eepurl.com/cBu4Sf Subscribers can download the free, second half of The very Worst Riding School in the World.

Web page: lucindaeclarkeauthor.com
Facebook: https://www.facebook.com/lucindaeclarke.author
Email: lucindaeclarke@gmail.com
Blog: http://lucindaeclarke.wordpress.com
Twitter: @LucindaEClarke
I love to hear from my readers.

Also by Lucinda E Clarke

A Year in the life of Leah Brand

The nightmare began the day the dog died. Leah's cosy new world is turned upside down as inanimate objects move around the house on their own, there are unexplained noises, and slowly she is driven to the edge of madness.
https://www.amazon.com/dp/B07WHJKGXF

A Year in the life of Andrea Coe

Andrea Coe was Leah's best friend; she was outgoing, outrageous and the opposite of quiet and shy Leah. What was the attraction? And is Andrea's friendship genuine? How well do we know our friends?
https://www.amazon.com/dp/B088KRQB67

Walking over Eggshells

The first autobiography which relates Lucinda's horrendous relationship with her mother and her travels to various countries.
http://www.amazon.com/dp/B00E8HSNDW

The very Worst Riding School in the World (free)

Who in their right mind would open and run a riding school when they can't ride, are terrified of horses, with no idea of how to care for them and no insurance or capital? Add to that two of the four horses are not fit for the knacker's yard. Yes, that would be me.

https://www.amazon.com/dp/B072TJT1YB

Truth, Lies and Propaganda

The first of two books explaining how Lucinda 'fell' into writing for a living – her dream since childhood. It began when she was fired from her teaching job, and crashed out in an audition at the South African Broadcasting Corporation. In a quirky turn of fate, she found herself writing a series on how to care for domestic livestock, she knew absolutely nothing about cows, goats and chickens. And it all continued from there.

http://www.amazon.com/dp/B00QE35BO2

More Truth, Lies and Propaganda

Tales of filming in deep rural Africa, meeting a ram with an identity crisis, a house that disappears, the forlorn bushmen and a video starring a very dead rat. You will never believe anything you watch on television ever again.

http://www.amazon.com/dp/B00VF0S3RG

Amie - African Adventure

A novel set in Africa, which takes Amie from the comfort of her home in England to a small African country. Civil war

breaks out and soon she is fighting for her life.
http://www.amazon.com/dp/B00LWFIO5K

Amie and the Child of Africa

As Amie goes in search of the child she fostered before the civil war broke out, she encounters a terrorist organization with international connections. She is not alone, but one of her friends will betray her.
http://www.amazon.com/dp/B015CI29O4

Amie Stolen Future

In one night, Amie loses everything, her home, her family, her possessions and her name. She has nowhere to turn, but she has no freedom for other people now control her life and if she does not obey them, they will not let her live.
http://www.amazon.com/dp/B01M67NRG4

Amie Cut for Life

A look and listen mission turns out to be a nightmare as Amie is left to rescue four young girls who are destined for the sex slave trade with a horrifying twist.
https://www.amazon.com/dp/B07545M9DB

Samantha (Amie backstory 1)

A light comedy as Amie's sister ventures overseas for the first time with her boyfriend Gerry – if it can go wrong, it goes wrong.
https://www.amazon.com/dp/B07HVNXV6F

Ben (Amie backstory 2)

Ben's story of his passage into manhood and the beginning of the civil war in Togodo.
https://www.amazon.com/dp/B07K352ZLQ

Unhappily Ever After

The real truth you've never been told before. In Fairyland, Cinderella is scheming to get a divorce with a good settlement from King Charming, and the other royal marriages are also in dire trouble. This year's ball is approaching, along with a political agitator hell bent on rousing the peasants into revolting against their royal masters.
http://www.amazon.com/dp/B01DPVB4M8

All Lucinda's books are available on Amazon in Kindle and paperback.

Reviews

A six star read, I can't wait for the next one. (**Leah Brand book 1**)

———————

A superb sequel to 'A Year in the Life of Leah Brand'. (**book 2 – Andrea Coe**)

———————

That Lucinda E Clarke can write and write well is not in question. This memoir left me breathless at times. She writes of her adventures, misadventures and family relationships in an honest but entertaining manner. I wholeheartedly recommend this book, (**Walking over Eggshells**) *buy it, delve in and lose a few days, well worth it.*

———————

This book was written with such consummate skill. I have enormous admiration for Lucinda E Clarke as an author. She not only knows how to write an edge-of-the-seat, well-constructed story that would make a brilliant movie – she does it using beautiful, spare, intelligent, and amazingly *descriptive language. By the time I got to the end of 'Amie' I felt as though I'd been to Africa – seen it, touched it, smelled it, heard it... loved it and hated it. Everything that is the truth of the country is there in this book. Can I give it six stars please? It deserves it. (**Amie an African Adventure**)*

---

*Lucinda E. Clarke takes the reader on another fast-paced African adventure full of suspense and twists and turns. The characters are so well developed that I felt as if I was watching a movie while reading this wonderful book. Mrs. Clarke both entertains and educates the reader about the African experience. The story never lags and quickly pulls the reader in this new adventure. (**Amie and the Child of Africa**).*

What a great book! I have so enjoyed this and love the tongue-in-cheek, self-deprecating humour with which Lucinda Clarke relates her experiences. It's quite fascinating to read how she becomes involved in writing and broadcasting, and also really interesting to realise how much easier it was to get in touch with decision makers in the days before the digital onslaught. Either that or Lucinda is being overly modest and making it look simple! I loved the descriptions of her early experiences in Libya - both funny and frightening. And of course, there are lots of memories for me here as I moved to South Africa in the early eighties and always listened to Springbok radio. The style is easy and fluid, and I have enjoyed every page, riveted by the quantity of writing she managed to do without any previous knowledge of the subjects. Amazing. For me, this is the best one of Lucinda's

316

yet in terms of keeping me pasted to my Kindle! I've read two of her other books before, and I'll definitely be reading the sequel to this one! (**Truth, Lies and Propaganda**)

I picked this one up purely on the basis of how much I enjoyed reading the first book and I was not to be disappointed. Lucinda E Clarke is one of those writers who can tell a story effortlessly in a way that just carries you along with her adventures. I have to say she is fast becoming one of my favourite authors. The book revolves around a period of her life as she returns to work in Africa and she uses her natural writing ability to not just recount events but to entertain along the way. Her skill is not in telling extraordinary tales but in making often ordinary real life stories come to life and it is in the smaller details of each story that I often found myself most enthralled. I cannot recommend this book and indeed the previous one highly enough. If your next book purchase is from the pen of Lucinda E Clarke you will have made a wise decision indeed. A thoroughly deserved 5 stars out of 5 from me. (**More, truth Lies and Propaganda**)

The author's imagination and humour are combined to create a story that makes your smile or LOL from beginning to end. It is a rollicking pantomime of dry wit and well-described imagery that works exceptionally well. Highly recommended. (**Unhappily Ever After**)

317

An excerpt from A Year in the Life of Leah Brand (book 1)

JANUARY

The nightmare began on the day the dog died.

It was New Year's Eve and, while Mason and I were out celebrating, my nemesis passed on to the big kennel in the sky. By the time we struggled out of the taxi, neither of us was in a fit state to notice the dog, dead or alive. Mason had to grab my arm as I caught my foot in the door jamb on the way out of the Uber. It was just as well the price of the fare would be billed automatically on the credit card; Mason was not sober enough to find the right notes to pay the driver.

We weaved our way up the path, arms linked, concentrating hard trying not to fall. It felt a long, long way to the front door. Mason propped me against the wall and then looked at me.

"Keys," he barked.

"I don't have them." Despite the pain above my left knee I couldn't stop myself from giggling. "Look in your pockets."

"I gave them to you." The fluorescent light from the

lamp post on the street near the gate illuminated the scowl on Mason's face.

"No, you didn't," I replied, but to placate him I fumbled with the clasp on my dinky evening bag as if to check. The problem was I needed both hands to undo the clasp and I swayed from side to side desperately trying to keep my balance. I didn't remember drinking all that much, but I couldn't even stand straight and I knew before I peered into my purse it only contained a small wad of paper hankies and a lipstick.

"I don't have them," I repeated.

Mason glared at me and began digging into the pockets of his dinner suit. He cursed loudly.

"Hush, you'll wake the neighbours!" Apart from Andrea we didn't know any of them all that well, but I often got the uncomfortable feeling they did not approve of us. Well maybe that was a bit harsh, but I'd tried to get to know them and had little luck.

"To hell with the neighbours," Mason shouted louder. "Happy New Year," he screamed. "Stuffy lot, in bed already? Night to celebrate! It's a brand New Year."

I grabbed his arm, as much to steady myself as to quieten him down. The pains continued to shoot up and down the leg that was no longer there as I made a valiant attempt to stay upright. I had a moment of clarity. "The spare key, it's under the middle flowerpot, over there." I pointed to the row of them arranged next to the step under the lounge window.

Mason staggered back, bent down and put his hand out as his legs gave way and he promptly fell over. He looked so comical lying there. The well-respected owner and head of the biggest law firm in town sprawled on the grass. Then I really got a fit of the giggles and laughed until the tears ran down my face.

One look at Mason's face helped sober me up. He did not appreciate anyone making fun of him. He took his dignity and his professional standing in the community very seriously. He turned his attention back to the flowerpots, lifting each in turn until he found the key.

"Yes!" He slipped the ring over his finger and twirled it around and I watched in horror as it flew off and landed in the holly bush halfway down the path.

The holly bush fought back, tearing at Mason's hands as he fumbled among the leaves to retrieve it. There were several futile attempts to insert it in the lock after which we both tumbled into the hall. Next hurdle was to navigate the stairs, fling open the bedroom door and collapse on the bed.

It took me a while to orientate myself as the ceiling revolved above me. Good heavens, how much wine had I drunk? I manoeuvred my way towards our bathroom by clinging onto the furniture. I tore off my black evening gown and my prosthesis, and hopped into the shower. I leaned against the wall and let the steaming water pour over me before I realised I was still wearing my bra and panties. But I was past caring. I think, if I remember correctly, I was beginning to sober up and questioning why I was this far out of it after less than half a bottle of wine. I don't drink all that often; I'd got out of the habit while taking the cocktail of drugs they poured into me after the accident. Everyone knows medicine and alcohol can be lethal. Now, I was down to a few daily tablets but I'd not taken any for a couple of days beforehand. I knew there would be plenty of booze at the party but maybe even the modest amount I had was enough to make me really drunk.

I clutched the shower door, grabbed a towel, sat on the loo and rubbed myself hard all over. My head was pounding but the biggest pain was in my leg, the one that wasn't there. How could my brain be so stupid? Consciously I knew the surgeons who saved my life had no option but to remove a limb crushed beyond repair. Five years later some of those complicated synapses told me it was still there and throbbing. I should take some of my pills but they were downstairs and I would never make it in my condition. I hopped back into the bedroom where Mason was comatose, spread corner to corner across the bed, arms akimbo, his dinner jacket crumpled and stained and his shoes covered in mud. He was out for the count.

I sighed. I knew that nothing short of a nuclear explosion would wake him, so I sank onto the bed, removed his shoes and rolled him over to his side. I pulled out my nightie from under the pillow and slipped it over my head, crawled under the duvet and, despite the pain, I remembered no more.

Loud, piercing shrieks coming from downstairs woke me. I flung myself out of bed, and tumbled onto the floor. In moments of stress I still forgot I can't walk. Swearing under my breath I rubbed my eyes and grabbed my false leg. Strapping it on, I dragged on my dressing gown and opened the bedroom door. It was no use trying to wake Mason; he was still dead to the world and not even the cries from below would wake him. I hurried down the stairs as quickly as I could. I knew who was screaming but I didn't know why.

Belinda was standing in the kitchen, still shrieking, when I shuffled in.

"What's the problem? Stop it. Calm down." A quick glance showed everything looked normal. The back door was still closed, the window panes intact, the counter tops as clean and tidy as I'd left them before going out last night. Everything in place, if you ignored the spilled cereal all over the floor where Belinda had dropped the corn flakes. They crunched under my feet as I went to hold her but she stepped quickly out of reach and backed up against the pantry door. She looked petrified.

* * *

Printed in Great Britain
by Amazon